THE
BARREN HILLS
OF
CREIGHTON

TRINA BROOKS

ISBN 978-1-7380-9070-9

Cover Illustration by Beren Davis

Edited by Allister Thompson

BOOM U Press, British Columbia, Canada

Printed and bound in Canada

www.trinabrooks.com

For my mom.
You inspired this book.
If you ever thought I wasn't listening when you shared the
stories of your life growing up,
this book proves I was.

ACKNOWLEDGEMENTS

Where does one start when it comes to thanking the people who helped make a dream, a passion, a compulsion since childhood come to reality? I will do my best, but this book would double in size if I listed everyone who ever supported or inspired me. To you all…you are a part of this story, and all the stories that follow.

First, Anya, my daughter. It wasn't until you were born that I picked up my pen to return to my passion of writing. I did so because I wanted you to be proud of me and show you that you can also do what you dream of, not what others dream for you.

On equal footing is Jim Valade, my partner in everything. You supported me in every way possible and have always been as enthusiastic and excited about my writing as me. Thank you for every coffee and lunch you slid on my desk during the writing phase. Oh, and your 37 years as a Canadian police officer also came in handy for my endless questions.

My mom, Gail Brooks. Without you this book wouldn't exist. It was your stories that inspired this story and I know you'll recognize parts of Rose from your own childhood in Creighton Mine and all the other places your colourful and nomadic family took you.

Those whose support made this book happen: My sisters, Lorri Skellett and Kelly Brooks, who gave me unwavering support and have the conviction that I am so much more talented than I ever believed. Jill McAbe, you were the first person to introduce me as an author and you never stopped pushing me further, mentoring me, and sharing what you know as an author and an entrepreneur. Diane Simpson, my author/illustrator friend whose shared conversations about craft and character over coffee impacted many of my creative decisions. Lynn McAuliffe, my cousin who grew up in Creighton Mine. It was like having my own personal historian on speed dial. Meghan Cooke, my dearest friend who never let me quit or make excuses for what I wanted to accomplish because you never doubted I could.

Those whose talents helped this book come to light: Beren Davis, the graphic artist who went into my brain and pulled out the cover of my dreams. Allister Thompson, my editor who went above and beyond, took my story deeper, and gave me confidence to keep going. Avan Patel, not only a talented photographer but a historian who shared his knowledge and passion of 1950's photography.

There are some people who impact your life and never really know it. One of those is Tanis Rideout, an amazing poet and novelist. As a writer-in-residence she took an interest in my writing, pushing me to not give up, which inspired in me the belief that I could do this.

To everyone I've worked with at LHSC who supported me by coming to see my plays, read my articles, and always asked, "How's the book going?" or "Let me know when your book comes out," well, since you asked…here it is.

PROLOGUE

VICTOR

July 11, 1951

Solving a murder isn't that hard. People are rarely killed by strangers, which is why I start by looking at those closest to the victim. I talk to their friends and family, apply a little pressure, and eventually the cracks begin to show. The real challenge is proving a murder. That's where the work comes in.

I rubbed at my eyes, not needing to look in the mirror to see how red they were. I was driving from Sudbury to a nickel mining town, aptly named Creighton Mine. It was day one of a murder case, and I'd only had four hours of sleep. I hoped the fresh air from the open windows would revive me. The drive to and from Creighton would be my routine most days until the case was solved. Hopefully this would be one of the easier ones – a jilted lover, a crime of passion, the usual story.

I let go with a yawn so wide it felt like I pulled a muscle. Nightmares were rare these days, but I probably shouldn't have listened to the news before going to bed. All the talk of the

Korean War was probably what dug up the old memories I preferred to keep buried.

Six years had passed since the Second World War ended. The world was moving on, focused on progress; new cars, new homes, and creating families to replace the millions of people we lost. I wanted to move on too, but the things I saw and did in France were hard to forget.

I loosened my tie a little. The day was warm, but I didn't mind. Summer was short in Northern Ontario, and before you knew it, you'd be waking up to frost. I'd only been in Sudbury a few years but quickly adjusted to the differences. After leaving the military, I wanted a change and thought a quieter life up north would be a nice change from Toronto.

The Sudbury Provincial Police hired me and even promoted me to Detective. But if I'd done my homework, I'd have realized Sudbury wasn't the remote and peaceful town I'd expected. It had a real Wild West feeling with miners, lumberjacks, gamblers, and prostitutes. Throw in some booze and you had a crime rate that rivalled cities twice its size.

I glanced at the piece of paper with the directions I'd been given. I'd just passed the last landmark. A sign that read Meatbird Lake. Up ahead I could see the top of a mine shaft which signalled I'd finally reached Creighton Mine.

As I turned onto the road leading into town, I was determined to solve this case quickly. With a population of about two thousand, it wouldn't be easy for a murderer stay hidden. Maybe if I focused on the case I could push those old memories aside, forget the past, and move on.

ONE

ROSE

July 1, 1951

"She's coming!" a boy's voice yelled from across the street. Everyone held their breath and waited for the car to come turn the corner, but when it did, it wasn't the one we were waiting for. My insides felt like they'd flown up high, then dropped really fast.

I flexed my toes inside my shoes. They were all cramped from standing in one spot for so long. School had only been out for summer holiday a few days, and already it felt uncomfortable to wear shoes.

A sturdy Packard stopped just past our house, and Hugh McLellan got out. He was wearing his usual pressed clothes without any stains, rips, or patches, and his hair was freshly buzzed. I could tell by the white line around the edges where the sun hadn't yet reached it.

"Hey, Mikey. Hey, Rose," he said as he passed by. Hugh was one of the few people who took notice of me and always said hi, but he didn't stop. He made his way straight over to my sister, Olive, and took a seat on the porch step beside her. I looked out over the street. There was a tingly feeling in the air like the last day of school or a carnival. Even people who didn't live in our neighbourhood came by.

We lived in an area called the Dardanelles. I always thought it was a pretty name. Like a lot of things in the town of Creighton Mine, it was brought from somewhere else. The Dardanelles were a place in Turkey. I heard it was the name of either a castle or a waterway, but the houses here definitely weren't castles, and the only water nearby was from the Albion Pond. It's called that because it was behind the Albion family's house, and they'd lived there forever.

I leaned my chin on the wooden railing and picked at the flaking paint. I couldn't believe so many people had come out to welcome my oldest sister Virginia back home. This was the biggest event to happen in Creighton Mine since our baseball team won the Monell Cup two years before. Our street buzzed with voices, people yelling from porch to porch, while little kids chased each other in circles.

Virginia had moved to Los Angeles, California four years earlier. I was only five years old at the time, and this was her first visit back home. I barely remembered her, and most of what I did know came from the occasional letters and postcards she'd sent home. June, my oldest sister, would read them out loud at the kitchen table. I'd close my eyes and try to picture the paved streets, palm trees, and homes with lawns, fences, and a car in every driveway that Virginia would write about.

4

"Is she here yet? Has your sister arrived?" Cheryl Gaston asked as her bike skidded to a stop in front of Olive and Hugh.

Mikey, June's son, which made him my nephew, piped up, "Oh, yeah, she's inside, and now we're all just waiting here for Santa Claus to come to town." He snickered and elbowed his buddy, Joey, sitting beside him. Olive turned around and pinched him hard.

"So, she's not?" Cheryl asked in her mouse-like voice.

Mikey rolled his eyes but kept quiet and rubbed the red spot on his leg.

"She'll be here soon," Olive said. I watched how the scarf tied about her ponytail bobbed when she talked. Olive always dressed smart, even though her clothes were old or hand-me-downs. She used the money she made working at the drug store to buy new buttons, ribbons, and other things to spiff up what she had. I'd snuck an old scarf from mom's drawer earlier that morning and tied it up in my ponytail just like Olive's.

"You must be ready to burst with excitement," Cheryl squeaked. "Can you imagine living in Los Angeles, California?" She drew out the words like it was a magical land that didn't really exist. "Your sister is the luckiest girl ever. I bet she knows loads of famous people. Can I come round for a visit while she's here? I am just dying to know all about her life."

"I'll see, but plenty of people want to visit, and of course she and I will be together most of the time. She's sharing my room, so I expect we'll stay up late talking all about Hollywood and all the famous people she's met," Olive said.

This was the first I'd heard about Virginia sharing mine and Olive's room. That meant I'd get to stay up late talking too. I was dying to find out if she'd ever seen Judy Garland and Mickey Rooney.

"She's coming! She really is this time. Look, here they come," a girl in the crowd yelled out.

Mikey's dad, Oscar, had borrowed his boss's car to pick Virginia up from the bus station in Sudbury. As soon as the car came around the corner, even more people came out of their front doors up and down the street and joined the crowd that was already there.

I was as excited as everyone else but also worried. What if Virginia turned out to be just ordinary, like me? What would everyone say then? She was only a Boyle, after all, and other than Olive, who was popular and pretty, the rest of us were nothing special.

The car slowed down and stopped in front of our house. I tried to smooth out the wrinkles in my dress, but I hadn't wanted to ask Mom to iron it, since she'd been so busy the past few days getting everything ready for Virginia's visit.

The car stopped right in front of me, and Oscar stepped out. He hustled over to open the door to the back seat. I held my breath along with everyone else. When my sister June, Oscar's wife, stepped out, a disappointed groan rose from the crowd. No one had gathered on our street to see June McFaye. Then Oscar reached back into the car, and a woman's white glove was placed into his hand. From where I stood, I saw a stockinged leg that ended in a bright red-heeled shoe appear.

The world was moving in slow motion. Then Oscar stepped back and completely blocked my view. I wanted to yell at him to move. All I could see was a tanned arm as it waved at all the people who were shouting greetings.

Finally, Oscar shifted to the side, and I saw the prettiest dress I'd ever seen in real life. It was white, with a full skirt, red roses around the hem, and a red sash tied around a tiny waist. Her hair was dark, like mine and Mom's, but styled in light waves. She reached into her handbag and pulled something out. Everyone started waving madly, and the kids yelled "Cheese!"

Then she turned around, and all I could see was the camera that blocked her face. I stared open-mouthed as she snapped a few pictures of us. Then it was gone, and I finally saw her, and, at that moment, I knew no one could ever say they were disappointed the day Virginia Boyle returned to town.

She was beautiful, like a picture in a magazine. I recognized a Boyle-ness to her, but she was like a perfect version of us; hair in the latest style, skin tanned in a way that just doesn't happen in Northern Ontario. She glowed like she saw summer all year long. I couldn't believe I was related to someone so glamorous.

Her eyes moved quickly over everyone on the front steps, like she was looking for something. The door squeaked open behind me, and Virginia's attention went straight over my head.

"Momma!" she called out and rushed past me, leaving behind the smell of flowers I couldn't name.

"Look at all the fuss you've caused, Ginny," my mom said, gesturing to the street. "Come inside. The whole neighbourhood is gawking."

7

Oscar pushed past me and knocked my shoulder with the luggage he struggled to carry. Mikey and Olive followed, each carrying a smaller case. I peeked into the trunk of the car, but there wasn't anything else to take in. I closed it and looked around the street, taking in the amount of people who'd gathered.

For the past few weeks, all everyone in town talked about was Virginia Boyle, who'd moved all the way to Los Angeles, where the movie stars and famous people lived. Growing up, lots of people talked about leaving Creighton, going on adventures to see the world, but very few ever did. Once, I asked June why she hadn't taken off somewhere like Virginia did. She said once you get married, you put your fanciful ideas away and get down to business of being a wife and mom. She seemed pretty happy being both.

I guessed that meant if Virginia got married, she'd move back to Creighton Mine. I couldn't picture a regular family living in Los Angeles. I thought it was only for movie stars and young pretty people, like I'd see in *Life Magazine*.

"Olive is the luckiest girl. I wish I had a sister like that," Cheryl Gaston said to Hugh. Over their heads, I could see the crowd had broken up. People walked back towards their homes in small groups. I knew for days, maybe years, people would talk about the day Virginia Boyle came back to town.

"Are you coming in?" I asked Hugh. He had an open invitation to come to our house anytime. He was Olive's oldest friend, and Mom and Dad liked that Olive hung out with him.

They thought he had good manners and hoped it would rub off on Olive and the rest of us.

"That's okay. I wouldn't want to get in the way; it's a special day for your family," he said, even though he looked at the door like he wanted to go in.

I shrugged and saw a group of kids playing in the street. I waved at them, but they didn't notice me. I climbed the front steps and turned the door handle to push it open, but it didn't budge. I tried again and leaned all my weight against it, but still nothing. It had to be blocked somehow because our front door didn't have a lock. I knocked and waited. Then I knocked again, but no one came.

I went down the stairs, around to the back of the house, and in through the kitchen. Laughter and raised voices poured from the front room. It sounded like a stranger's house. Normally ours was, well, not quiet, just not as light as it felt now. I slipped into the room, took a seat against the wall, and rested my chin on my knees.

Virginia sat on the couch, surrounded by my family. I couldn't take my eyes off her perfectly coloured red lips. Olive had of course claimed a spot beside Virginia, and for the first time she wasn't the prettiest girl in the room.

June was so excited that her knees were bobbing up and down. My niece, Maggie, who is only a year younger than me, sat tucked in beside June. She stared at Virginia's fancy dress with her mouth hanging open just a little. Dad laughed and swiped at some tears, which usually only happened when he was well into his cups. Even my brother Angus had stopped by for a visit, which didn't happen often because he worked for the mine one town over in Copper Cliff.

Everyone threw questions at Virginia, which she tried her best to answer, but I barely heard what was said. I was too caught up in watching her every movement, the way her hair bounced, and how her lips matched her nails, which matched her dress and shoes. It was so hard to believe she was my sister. I barely remembered her, since I was only five years old when she left. She seemed so much different than the rest of us. I never would have thought she came from Creighton; she was exactly what I thought a big-city girl would look like. But every once in a while, she'd say something, and her voice would tickle at my memory like, yeah, I did know her.

When I looked back up at her face, I was shocked to see her staring back at me with a kind of frown.

"Rose? Is that really you? You cannot be my little Rose?" She didn't say it like she was teasing me, more like she was confused.

"I'm nine," I said, caught by surprise.

Virginia tilted her head and studied me like she wasn't sure if I was telling the truth.

"Rose, go say hello to your sister," Mom said, so I pushed myself up off the floor and walked over to stand in front of her but stopped a couple steps away.

"Hi," I said, standing stiffly in front of her.

She opened her arms to me. "Can I have a hug?" she asked with a little smile.

I glanced down at my wrinkly dress with the dirt on the hem. It didn't feel right to brush up against her pure white one.

10

"For goodness' sake, Rose, hug your sister," Mom snapped from the doorway.

"It's okay." Virginia dropped her hands into her lap. "You know, last time I saw you, you couldn't pronounce my name and always called me Dinny."

"She probably still can't pronounce it." Olive smirked at me, and I felt my face heat up. I was used to Olive's jabs, but I didn't want her to make me look silly in front of Virginia.

"I didn't recognize you, sweetie. You're all grown up now." Virginia nibbled on her bottom lip. "It's okay," she said so quietly I wasn't sure if she was talking to me or herself.

Goosebumps jumped out on my arms when she called me "sweetie." I could tell she really meant it, and no one else called me that in such a warm voice.

Mom clapped her hands, which startled me. "Well, dinner won't make itself," she said and began giving orders to everyone. Oscar and Angus grabbed the suitcases from where they'd blocked the front door and took them to the back bedroom. Mom and June headed to the kitchen.

"I'll go change, then I can help with dinner too," Virginia called out, going towards my room but not before running her finger lightly down my cheek which made me shiver in a nice way. My feet automatically turned to follow her, but Olive stepped in front of me, crossed her arms, and looked down at me.

"Where do you think you're going?" she demanded.

"With Virginia. I'm gonna show her around our room so she knows where everything is," I said, feeling quite grown-up.

11

"Forget it. While she's here, it's her room and mine. You're sleeping in Mom and Dad's room on the trundle bed. So, stay out." She pointed at me. "And I've told you before, stop copying me." She eyed the scarf in my hair, then turned and walked away.

I reached up and yanked the scarf from my ponytail. What did I care? If I was going to copy anyone, it would be Virginia. She was so much better than bossy Olive.

I knew it wouldn't be any use trying to get into my room. I'd have to wait to get my own time with Virginia, and when I did, I would finally ask her all of the questions I had about her glamorous life in Los Angeles and why she left Creighton in the first place. And I'd study her, watch the way she walked, talked, and dressed so I could learn how to become like her. A person everyone wanted to be around and who no one would ever forget.

TWO

I held the sugar pie up to my nose and took a deep sniff. It smelled like warm sweetness. I moved a few plates to make room on the side table for the pie. I'd never seen so many delicious things in one place. There were baked goods and sweets from all different parts of the world. One of the best things about Creighton was all the different families who came to Canada to work in the mine. They came from places like Finland, Poland, Italy, Scotland, Ireland, Holland, and so many other countries, and they brought their cooking with them.

Our living room table was overflowing with baked goods from all these different places: pulla loaf, babka cake, cannoli, butter tarts, blueberry grunt, with still more in the kitchen. Virginia had only been home for a day, and so many women had descended on our house to welcome her.

I hadn't had a chance to say much more than good morning to her. Olive was glued to her side like she owned her. June and Maggie, who lived next door to us, were over for breakfast even before I woke.

I didn't expect it would be so hard to get time to visit with my own sister, and now our house was bursting at the seams with more people than I'd ever seen in it.

The older ladies sat in the kitchen with Mom and June. Even though June was only a couple years older than Virginia, she had a husband and a couple of kids, which made her seem much older than the young women who surrounded Virginia in the living room. I volunteered to answer the door. That way I could see who came and what they brought. I also really wanted to hear the conversations. I was pretty good at listening in. My favourite radio show was *The Shadow* about a mysterious crime fighter who could cloud men's minds to make himself invisible so the bad guys couldn't see him. I learned a lot about spying from him.

Normally, I wasn't too interested in what grown-ups said, but this was different because I got to hear Virginia talk about her life in Los Angeles. I found out she worked as a photographer's assistant there. It sounded really neat but the women who were visiting mostly wanted to know about men, shopping, and movie stars.

Virginia was dressed a lot different than the day before. She wasn't wearing bright lipstick or fancy clothes. A scarf held her hair off her face, tied at the side. Olive couldn't stop gushing about her denims. She said she'd only seen those kinds in magazines, and you couldn't even get them in Sudbury.

The front door opened, and a voice called out, "Toodle-oo." I rushed over to greet Paulette Carmichael. She looked fancy in a blue dress, like she was going to church, but her hands were empty. She was the first person who hadn't brought something.

"Hi, Rose." I recognized Miss Boone, whose head peeked out from behind Paulette. She had been my third-grade teacher until halfway through the year when she left to get married.

"Hi, Miss Boone…I mean Mrs. Clarke. Hi, Paulette."

Paulette brushed past me, but Mrs. Clarke held out a basket covered with a cloth. The bottom was warm.

"Follow me," I said. Paulette had gone ahead, but Mrs. Clarke let me lead her. She walked with a bit of a waddle because of her big belly, so I slowed down a bit. She had been my favourite teacher. She always smelled like honey, and when she laughed it felt like an invitation to join in.

"Lorelei! Paulette!" Virginia called out as soon as she saw the two women. She crossed the room with her arms wide open and a big smile. All three of them squealed and bobbed up and down.

"Oh my, Lorelei, look at you." Virginia patted Mrs. Clarke's belly. "And Paulette, you look as wonderful as ever. Come sit over here." She took them each by the hand to the sofa. "Lorelei, you look about ready to bust."

"I am, but I promise not to bust in your front room today," Mrs. Clarke said, and all the other women laughed.

"My head is spinning as I try to keep up with all the changes in Creighton. I want to hear everything from the both of you," Virginia said, grabbing a pillow to put behind Mrs. Clarke's back when she sat down.

Although Virginia had been mostly talking to Mrs. Clarke, Paulette jumped right in. For the next few minutes everyone listened to her talk about her job at the diner and breaking up with Swifty Hudzik. Then she went quiet and shoved her hand right in front of Virginia's face. My sister squinted at Paulette's hand and looked confused by what she saw.

15

"Don't you just love it?" Paulette gushed, and the room went silent. Everyone looked back and forth between the two as if they were waiting for something.

Virginia took a deep breath and folded her hands over her chest. "Well, Paulette, it is a lovely ring." I waited too because it sounded like she had more to say, but she didn't.

"I know, isn't it?" Paulette turned her hand around to admire her own ring, like she'd never seen it before. "That's right. I am officially engaged and very soon to become a wife and probably not long after a mother too." She reached over and patted Lorelei's belly.

"Gregory?" Virginia said, although it didn't really sound like a question.

"Someone already told you." Paulette pouted.

"Nope, just a lucky guess," Virginia said with a light smile. "Well, congratulations, Paulette. I'm so happy for both of you." Something changed immediately in Virginia, like when there's a laugh bubbling up in you. "And that is a beautiful ring."

Virginia then shifted in her seat to face Mrs. Clarke. "Well, Lorelei, I'd say your news is just as exciting as Paulette's."

"Well, where to start?" Mrs. Clarke blushed. "Dr. Worley says I have another two weeks, but I think it will be sooner. Obviously, I'm not teaching anymore, which I do miss, but getting the nursery ready, keeping house, and managing Jefferson keeps me plenty busy."

"Jefferson?" Virginia's voice dropped.

"Oh, yes, I guess I forgot that part." Lorelei laughed. "I am Mrs. Jefferson Clarke now."

16

"And soon you'll be wife to the principal when Miss Wallace retires," Paulette piped in.

"Oh, nothing is official, Paulette, but, well, Jefferson is well suited for the job." Mrs. Clarke beamed. "Since you left, Virginia, Jefferson was promoted to vice-principal. I'm so proud of him. He really is popular with the students."

"I must say, so many changes in these past few years that I'm having a hard time wrapping my mind around it all. And you, Lorelei, married our old teacher. Who would have guessed?" Virginia looked around the room, and some of the women raised their eyebrows like they were sharing a secret.

"Yes, but that was a long time ago. We were work colleagues for almost two years while I was teaching." Mrs. Clarke's cheeks turned a pretty pink.

"Well, congratulations on…everything. To both of you." Virginia waved her hand at Mrs. Clarke and Paulette. "Now, if you'll excuse me for a moment, I'll go check if there's more tea coming." Virginia walked straight to the kitchen.

Mrs. Clarke folded her hands and looked down at them while everyone else talked around her, Paulette loudest of all as she continued to show off her ring.

I took the still-warm basket into the kitchen and added it to the growing table of goodies. Virginia wasn't anywhere to be seen. I looked out the screen door and there she was, out back alone. I slipped outside.

Virginia stood near the outhouse, her arms folded, and I could see she was biting the inside of her cheek.

"Hey," I said softly, not wanting to startle her.

She turned to me. "Oh, hi, sweetie."

There it was again. The tingle.

"There sure are a lot of people who want to see you," I said and stood beside her. "You're really popular."

Virginia laid her arm lightly over my shoulders. I hesitated for a few seconds, then leaned into her; it just felt right.

"They just want to know about Los Angeles. It's not really me they're interested in," she said, but I didn't believe it for a minute. I knew I certainly was interested in her.

"Is it nice to be home and see all the changes that have happened?" I looked up at her.

"Well, it's seeing you and the family that makes me happy." She squeezed my shoulder. "But it's also kind of odd. Everything is so familiar, but I feel like a stranger, like I don't really belong here anymore. Some things have changed in ways I never would have guessed."

"But you do belong here," I blurted out.

"You are the sweetest girl ever, my little Rose." She pinched my nose lightly, which made me giggle. "Okay," she said and turned back to the house and clapped her hands. "As they say, 'Once more unto the breach, dear friends, once more.' Let's go." She strode back to the house like a soldier marching.

I stayed where I was. I'd had enough of grown-up talk, so I sat on the back step and turned my face up to the sun. I heard the door from June's house open.

"I snuck us some cannoli before they all disappeared." Maggie plopped down beside me and held out a pastry overflowing with sweet, creamy filling. "I hid a few at the back of the fridge for

Dad when he gets home from work. He loves them as much as we do."

"Thanks," I said, taking one for myself.

"We'll have enough sweets to last for weeks," Maggie said, then laughed. "Hey, that kind of rhymed."

I laughed too. Even though she was a year younger than me, Maggie was my best friend. You can be family and friends at the same time. In fact, that was the best way because they know you so well and they're always around. I thought of her more like a cousin or even a sister than my niece. It was the same with Mikey.

"Mom took Mikey home 'cause he ate so many sweets. She was afraid he would throw up everywhere," Maggie said.

I licked the last of the filling off my fingers.

"You wanna go and play on Slater's Rock?" she asked. "We can play Easter Parade. You can be Judy Garland and I'll be Margaret O'Brien."

Normally I'd have jumped at the chance. Judy Garland was my favourite movie star, but I just didn't want to leave the house. I knew it was dumb, but I had this fear that if I left, Virginia might not be there when I got back. I couldn't bear that thought.

"Not now. My tummy is a little sore too. Maybe I ate too many sweets," I lied.

"Okay." Maggie sighed then stood up. "Will you tell Momma I went to play, and I'll be back for dinner?"

"Sure. See ya."

Maggie skipped off in search of someone who wanted to play. She wouldn't have any trouble. All you had to do was wander any of the roads or go to the regular areas the kids hung out, and you'd eventually find someone else looking to play. Usually a whole group of kids.

I went back inside, grabbed a stool, and spent the rest of the afternoon watching Virginia. I listened to every detail of her life in Los Angeles. It sounded like the most wonderful place ever and so different from life here. I began to picture what it must be like and how great it would be to see it for myself with Virginia taking me to see all the sights. For the first time ever, I started to really think about the world outside of Creighton and that it might be worth exploring some day.

THREE

By late afternoon, the last of the guests were gone. I put a half-filled plate on the kitchen table when I heard the click of Virginia's camera. I looked up and saw it pointed at me.

"Sorry I didn't smile. I didn't know you were going to do that," I said and tucked the loose strands of my hair into the scarf I'd tied at the side of my head.

"That's the whole point, Rosey. I like to take pictures of people just going about their lives," Virginia said.

"But I wasn't doing anything interesting," I answered, secretly pleased at her nickname for me.

"Well, you are interesting to me," she said and quickly snapped another picture. "I'm going to be a famous photographer and have my pictures in *Life Magazine* someday, just like Dorthea Lange."

"Oh," I said, impressed, even though I had no idea who Dorthea Lange was.

"And you think *Life Magazine* wants a picture of Rose clearing the dishes?" Mom said, pursing her lips at me.

Virginia lowered her camera. The back door banged as June came in.

"How is Mikey?" Mom asked.

"I gave him a spoon of castor oil. He'll be fine, and maybe he'll learn not to make such a pig of himself," June said.

The camera clicked again.

"Stop it, Virginia. I'm a mess." June laughed and smoothed her hand over her perfectly pulled-back hair. She always wore it in the same tight bun. Her hair was the same dark colour as mine, Mom's, and Virginia's, but she was the only one who had inherited Dad's freckles. It was the one thing that kept her from looking older than she was. All my life June had been a grown-up, and I just couldn't picture her as a young person.

"Hey, Virg, want me to help you pick out something to wear for your big interview tomorrow?" Olive jumped in.

Before leaving for work in the morning, Dad had told Virginia that Eddie Szymanski, the local reporter for the *Inco Triangle* newspaper, wanted to do a story on her.

"Oh, Pop, no, I would really rather not. I don't have anything to say." Virginia stopped eating and seemed genuinely unhappy.

"My shift supervisor said the big bosses suggested it, which means I can't say no," he nodded at her, "which means *you* can't say no."

I couldn't understand why she wouldn't want to be in the *Inco Triangle*. People all the way to Frood and Copper Cliff would read about her and see her picture. I couldn't imagine anything better than being that famous.

I once had my picture in the *Triangle* when our class put on a Christmas play. I'd auditioned for every part and was eventually cast as a townsperson in *A Christmas Carol*. They wrote a story about our play in the newspaper, and in the picture, you could see half of me standing behind a fake lamppost. I saved the paper and kept it in the bottom of my drawer.

"Well, what do you say, Virg? Can I choose your outfit for you? You'll want to look super glamorous for the pictures," Olive asked again.

"Thanks, Olive, but I just want to get it over with. Regular clothes will do fine," she said, pointing at what she had on. "Unfortunately, this is the real me."

"There's nothing wrong with taking a little effort in your appearance, Ginny. You're representing our family, and I expect you won't say anything to embarrass us." Mom crossed her arms and stared at Virginia, who looked right back at her.

For my mom, embarrassing the family was the worst kind of sin. I sometimes thought she was more concerned with the neighbours seeing us doing something wrong than us actually doing it.

"You don't have to worry. I am perfectly aware of what is expected of me." Virginia turned her back and fiddled with her camera.

"How about we get all these goodies put away so we can start on dinner, eh?" June jumped in.

"I'll help," I said, wanting a reason to stay in the kitchen and close to Virginia. I moved to the other side of the table, where Olive was. She bumped me hard with her hip.

"Move it. You're always in the way," she sneered.

"Mom," I called out, even though I knew it wouldn't do me any good.

"Rose, go and fetch Maggie. Where is she?" Mom asked.

"She took off to play somewhere," I said.

"Go find her then."

I wanted to say no, but I didn't want Virginia to think I was a pest, and you just didn't say "no" to Mom.

"Hey, Rose."

I turned back to look at Virginia.

"I was wondering if you'd like to come with me for the interview on Wednesday? I'm gonna be pretty nervous and would feel a lot better if I had someone with me," Virginia said with the coolest wink I'd ever seen anyone make.

"I'll go with you, Virg. Rose won't be of any use. She barely speaks, and she's just a kid. You don't want to get stuck with her," Olive said.

Virginia straightened up, which made me realize she was at least a head taller than Olive. "I wouldn't be stuck with her," she said in voice that was as haughty as Scarlett O'Hara's in *Gone with the Wind*. "Well, Rose, what do you say? Will you come with me?"

Olive glared at me; her jaw clamped tightly. I'd never heard anyone but Mom put Olive in her place before.

My stomach and chest felt like someone had just blown up a balloon inside me. "Sure," was all I could squeak out, then I ran out the back door. My feet flew over the rocks as I leaped from one to another, seeking the usual spots where the kids of Creighton would play. At that moment, I felt like I could fly.

Virginia, the prettiest, most popular person in town, wanted me to go with her. For the first time ever, I got picked first. Out of all the people she could have chosen, she chose me. Now I knew what it felt like to be special.

FOUR

I found Maggie catching frogs at Albion's Pond with a couple of other kids. On the way home, I told her that Virginia asked me to go with her for the interview.

"Can I go too?" She pressed her hands together and jumped up and down.

The last thing I wanted was to share Virginia with anyone, even Maggie. "She's only allowed to bring one person to the interview, sorry."

I felt kinda bad lying to her, but Maggie got her own special days. Her dad would sometimes take just her to the candy store, and I know on rainy days she'd sit with June and they'd read books together. My mom didn't have time for things like that, and Dad was always tired after work. I guess it was because they were old parents who'd gone through more kids than Oscar and June had.

Maggie dragged her feet the rest of the way home but felt better when I told her we were having meatloaf for dinner. That was one of my favourite things about Maggie; she could never stay sad very long. She had too much happy in her.

After dinner, we all moved into the living room. Oscar stayed home with Mikey. The castor oil was doing its job and June said he puked all over himself. My older brother, Angus, also couldn't make it because he worked and lived in Copper Cliff, and he had already visited yesterday when Virginia first got here.

Everyone grabbed the place that was just theirs. Dad sat in his sturdy chair beside the radio, and Mom perched on the footstool onto which she'd cross-stitched flowers. June was at one end of the chesterfield, while Maggie and I sat criss-cross on the floor, waiting patiently. Virginia was also on the chesterfield with a collection of bags and boxes at her feet.

"Virginia, you know you didn't need to do this, wasting your money on gifts none of us need," Mom said.

"That's the point of a gift, Mom. It's because someone wants to give you something, not because they have to," Virginia said in a low voice. From a small brown paper bag, she removed something wrapped in tissue and handed it to Dad. He carefully unwrapped two short glasses and held one up.

"A friend of mine is a cigarette girl at the Mocambo Club. All the stars go there. She got these for me." She pointed at the words *The Mocambo* etched into the glass.

"Well, look at that, Helen. Won't I be the most sophisticated man about town? Thank you, dear." Dad held one of the glasses and rubbed his thumb over the etching.

"You're welcome. Now, Mom, you are so hard to buy for," Virginia said and picked up a large, circular box.

"Then why waste your money on me? I don't need anything."

"Still, you deserve a lot." Virginia handed the box to Mom, who just stared at it like the box was the gift.

"Go on, Mom. Open it," Olive said, bouncing up and down.

When she lifted the lid, I could see gold lettering that said *May Co. Wilshire*.

"Oh my," Mom said, staring inside.

"What? What is it, Grandma?" Maggie called out.

When Mom continued to just stare in the box, Virginia went over and took out a small flat black hat, which she set on Mom's head and fastened with a pearl pin. There was a dark green feather held in place by a rhinestone. Virginia pulled down the short black netting so it just covered half of Mom's eyes.

"Ohhhh, Mother," Olive gasped.

Mom sat stiffly. Then she reached up and touched it with her fingertips like it was made of glass and might break. I'd never seen her look elegant before. It drew attention to the bottom half of her face, which showed off her high cheekbones but hid the bags under her eyes.

"I want to borrow that!" June called out.

Then something amazing happened: Mom laughed. It sounded more like a cough, and she covered her mouth quickly, but not before I caught a glimpse of a smile.

The room felt light. I looked over at Virginia. She had made that happen. Somehow, she knew exactly what Mom must have dreamed of but would never say out loud to anyone. If I was given ten dollars and told I could buy my mom whatever she wanted, I would have picked out a new frypan or iron with a matching board. Never would I have picked out something pretty that didn't have a purpose other than looking good. It just wasn't Mom, but here she was with the most elegant thing I'd ever seen, and she liked it a lot.

"How do I look?" Mom asked, turning her head from one side to the other.

"You look like a movie star, Grandma!" Maggie yelled out.

"I think you look mysterious," I whispered, not recognizing the woman in front of me.

"It looks beautiful on you, Mom." Virginia's eyes sparkled, and with both her and Mom smiling, I noticed how similar their cheeks were.

"But where will I wear such a fancy hat in Creighton Mine?" Mom sighed, reached up, pulled out the pin, and took the hat off. "Virginia, you shouldn't have wasted your money on such an impractical gift." She stroked the feather lightly.

"It is possible someday you'll have an occasion to wear it." Virginia shrugged.

Mom grunted and placed the hat back into the box at her feet, but a ghost of a smile still hovered around her lips.

Virginia handed out the rest of the gifts. June got a blouse from the same store as Mom's hat. Maggie got a paper doll set with Hollywood-style gowns, and Olive squealed when she unpacked a sophisticated black and red purse. Gifts for Oscar, Mikey, and Angus were put aside for the next time she saw them.

I was really good. I acted happy for everyone else and didn't let on that I was going to burst as I waited for my turn. There was also a fear in the back of the mind that I wouldn't get anything. That when she was in Los Angeles, maybe she'd forgotten about me. Then Virginia reached down, picked up the biggest box, and put it on her lap. As she lifted it, I saw gold script that read *Madame Louise's Dress Shop*.

"Come on, Rose. Open it up," Virginia said, holding the box out to me.

At first, I didn't move. How could this be for me? The only gifts I got were usually socks and an orange for Christmas, and on my birthday June and Oscar would give me hard candies in a tin, and I'd eat just one a day to make them last. Mom didn't really believe in making a fuss just because it was the day you were born.

Everyone in the room stared with almost as much curiosity as me. I reached out and set the box gently on the floor. The tissue paper scrunched when I peeled it back layer by layer. I was already thinking about all the great things I could do with the box and the paper, and I hadn't even reached the gift part.

"Hurry up, Rose. I can't wait," Maggie said as she leaned over the top of the box.

Finally, at the last layer, I could see some red peeping through. I reached in and pulled out a dress. It was an exact copy of the rose dress Virginia wore the day she arrived.

"I hope you like it?" Virginia had her hands gripped under her chin.

"It's the most wonderful thing ever," I said, putting the dress back down to rub my hands hard against my shirt to remove any dirt from them. Then I stood up and held the dress in front of my body. I swung around in circles. The stiff material under the skirt made a delicious swishing sound. The sash was so silky. I couldn't stop myself from running my hand back and forth over it. I knew without ever going into the store that this dress was more beautiful than anything you'd find in Mrs. McGuire's shop in downtown Creighton.

"Can I put it on now?" I asked, looking between Mom and Virginia.

"Yes, of course," Virginia said, who looked as excited as I felt.

"Wait, bring it over here, Rose." Mom's voice sliced through my excitement.

I stepped over, and she pulled the sides of the dress tight against my waist. I looked down just as she yanked it from my hands. She reached inside, tugged at the tag, and frowned.

"What is it? What's wrong?" Virginia came over and kneeled beside Mom.

"What?" I asked, but no one paid any attention to me.

"It's too small." My mom held the dress out to Virginia like she'd done something wrong.

"What? Are you sure?" Virginia asked.

"I know Rose's size, Virginia. This is at least one size too small, maybe two. She'd bust the seams if she even tried to button it up, and there isn't enough material to alter it; it would just ruin it. Rose had a growth spurt over the past year."

Mom raised her eyebrows. I knew that look. It was when she was right and just waited for anyone to try to argue with her. At that moment, I wanted to. I wanted to tell her she was wrong, but instead I stood silent while tears immediately pooled and spilled down my cheeks. I looked at Virginia and saw her eyes were glassy and her nose had gone red.

"You could have told me," Virginia said, looking down at the dress, fingering the frill around the sleeve.

"Oh, so now it's my job, on top of everything else I'm responsible for? To keep you up to date every time someone grows an inch?" Mom pursed her lips.

"You know what I mean," Virginia said.

"It was an honest mistake. Kids grow so fast these days, you can't predict it," June jumped in.

"Virginia, you've been gone for years. Maybe if you'd asked me first, this wouldn't have happened," Mom said.

Virginia turned to me. "I'm so sorry, Rose. I should have known. I am the worst sister ever." She spoke softly, then hurried down the hall to my bedroom.

I looked at my dress lying in Mom's lap, and I was so mad at her. I was sure if she hadn't said anything, it would all have worked out. She didn't care how much this dress meant to me.

"Maggie, come over here." Mom waved her over.

"No, it's mine!" I blurted out, grabbing for my beautiful dress, but mom snatched it out of my reach.

"Rose, don't be ridiculous. It doesn't fit you. What do you want to do? Waste Virginia's money and keep it stuffed away in a box?" Mom snapped. "Whatever made her think a dress this fancy was a good idea for a kid?" She looked over at June, who stayed silent.

"Maggie already got the paper dolls. I won't have anything." I swiped at the tears that fell down my cheeks.

"Then you two trade. Maggie, give Rose the dolls, and you can have the dress," Mom said. "There, now everything is settled."

But it wasn't settled, and it wasn't fair. It wasn't just any dress. There were roses around the hem that Virginia picked out just for me. It was the most special thing anyone had ever given to me, and now Maggie would get it.

"Maggie, come," Mom barked like she was calling to a dog. Maggie glanced at me quickly, then away. She walked slowly over to the dress being held out to her. It slid easily over her head.

Maggie's hands moved back and forth over the silky sash at the waist. She tried to hide it, but I could see how much she loved the dress. How could she not? It hung loose on her and looked terrible.

"There," Mom said. "It's even a little loose, June, but that's good. She'll get a year or two from it. Maybe she could wear it for some of your special Catholic events."

"Sure, Mom. That'll be nice," June answered and kept her gaze from me.

No one looked my way, not even Olive, who would normally have called me a crybaby.

"Well, now that's sorted, I've got things to do. I can't sit around here all evening." Mom picked up her hatbox and took it upstairs to her room.

June lifted the dress over Maggie's head and returned it to the box, folding it gently. "Let's take this home, and we'll give Mikey his gift." Neither of them looked at me as they left.

"I'm going over to Cheryl's to show her my purse," Olive said, unable to hide the thrill in her voice.

I stood staring at my feet, unable to even lift my head that was so full of sadness. I felt all alone until a voice surprised me. I'd forgotten Dad was still there.

"I'm sorry about your dress," he said. "I know you feel bad, but I think your sister might feel even worse. Why don't you go tell her how much you like the paper dolls?" He gestured to the chesterfield, where Maggie had left the book behind.

I'd forgotten all about Virginia at that moment, and I didn't want her to feel bad too; after all, it was my fault for growing too much.

FIVE

I knocked on the bedroom door, even though it was my room.

"Who is it?" Virginia's voice sounded deeper and heavier.

"It's me, Rose." I pressed my mouth against the gap in the door, not wanting to raise my voice.

"Come in," she answered.

Virginia was lying on the bed with her arms wrapped around a pillow and her legs drawn up. I crawled onto the bed and laid my head on the pillow beside her.

"Thanks for the dress," I said. "It sure is pretty."

Virginia pulled the pillow over her face and mumbled something.

"What did you say?" I said.

She spoke again, but I still couldn't hear her, so I picked up the corner.

"I can't hear you, Virginia. You're all muffled."

She took the pillow off her face and looked at me with her puffy eyes.

"I said I'm sorry I'm such an awful sister."

"You're not an awful sister. The dress was perfect. I just ate too much this year," I told her.

She hiccupped, laughed, then opened her arms wide. I crawled in and laid my head between her neck and shoulder. I fit perfectly, but I wasn't really sure what to do.

"You're like a piece of wood, Rose." She laughed and pulled me in a little tighter.

We stayed like that for a while with her heartbeat loud in my ear. No one had ever held me like that before. If I skinned my knee, as I did a lot, I'd just wash it off and put a bandage on it myself. No kisses, hugs, or cuddles.

I never knew how wonderful it felt to curl against someone else. My body went all liquidy, like honey. I listened to Virginia breathe and tried to match mine to hers, in and out at the same time, like we were one person.

"You smell like a garden," I whispered, so relaxed I could have fallen asleep.

"Thanks, sweetie," her voice rumbled from her chest. It sounded funny, like she was speaking underwater. "It's called L'Air du Temps," she said. "Don't tell Mom, but an old boyfriend bought it for me. It's the bottle over there with the birds on it. You can have it if you want."

I thought about it for a second, but I liked how it smelled on her. "Thanks, but Mom says bugs are attracted to perfume, and blueberry season is coming, so I better not."

"I sometimes forget how different life is here. Still, I do feel awful about your gift. I have to make it up to you somehow."

"It's okay. Mom fixed everything. Maggie will have the dress, and I get the paper dolls." I tried to sound like I thought it was a good idea too.

"Yeah, Mom sure is good at fixing problems, isn't she?" She picked at a feather that was poking out of her pillow.

"I guess, but that's a mom's job: fixing and taking care of stuff."

Virginia reached over and tucked a loose strand of hair behind my ear. Her touch caused a delightful shiver.

"Yes, Rose, that's what they're supposed to do. You know what? I think I do have something I can give you." Virginia jumped off the bed and grabbed a black silk box with pink flowers on it from the dresser. She put it between us and opened the lid. Inside was a wonderful collection of sparkly jewellery. She dug through and pulled something out.

"My friend Sally and I like to go to the flea market on Saturdays. It's a great place to find a bargain. One time, Sally found this." She held out a necklace. It was a gold locket, round with a raised design on the front.

"What is that?" I pointed at the delicate image.

"It's a mermaid in the ocean. It's cute, but that's not why I bought it. Turn it over." She placed the locket in my hand. On the back in fancy letters were the initials *V.B.*

"See, it was meant to be. Virginia Boyle. Sally and I made stories up all day about who could have owned it. Virgil Buford. Vanessa Beauchamp." She lay back on the bed. "We had such fun that day. If you ever come visit me in Los Angeles, I'll introduce you to Sally. She works as a cigarette girl at a fancy club, and twice she sold cigarettes to Clarke Gable."

I couldn't stop my mouth from falling open. Clarke Gable was a real movie star, but even more amazing was what she had said: "If I ever visited her." Could it be possible?

"Here." Virginia held out her hand for the necklace. "Turn around and lift your hair."

I did as she said.

"You have beautiful hair. It's a lot like mine, if I do say so. There now, what do you think?"

I looked down at the locket. It was shiny, like a real treasure.

"Can I keep it?"

"Yup, it's all yours. You can keep VB right next to your heart." Virginia tapped on my chest.

"Neat. No one else will have anything like it." I was already planning on wearing it to school on the first day back.

"That's right. It's unique. Just like you." She touched the end of my nose, and I couldn't help laughing. Happiness was bubbling inside me, and I didn't even care about the dress anymore — well, not too much.

"Can I go show Maggie?"

"Sure, sweetie." Virginia leaned over and pulled me into a hug so tight, I could barely breathe, but I didn't mind. She let me go just as quickly and I jumped off the bed.

"Wait, Rose…"

I turned around and Virginia's head was tilted like she was thinking really hard about something. I wondered if she had changed her mind about giving me the necklace.

"What is it?" I asked.

"Rose, there's something…" She shook her head and laughed like she was being silly. "Never mind, go show Maggie your special necklace."

SIX

It felt like the sun was shining only on me and I was ten feet tall as I walked into the main shopping area of Creighton, just me and Virginia. On our way to the diner, we waved at Mr. and Mrs. Valenti, who owned one of the grocery stores in town. Virginia pressed the button on the camera that hung around her neck.

"Don't you have to look through your camera to take a picture?" I asked.

"Not with this one. I just shoot on instinct. Hey, if you'd like, I could teach you how to take pictures while I'm here. It's good to have other skills for when you go out in the world."

I wasn't quite sure what she meant by that; we were already out in the world in downtown Creighton Mine. I looked up at Virginia, still in awe that I was related to someone so pretty, kind, popular, and special.

"Do you take your camera everywhere you go?" I asked.

"Back home, not as much, but I'm hoping to do a retrospective on life in a mining town. Sort of like the town time forgot. *Life Magazine* loves that kind of thing." This time she took a picture of a couple of men in their overalls heading to Three Shaft.

I wasn't really sure what a retrospective was, but it explained why she disappeared for a few hours most afternoons with her camera. She must have been taking pictures. I couldn't imagine what would be very interesting in Creighton; other than Tank Hill or Slater's Rock, there wasn't much to see.

"Don't worry, we won't be here long," Virginia said as we got near the diner.

"I don't get why you aren't excited to be interviewed for the *Triangle*. Everyone will see your picture and read about you. You'll be famous," I said.

"I don't want to be famous. I want to be a professional photographer, and for that I have to be able to blend in and not be noticed."

"You mean like *The Shadow?*" I asked.

"Who?" She looked confused.

"You don't know *The Shadow?* It's only the best radio show ever. Lamont Cranston is a rich guy, but his alter ego is the crime-fighting Shadow who uses hypnosis so people can't see him."

She laughed. "Oh, I see. Well, I guess I'm a bit like The Shadow, but I'm not fighting crime. Instead, I want to expose the plight of the average person with my pictures."

"The average person? Don't you want to take pictures of movie stars?"

"Goodness no. They are the worst," she said.

Before I could ask any more questions, we reached the diner.

It was midafternoon and not very busy. I pulled Virginia over to a booth by the window so that anyone walking by would see me with her.

41

"Can I get a milkshake?" I asked Virginia.

"Of course. Anything for you, my little Rose."

From the corner of my eye, I saw a man get up from one of the seats at the counter and move towards us.

"Well, if it isn't little Ginny Boyle."

It was Gregory Hansen, the one who'd given the ring to Paulette Carmichael. A lot of the girls in town called him Gregory Handsome because of his blond hair and blue eyes.

"Hello, Gregory," Virginia said, but her voice sounded like it was caught in her throat.

"I wondered if we would run into each other." He didn't seem to notice me. He just stared at Virginia like he was searching her face for something. I wondered if she looked much different than when she used to live here.

"How are you?" Virginia said, sounding strangely formal.

"I'm good. Working for Inco, of course, but in the office. I'm planning on getting transferred to Sudbury soon. So, I guess you won't be the only one to get out of Creighton." He crossed his arms, and I noticed the muscles on his upper arms twitched occasionally.

"That's great, Gregory. I'm really happy for you."

I hoped one of the waitresses would show up to take my milkshake order.

"I'd like to hear about your adventures," Gregory said and gave her a sort of half smile, half frown.

"Oh, yeah, of course, that..."

A voice cut her off before she could finish.

"Hey, Virginia, what a nice surprise." Paulette Carmichael came over and slipped her arm into Gregory's. She was wearing her pink waitress's uniform that looked a bit too small for her.

"Hi, Paulette," Virginia said.

"What do you think? Don't we make the cutest couple?" she said and laid her head against Gregory's shoulder.

"You sure do," Virginia answered. Gregory kind of grimaced, like maybe Paulette was hanging on to him too tightly.

"Just last night I was telling Gregory about how exciting your life is in Los Angeles and how you couldn't wait to get back there. Creighton must feel like such a bore to you now. Oh, and how shocked were you to hear Lorelei had married Mr. Clarke? I can tell you it raised a few eyebrows in town when it happened, what with the age difference and all. Didn't it, honey?"

Paulette looked at Gregory, who wasn't paying attention and didn't answer her.

"I can't remember if I showed you my engagement ring or not." Paulette thrust her hand in front of Virginia and wiggled her finger with the small ring on it. "It will be nice to finally hang up my uniform so I can be a wife and, of course, mother."

Gregory grabbed Paulette's hand and shoved it down. "No one cares about your ring, Paulette. Come on, let's go."

Paulette's cheeks went red. "It is getting late, and I have a meal to make." She shrugged at Virginia.

"Paulette?" I spoke up, since no one seemed to have noticed me. "Can I get a strawberry milkshake?"

"My shift is over. You'll have to wait for your waitress," she said with pursed lips. "Anyway, we were just leaving. You know it's too bad you live so far away, Virginia, otherwise I'd invite you to the wedding."

Paulette had to hurry to catch up with Gregory, who was already opening the door. Just as she walked through, he turned his head to look back at the table, so I waved goodbye.

"I liked her ring, even though it's really small," I said.

Virginia smiled, leaned forward, and whispered, "Wanna know a secret?"

I nodded. No one ever shared secrets with me, except Maggie, and they weren't very interesting.

"Promise not to tell?" she said, holding up her pinky finger.

"I promise," I said, wrapping my finger around hers for an unbreakable pinky swear.

"That ring used to be mine," she said and sat back with a sneaky grin.

I couldn't stop my mouth from dropping open.

"In high school, Gregory was my boyfriend, and he bought that ring for me, but when we broke up, I gave it back. Maybe I should have kept it. It is very pretty." She looked down at her hand. I thought she was maybe imagining what it would look like on her finger. "Okay, let's get you that milkshake."

And all thoughts of rings and boyfriends went out of my mind as Virginia waved the waitress over for my order.

SEVEN

Just after the pink, frothy drink was put down in front of me, the bell over the door tinkled again. I turned around to see Eddie Szymanski limp in. He was the reporter from the *Inco Triangle* and easy to recognize. Eddie was a grown-up, at least twenty-something years old, but he looked more like sixteen. He was skinny and wore a brace on one leg from when he had polio as a kid.

"Hello, you must be Miss Boyle?" He bobbed his head at Virginia.

"Yes, I am, and this is my little sister, Rose." Virginia pointed at me.

Eddie turned to me. "Of course. Hi, Rose," he said, but I guessed he would never have known my name or who I was if Virginia hadn't told him.

He slid into the booth beside me, pulled out a notebook, and placed his camera on the table.

"Thanks for doing this, Miss Boyle." He continued to nod as he spoke, like he was agreeing to everything that was being said.

"Please call me Virginia. So, I see you use a Rolleicord camera too?" she said, pointing at Eddie's beat-up camera on the table and set her own beside it.

Eddie's eyes widened. I didn't know anything about cameras, but I could tell Virginia's was newer and in better shape than Eddie's. They immediately started talking about taking pictures, cameras, film, and other stuff I didn't understand. Virginia's face brightened, and she used her hands more when she talked about photography. It was like the way some boys would get really excited when they talked about their favourite hockey teams.

I paid more attention to my milkshake than their conversation. It was only the second time I'd had one at the diner. The first time was last year when Oscar brought Mikey, Maggie, and me here for dinner. There had been an accident at the mine, and one of the men on Dad's shift got killed. June told Oscar to get us out of the house and feed us. Any other time, Mom would have said it was a waste to buy food at a diner when we had perfectly good food at home, but this one time she didn't protest.

"So, is it okay if we get to the interview part now?" Eddie asked. He grinned like was having the time of his life.

"If we have to." Virginia looked over at me and made a funny face, which made me giggle.

Eddie asked her a whole bunch of questions that I'd never thought of asking but was really interested in hearing.

"When I first moved to Los Angeles, I got a job at a photography studio as a receptionist. He's an Austrian man, very temperamental. He had a new assistant who wasn't very good. One day he fired him, right on the spot, and I was the only one around, so I jumped in and helped with the shoot. From that day on he began training me as his assistant. I just love it. We mostly do portrait pictures in the studio, and I'm learning so much from him," Virginia said.

"Have you ever taken portraits of any famous people?" Eddie scribbled in his notebook as he spoke.

"Sure, we take portraits for some of the studios. Let's see, I've met Humphrey Bogart, Lauren Bacall, Claudette Colbert, Bing Crosby, Glenn Miller, and Ella Fitzgerald."

"Wow. What are they like?" Eddie asked the same question I was thinking.

"Mostly they're smaller in real life than you expect. After about ten minutes, they stop being movie stars and just seem like normal people. Some are shy, but some are rude or ignore you altogether."

"Who was the rudest one?" Eddie asked. His pencil hovered over the paper.

"One of the things you learn working in Hollywood is, if you want to keep your job, you never gossip or speak about the clients, especially the famous ones."

"Oh," Eddie and I said at the same time.

Eddie cleared his throat and looked down at his notes. "So, are you engaged or have a beau back in Los Angeles? Maybe an actor or something?"

Virginia pursed her lips like she was thinking about how to answer. "For the sake of the story, you can say I am not married or engaged at this time."

Eddie looked up at Virginia and smiled.

He asked a bunch more questions, mostly about how much she missed Creighton, her favourite memories, and the best part about being home. I was more interested in her life outside of Creighton. My drink was long gone by the time he asked his last question.

"Okay, I think I got everything I need for the story. Could we get a couple pictures outside?" he asked.

"All right. Let's get it over with," Virginia said but with a kind smile.

Outside, Eddie suggested Virginia should stand by the window of the diner.

"That could work." She squinted up at the sky. "But you'll most likely catch your reflection, plus the lighting is going to throw shadows all down my left side."

"Oh, right," Eddie said, his cheeks turning red. He looked around but couldn't seem to decide where to go.

"How about around the corner there? You'll be able to use the natural light." Virginia pointed to the right of the diner.

"Yeah, okay," he said.

I followed them around the corner. Virginia went to stand by the diner wall. "Rose, come here. Eddie, would you mind taking one of Rose and I together?" She tilted her head at him and smiled.

"Sure, of course, yeah," he said. I gave my best smile.

"Here, Rose, would you hold my camera?" Virginia lifted it over her head and held it out to me.

"Can I take a picture too?" I asked.

"Sure, hon." She showed me where to look and what button to press then stepped back against the wall. "How about this?" She said and stuck her tongue out the side of her mouth and crossed her eyes. The camera shook as I took the picture because I couldn't stop laughing.

Virginia leaned back against the building. Eddie took a couple of pictures on one side, then moved to the other. He was much more serious when he took pictures than Virginia was, and no one spoke.

There was a faint click, he'd wind the film, and then take a step forwards. Click, wind, step, over and over, as he got closer and closer Virginia. Her smile became tight, and her body stiffened until Eddie was only arm's reach away. Then she suddenly pushed herself from the wall, causing him to stumble back a bit.

"Okay, I'm sure you'll be able to find at least one picture that will work." She looked over at me and opened her eyes wide. I knew it was some kind of signal, but I wasn't sure what she was trying to say.

"Yeah, that's great, Virginia. Thanks. Um, I was hoping, maybe you and I could meet up sometime while you're in town, you know, to talk about photography and stuff," Eddie said, fiddling with his camera.

"Oh, gee, Eddie, I'm not sure I'll have much time. My family has me completely booked up with visits and such until I leave. Isn't that right, Rose?" Virginia said.

I racked my brain, wondering what visits I had forgotten about but not wanting to look dumb. "Um, yeah. Loads of them."

"Sorry, Eddie. You know how it is." She shrugged and gave Eddie a super-sweet smile.

"Yeah, I know how it is," he said, sounding like Mikey when June wouldn't let him do something he wanted to. Eddie bent over, snapped open his bag, and shoved his camera into it. "Thanks for your time." Then he limped around the corner like he was in a hurry to get somewhere.

As soon as he disappeared, Virginia sighed. "Well, that wasn't too painful. Come along, my little Rosey-posey. Let's get home before we run into anyone else."

She held out her hand, which I grabbed happily. We walked all the way home swinging our arms and singing Judy Garland songs like the two best sisters we were.

EIGHT

"Psst, Rose, Maggie. I need your help."

Maggie and I turned to see Virginia peeking at us from behind the screen door. She was looking out from the kitchen.

"Who are you hiding from, Virginia?" Maggie asked.

"Shhhh." Virginia motioned us into the house.

We left our marbles on the ground where we'd been playing. Once inside, we heard a knock at the front door.

"I'll get it!" I hollered and went to leave, but Virginia grabbed my collar and yanked on me. "Hey!" I stumbled backwards.

"Sorry, but it's Eddie Szymanski at the door. I need a favour from you girls." She paused, and Maggie and I both nodded. "Great, I need you to answer the door and tell him I've gone out, but you don't know where or when I'll be home. Can you do that?"

"You mean lie?" Maggie asked.

"Well, I guess but…"

"No problem." I cut her off. "The Shadow lies all the time, but it's always for good reasons."

"Exactly," Virginia said, "just like that."

There was another knock at the door, only harder this time. Virginia gave us a little push into the hall while she stayed hidden in the kitchen.

Eddie seemed surprised to see us when we opened the door. I was surprised to see him with his hair slicked back. He'd never worn it that way before, and it looked like it'd never move, not even in a tornado.

"Hey, Eddie," I said, while Maggie just stared at him.

"Oh, hi, um, is your Aunt Virginia in?" he asked.

"She's my sister, not my aunt," I answered.

"She's *my* aunt," Maggie piped in.

Eddie looked a little confused, but people often got that way about our family.

"Okay, well, is your sister," he looked directly at me, "is she home?"

"No," I announced.

He seemed to expect more, but I didn't know what he wanted.

"Okay, do you know where she is?"

"No," Maggie answered, just like I had before.

"You know, it's kind of funny that Creighton Mine is such a small town, yet it sure has been hard to find your sister. I'm starting to wonder if she's avoiding me," he said and looked back and forth between me and Maggie.

At first, I felt important because Virginia asked me to do this for her, but then I felt a bit bad. I knew what it felt like when other kids didn't include you or pretended they couldn't come out to play. I hoped that maybe grownups didn't get hurt feelings like kids did.

"She's pretty popular. Everyone wants to hang out with her," I said and hoped he would just think she was out with friends somewhere.

Eddie looked down at his shoe. "Yeah, I bet she is. Well, will you tell her I stopped by, again?"

"Yeah, okay," I said.

Maggie and I watched him shuffle down the road with his head hanging like an old basset hound.

"Is he gone?" Virginia's voice came from the kitchen.

"Yup, all gone," Maggie called, skipping back down the hall.

"Well, that deserves a reward. Come on, and I'll get you each a piece of pie."

Maggie and I sat down while Virginia fetched us a piece of pie from one of the many leftovers. We were doing our best to finish them all up before they went off.

"Hey, Virginia, don't you like Eddie?" I asked, still feeling bad for him.

"Sure, sweetie, I like him well enough, but there are some boys that, if you are too kind to them, get confused and think you want to be their girlfriend. They don't always know how to take a 'no.'" She gave us each a glass of milk to go with our pies. "You'll understand when you get older and the boys start chasing you for kisses."

Virginia bent over and gave Maggie a great big sloppy kiss on the cheek, which made her squeal with laughter.

"In less than a month I'll be sixteen years old. That's old enough to move out and get a job!" We all turned at the sound of Olive's raised voice coming in the front door. "Mom, please,

Virginia promised to help me get a job. I don't want to stay in Creighton forever."

"Oh, boy, here we go," Virginia said quietly.

Mom and Olive came into the kitchen, each carrying a bag from their trip to Valenti's grocery store.

"You are not mature enough to go running off to Los Angeles. Virginia was twenty when she left. I don't want to discuss it anymore. That's final." Mom pulled stuff from the bag and slammed them on the counter. The cans were especially loud. Maggie looked at me with raised eyebrows. I shrugged back. We knew enough to stay quiet if we wanted to hear what was going on.

"Will you talk to her, please?" Olive said to Virginia while pointing at Mom. "She doesn't understand. I can't live my life here. I need to get out of Creighton."

"This is your doing," Mom said, pointing a bunch of carrots at Virginia.

"It was Olive's idea, but, yes, I did say if you were okay with it, she could come live with me." Virginia spoke in a tone I would never dare, like she was challenging Mom.

"Well, you've been here exactly one week, and you're already mucking things up. That is so like you." Mom turned her back and continued putting things away.

"What's that supposed to mean?" Virginia folded her arms over her chest.

"You," Mom said without turning around, "have a habit of leaving messes behind for other people to clean up. This is just another example."

Virginia's arms dropped to her sides as she stared at Mom's stiff back. I thought she was going to say something, but instead she walked out of the kitchen. The only sounds were her footsteps going towards my bedroom and Mom angrily folding the paper grocery bag.

"Knock-knock." Everyone turned to Hugh, who had just come in the back door, smiling, not knowing he'd just walked into the middle of something. Although what it was, I didn't know. "Hello, everyone?"

Mom just shook her head and left the kitchen. Olive stood with her arms crossed, glaring after her.

"What's going on?" Hugh directed his question to me.

"Olive wants to go to Los Angeles and move in with Virginia," I said and pointed at Olive.

I picked up my plate of half-finished pie and threw the rest in the garbage, having lost my appetite. It couldn't be real. I was Virginia's favourite sister. If anyone should go to Los Angeles to live with her, it should be me.

"Is this true, Olive?" Hugh asked softly.

"Well, I wanted to, and Virginia wants me to, but Mom is being absolutely horrible and won't let me to go." Olive's eyes welled up.

Hugh let out a big sigh. "Well, mothers know best. But, hey, maybe you can visit her sometime. That would be fun. How about we take a walk, and I'll buy you an ice cream?"

First Los Angeles and then ice cream. Why did everything happen for Olive and never for me? Olive didn't say anything but stomped out the back door while Hugh scurried after her.

"Wanna finish our marbles?" Maggie asked, licking the cherry from her plate.

"No. I don't wanna play anymore," I said.

"Well, what do you want to do then? We could colour or play with the paper dolls Virginia brought."

"I don't want to do anything right now."

What I really wanted was to go and talk to Virginia and convince her to take me instead of Olive, but I needed to get her alone for that.

"Fine, I'll go see if Dottie's home. She's always fun." Maggie slid off the chair and left.

I slipped down the hallway to talk to Virginia but heard Mom's voice coming from my bedroom.

"She could have a good life here, you know. If you hadn't noticed, Hugh comes from a good family. He would provide well for her."

"Provide well? Mom, this isn't the Middle Ages. Women aren't chattel," Virginia responded.

"Oh, I forgot. You're a modern woman with no husband, living in a boarding house. You've got it all figured out," Mom said.

"I don't expect you to understand, but I am happy. And Olive could be too. There's a whole world out there with opportunities. Things have changed since the war. Girls can have more than this."

"This? So now you're too good for this life? Don't forget the sacrifices other people have made so you could have your better life." I could picture Mom with her hands on her hips as she spoke.

"How could I forget? You've reminded me of it every day since I got here," Virginia sighed. "Look, Mom, I would never have agreed if Olive was a different kind of girl, but you know she's too big for Creighton. She's not like Maggie. I can already tell Maggie will grow up just like June, content to stay here the rest of her life."

What about me? I wanted to know what kind of girl she thought I was. I know I was meant for something bigger, something special too, and yet I'd never pictured myself anywhere but Creighton – at least not until now.

"Well, you've really opened a can of worms here, Virginia. This is all your father and I are going to hear about from Olive from now on. She won't let this go, and there won't be any peace in this house because of it," Mom said, her voice dropping. "I'll speak to your father and see what he thinks. But, Virginia, if you start getting any ideas about taking Rose, forget it. She stays here, do you understand?"

I scrambled back into the living room before I could hear what Virginia had to say. I pretended to read the Sears catalogue, but Mom just walked back into the kitchen without noticing me.

It wasn't fair. Olive was mean and always got her way. I never bothered anyone and did what I was told, so why didn't I get rewarded? I wanted to see Los Angeles too, but more than that, I wanted to be with Virginia. She was the only person who noticed when I was around. Why would Mom insist I stay here except to be mean? She'd never notice or care if I was gone.

NINE

It felt like there was a battle going on inside me ever since I heard Mom tell Virginia I couldn't ever leave Creighton. I felt trapped and kind of mad, but on this day, I also couldn't stop the happy inside me. It was the first official day of blueberry-picking season, which was a big day in Creighton. The whole town would come out to get their fill.

Every hill would be staked out on a first-come basis. People had gotten in fights over prime picking spots, and every year there were rumours about a motherlode of berries in this area or that. After Christmas and Easter, it was the day I looked forward to the most. Best of all, I'd asked Virginia to come picking with me and Maggie, and she'd said yes.

The banging of tins and pots rang through the house. Mom and June were pulling out all the jars, pots, and pans they'd need for cooking and canning.

Olive came into the kitchen wearing a pair of faded denim pants and an old shirt tied tight at her waist. No one wore nice clothes berry picking. Even so, Olive still managed to look fresh and pretty with her hair pulled back under a kerchief that matched her top.

"Good morning, Maggie. Hi, Rose." Olive patted Maggie on the head as she passed by.

Maggie looked over at me with wide eyes. I shook my head. For the past few days, Olive had been like a bear with a thorn in its paw, snapping at everyone. We had no idea what had changed her mood, and it made me suspicious.

Hugh came in the back door carrying an empty Crisco tin and wearing a crisp, clean shirt. I don't think Hugh owned hand-me-downs or what we called play clothes. The ones that had stains or holes in them, so you didn't have to worry about getting any more. I couldn't figure out if he never got dirty or if his mom just bought him new things if he messed up his old clothes.

"Hey, Hugh, are you picking berries or meeting the Queen?" Mikey said, then laughed at his own joke.

Hugh tugged at his pressed shirt. "Aww, go on with you."

"Don't mind him." Olive went over to Hugh and put a hand on his shoulder. "If we let him, Mikey would wear the same clothes everyday until they rotted off him. I like your shirt."

"Smile, you two." Virginia pointed her camera. Olive posed while Hugh smiled painfully. "I like your shirt too, Hugh. It's pretty spiffy."

Hugh's ears turned pink at the tips. Sometimes I thought he and I were a bit alike. Like me, he wasn't popular or good at sports, except he had something I didn't: an in with the popular kids. If he didn't have such a close relationship with Olive, I doubt the other popular kids would have included him. I knew this because I'd heard people say it.

For as long as I can remember, Hugh had been Olive's sidekick, as my dad called him. I thought he was nice, but he wasn't like Olive's other friends and he and Oliver were completely opposite, but Hugh could sometimes get his parents' car and, because he got an allowance, he'd often pay Olive's way at the movie theatre. I guessed the thing Olive liked most about Hugh was that he never said no to her. I couldn't imagine what that was like. I heard "no" way more than I ever heard "yes."

"You'll never guess what's happened, Hugh." Olive swung back and forth in front of him. "It's the most wonderful thing ever." She paused and looked at Hugh, who just shrugged. "Mom and Dad are letting me go to Los Angeles in September." She squealed and jumped up and down.

"Wow, that's really neat, Olive. I bet you'll have a great time. Hey, I can lend you my camera so you can take loads of pictures to show us when you get back?" Hugh said, smiling warmly.

"No, silly." She slapped him playfully on the arm. "This isn't a vacation. Virginia and I are going to live together. She's going to help me find a job, maybe take some night classes if I need to. I'm moving there, getting out of Creighton Mine. Isn't that the most exciting thing you have ever heard?"

Olive squealed, wrapping her arms around herself like she was giving herself a hug. Hugh's mouth opened and closed a few times, making him look like a fish out of water. He looked over at Virginia, then Mom, and around the room at each of us as if he hadn't quite heard right and was waiting for someone to clear things up, but none of us spoke up.

I was as shocked as Hugh. When Mom had said no a few days ago, I thought that was it. Even when she told Virginia she'd talk to Dad, I didn't think anything would come of it. Mom never changed her mind, at least not for me.

"Well, that's big news, isn't it? Mrs. Boyle, are you okay with Olive going so far away? Isn't she still kind of young to leave home?"

Mom shook her head and flicked a dishtowel in her hand in Olive's direction.

"How can I say what's best for a sixteen-year-old girl? I've lived in Creighton my whole life, so apparently, I know nothing of the outside world," she said, looking at Virginia. Then she turned around and plunged her hands into the soapy dish water.

"Young? I'm old enough to work at the drug store, so I must be old enough to move out." Olive put her hands on her hips. "I can't wait to see the look on Cheryl Gaston's face when I tell her. Just think, indoor plumbing, paved streets, and no more snow. And guess what, Rose?" Olive said as she looked over at me.

"What?" I answered warily.

"You'll have the bedroom all to yourself."

For one moment, there was a silver lining, but then Mom spoke.

"Don't get too excited, Rose. We may end up renting your room out. There are always men who would rather live in a home than the rooming houses in town. Your father and I discussed it, and there's plenty of room for you on the trundle bed."

So, Olive would get to move to Los Angeles with Virginia, and I would have to sleep on the trundle bed for the rest of my life, listening to Dad coughing all night and Mom turning the lights on at 5:00 a.m. It was so unfair, and even Olive looked like she thought so too, although she didn't say anything, of course.

At that moment, I didn't know who I was angrier at: Mom for taking away my bedroom with no care for my feelings, or Olive for getting everything she ever wanted, even though it ruined my life. I put my head down and focused on my breakfast, biting my lip to keep from crying in front of everyone.

Other than Mom rattling pots and pans, the room was quiet as everyone settled into the news they'd just heard.

June broke the silence and jumped in with her overly cheery voice. "So, where is everyone going to pick today?"

"Cheryl heard from her dad that Five Shaft was looking good." Olive pointed at me and Maggie. "And don't you kids even think of going there." But her voice didn't have its usual bite.

"Naw, Five Shaft isn't any good," Mikey spoke up. "Everyone knows this year it's either Up-by-the-dump or North Star. Besides, what do you care? You teenagers spend more time smooching than picking."

Olive reached over and yanked his hair.

"Owww... Grandma!" Mikey hollered.

"Olive, if you can't behave like an adult, you won't be going to Los Angeles or anywhere else." As soon as Mom said that, I knew it would be the threat we'd hear for the rest of the summer.

"Virg, you wanna come with Hugh and me?" Olive slipped her arm through his, which made him stiffen.

"No, she's coming with me! Aren't you, Virginia?" I snapped.

I felt everyone's eyes on me, including Virginia, who came and knelt down beside me.

"Well, that depends. It's been so long since I've picked. Do you think you could stand being seen with a nit-picker like me?"

"Are you kidding? You're a Creightoner. Blueberry pickings in your blood, even if you haven't done it in a while," Mikey said.

"In that case, I'd love to join your group, Rose." She slipped into the chair beside me. "God, I remember how serious I was about picking when I was your age." She tapped my nose. "Paulette and I would go together, and at the end of each day, she'd record our amounts on a piece of paper. At the end of the picking season, we'd add them up to see who'd won. It was always Paulette, until the year we turned thirteen. I looked closely at the numbers and noticed smudges…but only on my numbers." She looked at each of us, wide-eyed. "Paulette had been erasing and lowering my numbers."

"She cheated?" Maggie's eyes were big as saucers. Cheating on your count was considered the worst kind of dishonesty.

"Yup. It took me a long time to forgive her. Then when we got older it was more about hanging out with our friends, trying to look cute while we picked." She winked at Olive, who smiled back. "We ended up eating more than we brought home," Virginia said.

"That's true. I remember when you were fifteen. That year I barely got five jars canned because your picking was pitiful," Mom said.

"I promise I will do much better today. What about you guys? Are you pros?" Virginia asked.

"We're pretty good," Maggie spoke up for the group, "but nowhere near as good as the Finns."

The Finns were legends when it came to blueberry picking. The ladies originally from Finland were serious pickers. They would return at the end of the day with eleven quart containers overflowing. They'd have one in each hand and another one balanced on their heads.

Mom was always amazed at how they were able to do that. She said they saved all the money from their pickings so they could send their kids to university. For some reason, they didn't want their boys to follow their fathers into the mines.

As the talk turned to picking, I began to feel a bit better. At least I had the day to look forward to, and I'd worry about the other stuff later.

It was hard not to get caught up in the excitement. Blueberry season was like a carnival. Everyone in town came out. Picking was one of the few things anyone could be great at. You didn't need to be big or strong, and there wasn't any fancy equipment that would give you an advantage. It all came down to hard work and a little bit of luck. Anyone could pick, from small children to the oldest grandmas.

Then the smells of pies and jam cooking would float out of kitchen windows and fill the air of Creighton with a sweetness that didn't exist any other time of year. At the end of each season, tales would be told and the size of people's pickings would grow with each telling. There would be stories of people stumbling upon bears or catching a glimpse of a ragged hermit who lived in the hills. Berry-picking season was the official kick off to summer.

And this year's would be extra special because I got to do it with Virginia. It wasn't just getting to spend time with her that I looked forward to; it was time alone with her that I really wanted. I had some very important things to discuss with her.

TEN

"Come on, it's just over the rise." Maggie trotted up the hill ahead of us, her empty bucket swaying back and forth. Mikey and his friend Joey had already run far ahead while I walked at Virginia's side.

"Whew, I am not used to all this climbing anymore. The boulevards in Los Angeles are wide and flat, and the bugs here," she swatted at a swarm, "black flies, deer flies, horse flies…ugh, am I missing any?"

"Just mosquitos." I giggled. The bugs were annoying, but I was used to them. "Hey, Virginia?"

"Yeah, sweetie?"

"Can I come and visit you sometime…in Los Angeles?"

She frowned and didn't answer right away. "Rose, I would love for you to come visit, if Mom will allow it."

I felt myself sink. Mom wouldn't let me go. I already knew that.

"But you know what? I'm going to try to come back and visit as much as I can. Especially with Olive coming to live with me. I'm sure you're all going to miss her a lot."

"Nope, not at all," I answered without much thought.

Virginia laughed. "Okay, I get it, but I am serious about coming home more often. Do you know what I'd really like?" She stopped walking and looked down at me. "I'd really like it if you'd write me letters. You can tell me what's happening here in Creighton and what's going on with you. It's really important to me that we get to know each other better." She squeezed my hand, which I squeezed back.

"Virginia..." I hesitated but knew I might not get another chance. "When I turn sixteen, can I come live with you too? I know Mom said I couldn't, but you promised to teach me photography, and I wouldn't take up much space, and I would help you with all the chores."

"How do you know Mom said you couldn't come live with me, hmmm?" She folded her arms but didn't look angry.

"I heard her say so." I decided to come clean. "I was listening outside the door."

"Just like The Shadow, eh?" She smirked, but then her face turned serious. "Can you keep a secret, Rose?"

"Of course. I haven't told anyone the secret about the ring Gregory gave you."

"That's good. Okay, well one day, I'm not sure when, but I have every intention of making sure you get the chance to leave Creighton, just like Olive. I want you to be able to do whatever you want in life. But we have to keep it just between us. Mom can't know because it would make her sad."

"Mom wouldn't miss me. She doesn't pay any attention to me," I said.

"Don't be too hard on her. First, I left, now Olive…" she hesitated, "and you know about Francis, don't you?"

"Yes." I had heard about poor Francis, who was even more ignored and forgotten in the family than I was. His name was never mentioned, and whenever I snuck a look at the one picture on Mom's bedside table, I'd feel sad. It was like he never really existed.

He would have been twenty-one now, but he died when he was only a year old. All I knew was what I heard Dad say, one night when he was in his cups, how Francis got sick with a fever in the winter. Doctor Worley was in Sudbury and couldn't get back because of the storm. He finally came two days later, but it was too late. I imagined if he lived, Francis would have been a really great big brother, more like Virginia than Olive. I wanted to visit his grave one day just to prove to myself that he was real, but the cemetery was far down the road past Meatbird Lake.

"When we go away," Virginia said, as she squinted up at the sky, "it must feel a bit like she is losing us, so don't be too hard on her. Everything she does is for the family. Okay?"

"Okay." I tried to look serious when really, I was busting with happiness because one day I'd get to go live with Virginia.

"Here it is!" Maggie ran back to us, waving her arms at a large patch of undisturbed berries.

Virginia laughed. "Okay, you two, I'm going to go over there." She pointed farther up the hill to a spot with a few spindly trees and some shade. "I want to get out of the sun a bit. I have lunch here." She held up a basket Mom had packed for us. "Come and get it whenever you want."

I had brought a really large basket because I was determined to make this my biggest haul ever. The day felt golden, and I had the most exciting secret that someday I'd get to leave Creighton, see the world, and be with Virginia.

"Hey, Virginia?" I called out.

"Yeah, honey?"

"Isn't this the most perfect day ever?"

She flashed the biggest smile at me. "I'll never forget it as long as I live," she said.

"Yeah, me either." I took off running to catch up with Maggie.

ELEVEN

Other than a quick stop for sandwiches at lunch, I spent the day focused on my work. I'd pick all the berries from the small bush at my feet, shimmy my bum over, extend my reach to another spot, pick some more, shimmy, pick, shimmy.

While my hands worked without thinking, I sang through all my favourite songs from movies and the radio. When I finished singing the last Judy Garland song, I could tell it was time to head home. The back of my neck was warm and tender from the sun, and my knees were aching. The tips of my fingers were stained a pretty blue. My old shirt had streaks of blue juice I knew would never come out. My back made a satisfying crack sound when I stood up and stretched. I searched for a glimpse of Maggie but didn't see her.

I cupped my hands around my mouth and hollered, "Yoo hoo!" There was a faint response from over the hill: "Hoo yoo!" It was my and Maggie's signal to each other. At lunch, we had agreed to meet up back at the shady spot where Virginia would be waiting for us.

As I walked, I looked around, wondering if I'd miss any of this when I left Creighton. I wasn't sure if they had blueberry picking in California. I'd have to remember to ask Virginia. I hadn't realized how far away from our meeting spot I'd travelled until I had to make my way back. My basket was overflowing, and my arms ached. The worst thing that could happen now would be if I dropped my haul. I finally reached the trees and thought about sneaking up on Virginia to scare her, but I was too tired to try.

"Hey, Virginia, I'm back," I called as I rounded the corner.

Virginia was stretched out on the flat stones. If anyone else found out she'd taken a nap during picking, they'd tease her something awful. I would keep the secret for her; after all, we had plenty of secrets between us already.

"Virginia, sleepy head, time to wake up."

I stepped closer and thought it odd that she slept on her back with her arms flung wide open. I put my basket down and knelt beside her.

"Virginia, wake up." I shook her shoulder, but her eyes stayed closed. Her head flopped to the side like she had no bones or muscles. My hand landed on something wet on the stone. I thought it was juice from the berries scattered around her, but the colour was wrong. It was darker and sticky.

"Virginia!" I called and shook her harder. This time her limbs flopped too, but it didn't wake her up. Something was wrong. I pushed, poked, and shoved at her, trying to get a response, and I called her name over and over. I wished for someone else to come along, someone older than me.

"Help!" I called, hoping other pickers nearby might hear me. "Help!"

"Rose?"

I whipped my head around. Maggie's eyes were wide as she stared past me.

"What happened?" Her voice was barely a whisper.

"I don't know! She won't wake up."

The trees opposite me bent as a group of women and kids pushed into the clearing. I was relieved to see grown-ups. They'd know what to do. Two of the women came over, asking the same question Maggie had.

"I don't know. She was just lying here when I got back."

They began talking quickly to one another in their own language. Just to the left of us, Mikey and Joey burst into the clearing, panting, obviously having run when they heard the yelling.

"What's happened? Is someone hurt?" Mikey yelled to no one in particular.

I was grabbed from behind, stood up, and pushed to the side. The women who knelt beside Virginia also kept trying to get her to wake up. One of the women pointed at a girl about my age who I recognized from school. She shouted something, and the girl took off flying down the hill.

"What happened? Is she all right?" Mikey yelled at me, but I didn't have an answer for him.

All I wanted to do was go to my sister's side, to feel her warmth, her heartbeat, to know she'd be okay, but an older woman came around and blocked Maggie and me.

"It's okay, sweeties. It'll be okay," she said with a strong Finnish accent.

But it didn't feel like it would be okay. Mikey kept asking questions that nobody would answer. The women's voices began to rise, and they waved their arms frantically at one another, but Virginia didn't move, not even a breath. They slapped her face lightly and put their ear to her mouth. Even though their voices were high-pitched and distressed, it still sounded as if the world had gone silent. As they spoke, their sound was muffled, and it felt like I was far away just watching a scene that wasn't real.

Beside me, Maggie whined like a puppy calling to its mother. I stayed silent while my whole body trembled. The doctor, I thought. They just needed to get her to Dr. Worley's office, and he would make her all better.

Moments later more panicked voices flowed up the hill. I recognized them before I even saw their faces and felt a rush of relief. They'd know what to do. Seconds later, Angus burst over the rise, calling out Virginia's name. He was running full out, not even breathing hard. His face was set in stone, while behind him Mom struggled over the rocks with June, who grabbed her arm to steady her. They both still had their aprons on.

As more people filled the small clearing, Maggie and I were pushed further out of the way, and I stumbled over something. It was Virginia's camera. I picked it up and held it close. She would want me to take care of it until she needed it again.

The ladies shifted out of the way when Mom arrived and fell to her knees. Her hands shook as they brushed over Virginia's face, pushing her hair back, but instead of trying to wake her, as everyone else had done, she collapsed on to Virginia and let out a cry. It felt like a spear in my chest. I'd never heard such an awful sound before.

Maggie gripped my hand painfully and buried her face into my neck. I looked down and saw a dark puddle spreading out under our feet where Maggie had wet herself. I hung on to her with one hand, and the camera with my other, while rocking back and forth.

Then a face appeared. June dropped to her knees in front of Maggie and me and swept us up into her arms. I clung to her with all my strength and closed my eyes so I didn't have to see anything anymore, but I couldn't block out the sounds of so many voices, and above it all, my mother howling. It was a sound I didn't just hear but felt deep inside me, and it stole the last bit of hope I had.

TWELVE

I had no idea how I got back down the hill, but once in the house, someone set up the metal washtub behind the screen in the kitchen and put Maggie and I into it. The hot water didn't stop my shaking. We just sat there in silence with our knees drawn up under our chins. No one scrubbed us or came to check on us, not even June.

From behind the curtain, I watched the shadows of women coming in and out of the kitchen, speaking in hushed tones. The kettle was continually being boiled to make pot after pot of tea. From the living room, more voices drifted in. It was like a soft hum without actual words. The front door squeaked open and shut, over and over.

The kitchen was dark with only one light on. I was grateful for that because my head felt strange. I tried to convince myself it was just a bad dream that I'd soon wake up from. Any time my mind drifted back to the hill, I'd squeeze my eyes shut, real tight, and shake my head. I didn't want to remember anything.

I don't know how long we sat there, but eventually the water turned cold and Maggie's teeth began to chatter. I climbed out, wrapping myself in a towel, then I helped Maggie out, making sure she was covered up too. The kitchen was empty when I lifted the curtain. Half-filled plates of cookies sat on the table, and unwashed teacups cluttered the counter.

Maggie followed behind me as we dripped a trail of water out of the kitchen and into the living room. There were about as many people in our front room as when all the ladies had come for tea and desserts to visit Virginia, but this was different. Mom, Dad, Angus, June, and Oscar were seated around the front room. Officer Kowalski, one of the Inco mining company's police officers, was there, but not in his uniform. He sat beside my father with his hand on Dad's shoulder. I recognized him from around town, but he'd never been in our house before, as far as I knew.

Reverend Joyce from the United Church and Father Mancini from the Catholic Church talked quietly in a corner, sipping tea. The rest of the people were neighbours and some who worked on the same shift as Dad. I couldn't find Mikey or Olive anywhere.

"Mom," I whispered, not wanting to be noticed but needing her attention. I tried willing her to turn and see me, but her gaze was stuck on her hands, which she gripped in her lap. "Mom," I said a little louder and waited but didn't get any response. I tried once more, only this time louder. "Mom."

Every head in the room snapped around to look at me. Maggie squeaked and stepped behind me. With every eye on me, I forgot what I wanted to say. What was there to say at this moment?

Finally, I asked, "Mom, where is Virginia? I want to see her," realizing that was what I wanted most. To see her again. I couldn't stand the thought of her being alone somewhere.

Mom's mouth fell open, but nothing came out. She just stared at me. Everyone's head dropped to look at the ground, except for Dad, whose lips were pushed so tight together, I could see a white outline.

"Come on, let me get you girls settled." Mrs. Valenti, Mom's best friend, scuttled over to us and pushed us towards my room. At that moment, she could have walked me off the edge of Slater's Rock and I wouldn't have protested.

"Raise your arms," she said when we got to the bedroom and a nightgown slid over my head. It was one of Olive's and too long, but I didn't care and kept quiet. Maggie was dressed in one of mine. Then Mrs. Valenti lifted each of us into bed, even though I was too big for such a thing.

"Where's Mikey?" My voice was startling to my ears; it didn't sound like me.

"He's over at his friend Joey's tonight." Mrs. Valenti tucked the blanket under my chin.

"And Olive?" I asked.

"She's spending the night at Cheryl Gaston's. Now you two sweeties try to sleep, okay?" She brushed our hair off our faces and gave each of us a kiss on the forehead, like I'd seen parents do in movies. She left the bedside lamp on and went to the door.

"Did she fall?" I asked.

"What's that, Rose?"

"Virginia. Did she fall down? Is that what happened?"

Mrs. Valenti's face crumpled a bit. "Don't think about it, sweetie. Just sleep." She blew us each a kiss then closed the door behind her. Under the blanket, I reached out for Maggie's hand to make sure she was still with me.

"I won't ever stop thinking about it, Rose," Maggie whispered once we were alone.

"Me either," I said. "Not for the rest of my life."

THIRTEEN

I stared at Virginia's camera sitting on the dresser. That and the locket that still hung around my neck made me feel connected to her. I'd barely registered that I was back in my old room instead of on the trundle bed in Mom and Dad's. Maggie slept beside me. I slipped out of bed, careful not to wake her. I didn't want to see her go through the same remembering I did when I woke up.

I could tell by how the sun came through the window that the morning had passed, but I still felt like I could sleep another three days. My head felt like it was full of wool. I remembered what had happened the day before, but it was like looking at it through a piece of cheesecloth. I shuffled down the hall, not sure if I wanted the living room to be empty or full when I got there. The voices that met me were just like the night before, hushed, but there were fewer of them.

Mom and Dad sat in the exact same spots they had the night before. I wondered if they had moved at all. June and Oscar leaned against one another on the chesterfield, her small hand clasped in his.

All heads were turned towards Officer Kowalski, the Inco policeman. I would have preferred him in his regular clothes from the night before instead of the uniform he was wearing. He looked out of place sitting on a kitchen chair in the middle of our front room. His freshly pressed clothes stood out compared to the rumpled ones of the rest of my family. No one noticed me until I slipped in between June and Oscar, needing someone else's warmth because mine was all gone.

Officer Kowalski balanced a notebook on his knee. He wasn't a large man and didn't have that gruff manner police in the movies often had. He looked like any other miner. I'd heard Mom once tell June he was a fair man. Everyone knew on payday he'd wait at the bank when the men cashed their cheques. A few of them would drink the money all away if he didn't make sure their wives were given some of it.

I listened as the grown-ups talked around me without paying attention to their words, not quite ready to hear any truths. I came back into focus when Officer Kowalski spoke my name.

"Rose, can I ask you a few questions?" He leaned his elbows on his knees to get closer.

When I nodded, he turned to Mom, who also nodded but seemed unsure.

"Rose, I want to find out what happened yesterday, and I know you were there."

"When Virginia had her accident?" I asked.

June began to quiver beside me, and Oscar passed her his handkerchief. The air in the room changed, and Officer Kowalski shifted in his seat.

"Well, yes," he drawled, "but we are also looking into the possibility that it might not have been an accident. That someone may have hurt her on purpose."

"No!" All my manners were forgotten, and I shook my head at him. Virginia was the nicest person in the entire world. No one would ever want to hurt her, not on purpose.

"It's not for sure yet. It is possible she somehow fell and hit her head, but there were a few," he coughed, "marks that are a little suspicious. We just want to make sure we have the whole story. Okay, Rose? And that's why I want to ask you if you saw anyone else while you were picking yesterday."

My mind went blank. Someone might have purposely hurt Virginia? It was too horrible to think about. Things like that didn't happen in Creighton Mine. It was something in movies or big cities far away. And not to Virginia — there'd be no reason.

"Rose. I know this is hard, but I need you to think. Did you see anyone yesterday?"

"No. Just me and Maggie. Mikey and Joey started with us, but they took off to their own spot. I didn't see anyone else."

I would have been able to hold it in if Officer Kowalski hadn't been looking at me with the kindest eyes and a bit of pity, but he did. My chin began to tremble, and my eyes prickled. June's arm slipped around me, and I collapsed, my head on my knees soaking my nightgown as I cried for the first time since it all happened. I fought really hard to stop my tears and not cause a scene. It took a few hard swallows and deep breaths. I even pushed my nails into my palms so I could focus on the pain in my hand, not in my chest.

I wiped my tears away and pushed myself back up. The crying took away all the energy I had. Now I just wanted was to crawl back into bed, pull the covers up, and not hear anyone else's words. I wanted to go back to being invisible. Being unseen, even in front of people, was preferable to this.

When my eyes cleared, I saw Maggie in the doorway, wrapped in a blanket. My crying must had woken her up because she looked frightened.

"That's enough for today, Gene," Dad said to the officer, who nodded and slipped his notebook away.

Maggie took a seat beside Oscar, laid her head on his lap, and sucked her thumb, something she hadn't done for a few years.

"Connor, we've put a call in to the Sudbury OPP department. They'll be sending out a detective tomorrow," Officer Kowalski told Dad.

"I trust you to do the job, Gene. You're one of us," Dad said.

"Well, I appreciate your faith in me, but it was only a few years ago I was down in the mines just like you. I don't have the kind of training needed for an investigation like this. And with Officer Greene out of action with his broken leg, I'm all alone." He stood up with his hat in his hand and nodded at each of the grown-ups. "I'm sorry, Connor, Helen, June, Oscar. In the meantime, I'm asking everyone in town to lock their doors and keep a watch for anything suspicious."

Locked doors? Our doors didn't lock; at least I didn't think so. There was never a need to until now. No one moved from their spot to walk him out. I looked around at each of the grown-ups, waiting for some sign of what we should do, how to make sense of this all, but it didn't come. They looked as lost as I felt, which scared me even more.

Just after the officer left, the front door opened again. This time Olive, Hugh, and Mikey came in. They stopped at the entrance to the living room like strangers waiting for an invitation. Olive's eyes looked puffy and painful. Hugh's hand on her back seemed there to make sure she stayed steady. Mikey shuffled into the room and took a seat at June's feet, wrapping his arms around his knees.

"Thanks for walking Olive and Mikey home, Hugh. We really appreciate it," June said.

Hugh nodded and dropped his arm away from Olive, pushing his hands deep into his pants pockets.

"She was killed," I blurted out.

"Rose!" Mom hissed at me, and I sank back into the chesterfield.

"What did you say, Rose? Mom? I thought Virginia had an accident." Olive reached behind herself. Hugh stepped forward and grabbed her hand.

"It's most likely, Olive. Officer Kowalski was just here, and there were some marks on her body that make them think someone did this to her," Oscar said, which showed how upside down everything had become. Oscar was the quietest person ever, but when he did speak, his voice was soothing and calm. It was what we needed.

Olive turned to Hugh as if he could make sense of it all for her.

"Do they know who did it?" Hugh voiced the one question none of us had so far.

"No," Oscar answered. "There's no suspects yet."

June took a big, shaky breath and stood up. "I'm going to make a pot of tea. Will you join us, Hugh?"

"No, thank you. My mother wants me to come straight home. I'm really sorry for you all." He sounded on the verge of tears himself.

June sighed. "Thank you, Hugh."

He put his hands on Olive's shoulders and spoke to her like she was a child. "Would you like me to come by later this afternoon to keep you company?"

"Mmmhmm." Olive nodded.

The back door slammed, which made all of us jump. Angus came in through the kitchen. He looked awful, like he hadn't slept, and from where I sat, I could smell stale beer and sweat. His red-rimmed eyes took in each of us one by one. He walked over to Mom, fell to his knees, and sobbed into her lap. Mom patted his back absently as if comforting a toddler who had spilled their milk.

Nothing was like it should be: strong and stoic Angus sobbed, silent Oscar had spoken, and Olive needed Hugh for comfort and strength. Each of us was broken, and I didn't know how we'd ever get better from this. Why were the grown-ups so lost? This wasn't the first time for them. They'd gone through this before when little Francis died. Was it the same then? Did they eventually just get back to normal, or was it different to lose a child from illness instead of murder?

A knock on the front door made Mom lean back and lift the curtain. She sighed loudly and looked at Dad.

"Connor, get ready. They're coming." She stood up and looked around with a puzzled expression.

June jumped up from the couch. "Angus, go upstairs and either put yourself to bed or clean up. You girls get dressed," she said to Maggie and me. "Olive, you let the visitors in, and Oscar, can you—" Her voice hitched like it got caught on something sharp. Oscar came to her side. "Can you get something strong? I think we'll need it to make it through the rest of the day."

Up until the sun set, the people of Creighton came and went through our home, bringing casseroles and meals. They wore their Sunday best and spoke softly while patting my parents on their shoulder or forearm.

Hugh returned, like he said he would, and Olive never left his side. No one noticed when Maggie, Mikey, and I slipped off to their house. It felt better to escape the stares of pity and pats on the head with "you poor lamb" or "you dear wee soul." They meant well, but it didn't bring us any comfort.

The three of us gathered around the radio and listened to shows that usually entertained us. Even the funny ones couldn't make us laugh. I didn't know about Maggie or Mikey, but I wondered if I'd feel happiness or anything other than the sharp pain in my chest ever again.

FOURTEEN

VICTOR

The town of Creighton Mine was easy to find. All I had to do was watch for the mine shaft. A mishappen building that towered above everything else in town. It was their landmark. Not quite as impressive as when I saw the Eiffel Tower, but it got me where I needed to go.

I was convinced this case would be an easy one. With a population of just over two thousand, finding out who killed a young woman shouldn't tax my skills much. I'd planned to round up the usual suspects, family members, and boyfriends, and within a week I'd have the most likely culprit and motive figured out.

Besides hoping for some time off, I was also motivated to solve this crime quickly because I wasn't looking forward to the drive between my home in Sudbury out to Creighton Mine most days for the investigation.

This was my first time in Creighton, but I'd been to a few of the other mining towns. The mining company, Inco, had their own police force in each of the company towns, but when it came to murder or other serious crimes, they usually called us in.

Sudbury was the closest Ontario Provincial Police department in the area, and for this case, I drew the short straw.

All the Inco towns looked the same to me, like I'd stepped back in time about thirty years. They were still using outhouses, wooden slat sidewalks, and not many people had cars.

"Goddammit." I lurched forward and almost hit my nose on the steering wheel from slamming on the brakes. I narrowly avoided running over a man and his horse hitched to a wagon.

The man was unfazed and waved at me. They passed by as if they had weeks to make their deliveries instead of an afternoon. The wagon was half full of sacks of flour and other grocery items. I guess someone forgot to tell Creighton Mine that it was 1951, not 1921.

I manoeuvred my car around the man and his horse, moving through the town to get a quick feel for it before heading to the police station. I followed the gravel road as it wound through neighbourhoods of a few houses here and there, coiling around clusters of rocks. People stopped and stared as I passed. A stranger in town was considered big news, almost as big as a murder.

I found a flat spot, parked, and got out. My right knee told me rain was on the way. Ever since I injured it jumping out of a plane over France, it had become my weather forecaster. It was the same jump that gave me the C-shaped scar at the corner of my right eye and onto my cheek.

Back in Toronto they had a whole city department devoted to town planning; here the only one dictating where building and roads went was Mother Nature. Each house looked like it had been dropped into place, onto a slab of rock, and landed at an odd angle. Giant rock wedges jutted up between the homes. It reminded me of a child's drawing, with everything slightly askew.

When I first moved here, I found the scenery bleak and harsh. The landscape was like a watercolour: pale and washed out with bedrock as its main feature. Back when copper and nickel were discovered, the first thing to go were the large trees to fuel the ore smelting. Then whatever it was that spewed from the chimney stacks killed off most of the surrounding forests. The few trees that insisted on scraping out an existence were spindly but hardy, plunging their roots where they could. There weren't any of the mighty oaks or broad maples I grew up climbing.

I looked out at what I could see of the town. Even up on the hill I could hear a deep pounding from underground. I wondered if the people who lived here even noticed it or had become immune to the sounds. It wasn't as if the mine was somewhere off in the distance. The homes were built beside, in front, and around the mine shafts, so all the drilling and blasting happened beneath their feet.

A whistle pierced the air. I glanced at my watch. It was twelve o'clock on the dot. Time to meet up with the Inco police and see how far they'd gotten on the case. Somewhere in this town was a murderer, and if I was going to catch him and close this case quickly, I'd better get to work.

I pulled up in front of the smallest police station I'd ever seen on the only paved street in town. It didn't look like the building was ever intended to be what it was, like the previous occupants

89

had left and the police scurried in, claiming the space as their own.

Then again, I reminded myself, it kind of fit because the men inside weren't real police officers. From my experience, Inco police were just miners in different uniforms. They got some training, but their power only extended over the other workers and families. Their daily duties ran more towards stolen bikes, drunks, and mischief. Even bootlegging, which was illegal, was mostly given a pass as long as they didn't cause a problem.

The station's door was propped open, and considering a murder had occurred only forty-eight hours earlier, there was a disturbing lack of activity. Inside, a lone officer sat at his desk reading a newspaper. When he saw me, he jumped up and smoothed down his well pressed uniform.

"You must be the man from Sudbury. Gene Kowalski, Inco police, pleased to meet you." His smile was warm and welcoming, more like a grocer than an officer.

"Detective Victor Lapointe." We shook hands.

"I'm glad to see you. This is a real tragedy for our town, and I'm not embarrassed to admit a murder is well over my head."

His handshake was firm and quick. He wore his hair greased down, but even that couldn't hide the waves that, given an inch, would spring into red curls.

"Is there a desk I can use as my own?" I asked, ready to get started.

"Sure, just over here." Gene scooped a few papers off a desk in the corner.

"I'd like to get started right away," I said and took a seat, grabbing a fresh notebook from my briefcase.

"Yes, of course." The officer shoved his hands in his pockets and rocked back on his heels. "So, what exactly does that mean? What do you need?" He grinned slightly.

"I'll need you to fill me in. My Detective Sergeant didn't give me much to go on, but first I'd like to visit the crime scene before the evidence begins to disappear. It's likely going to rain soon, so we don't have much time," I said.

The officer rubbed the back of his neck and grimaced slightly. "Yeah, about that. The young lady," he cleared his throat, "the victim, was found by her little sister, then a group of ladies came upon them who sent for help. All that chaos and yelling brought more people. It's a small town, news travels fast, which brought even more people…" He trailed off.

"So, the crime scene was compromised." I rubbed my forehead to chase off the headache I felt brewing, "Okay, what about the body?"

"She's at the doctor's office for now." He nodded towards the door.

"That's nearby then?"

"Yeah, we can walk over there if you'd like," he said.

On the way over, Officer Kowalski gave me a quick rundown on what happened. I was surprised to find out she wasn't a resident of the town, having only been back for a short visit. He had no motive, suspects, or ideas as to who could have committed the crime.

"Okay, so we're starting with a ruined crime scene, no clues, no suspects or witnesses, and the first person to come upon the body was a nine-year-old girl?" I stopped and faced the officer.

"That sounds about right."

"Is there any other good news you want to share with me?"

"My partner broke his leg sliding into second base, so you and I, we're it." He shrugged.

Things were looking bleaker by the minute, and my plans for a straightforward case were beginning to fade.

It took us all of five minutes to reach the doctor's office. At first, I thought it was just a house, but a plaque hung over the door with the name *Dr. Ernest Worley* engraved on it. I followed Gene up the steps and inside. We passed an empty waiting room and continued down the hallway to a back room.

"Doc? It's me, Gene," he called out.

We found the doctor sitting at a metal desk, eating what smelled like sausage and sauerkraut. He wiped his hands on a napkin and stood up when we entered. Gene quickly introduced us.

"I'm glad to see you both. I was about to send for you, Gene. The coroner will be coming this afternoon to take her to Sudbury, and I knew you'd want to take a look." The doctor glanced over the top of his glasses at me. He was overweight but in a solid way and sported an impressive white moustache that hid his top lip. "I'm afraid I don't have much light to shed on the situation. My examination was strictly exterior."

"I'd still be interested in your initial thoughts," I said.

"Sure, have a seat." He sat back behind his desk. "She was strangled, that's for sure. The bruising around her neck shows considerable force was used, and there's multiple scratches down the front of her throat."

"So, she was choked to death?" Gene shook his head.

"Actually, I don't think so. My theory is she was standing up when she was being strangled, and at some point, she'd have lost consciousness. The person who did this wouldn't have been able to hold her up, so she'd have dropped pretty darn hard and there's a significant wound to the back of her head, consistent with hitting something hard and pointy. But that's just my theory, and until the autopsy results, it's just a guess." The doctor shrugged.

"Could the wound have been caused by a blow to the head instead of a fall?" I asked.

"Perhaps," the doctor said, though seemingly unconvinced, "but they would have had to strike her up and under at the base of neck. It's in an awkward spot. Normally, a blow to the head would be on the side or the top. But this isn't really my area of expertise."

"Can we see the body?" I asked.

"Yes, of course," the doctor said.

"Is that necessary?" Gene asked, looking a little pale.

"Yeah, it's necessary," I said and followed the doctor into a small examining room.

The corpse was on a table normally reserved for live patients. A sheet covered her body and face, leaving only her feet exposed. Red polish stood out starkly against her pale skin. Doctor Worley

93

turned the sheet down to just above the chest, laying it gently as if not wanting to wake her.

I sucked my breath in. There was something familiar about this girl with her matted dark hair. Small twigs and a few leaves were caught up in her curls. She bore a disturbing resemblance to someone else I'd known and, at this particular time, didn't want to remember.

I leaned over the victim, pretending to take a closer look, when what I really needed was a moment to collect myself. I didn't want to see Margaux's face in this other woman's, so instead I focused on the details in front of me. There was a small scratch mark on her cheek, but that was the only visible sign on her face, which even in death was beautiful.

"How old was she?" I glanced over at the doctor.

"Twenty-five," Gene answered from the doorway.

The deep scratches on her neck were caked with dried blood, and the smudges there were either light bruising or dirt. I had a lot of experience with trauma to bodies, and this one showed very little outward signs of what happened.

"This is what I believe was the cause of death." The doctor stepped forward and lifted the woman's head, turning it to the side just enough to see the dried blood crusted there.

"If she died from hitting her head, it's possible whoever did this might not have intended to kill her?" I said more to myself, really.

"What did he expect would happen when he was strangling her?" Gene spoke quietly.

"What about sexual interference?" I asked, turning to the doctor.

"It doesn't appear so." He shifted uncomfortably, looking away from the girl.

"But you don't know for sure." In a murder case, I needed definitives, not guesses.

"Her undergarments were all intact, so..." Dr. Worley shrugged.

"I assume you have her clothing somewhere?" I asked, looking for a reason to leave the room.

"Yes, back in my office. You know, I was her mother's doctor. I helped bring her into this world." He shook his head.

"Then you must have known her very well."

"Somewhat. I could tell you about her childhood illnesses and such, but that's about it." He led us back into his office.

From a paper bag in the bottom drawer of his desk, the doctor pulled out a pile of neatly folded clothes. I picked up a top and spread it out on the desktop. It had been white with small blue flowers embroidered on the collar, but the front was stained a dark purplish-blue hue.

"It's the blueberries," said Gene. "One of the toughest stains to remove, or so my wife says."

"She was picking berries when she was killed?" I asked.

"Yes, it was the first official day of the season, which is a pretty big deal around here. It's an important source of income for some of the families, which proves how upsetting this all was. From what I hear, no one went out picking the next day," Gene explained.

"Are there any serious rivalries in regard to the berries?" I asked.

"Detective, you can't think someone would be killed over blueberries." The doctor chuckled.

"Money or love. Those are usually the only reasons people kill," I said.

"Really, that's it?" Gene asked, looking over my shoulder at the stained clothing.

"Mostly," I answered.

"Well, I'm pretty sure the Boyles pick for their own uses and not to make money," the doctor said.

I shrugged. "Then that leaves love."

"You don't kill someone if you love them." Gene folded his arms across his chest.

"Are you kidding?" I said, facing him. "I'm surprised it doesn't happen more often."

FIFTEEN

ROSE

I never realized how many sounds a silent person makes until I sat at Mom's feet, feeding her yarn to darn socks. She pushed her breath out her nose while her lips stayed pressed tightly together.

Dad should have been at work. He told Mom he'd go back tomorrow or maybe the next day. As for me, my stomach made gurgling noises; not like it was hungry, more upset. I'd made more than my usual trips to the outhouse, and I couldn't eat much, even with all the good food people had dropped off.

Three days had passed since Virginia left us. I still couldn't believe it was real. I had no idea what I was supposed to do or how I should act. Everyone was wrapped up in their own sadness, and each person's looked different. Maggie sucked her thumb and hung on to June all the time. Mom stared off like she could see something far away that no one else could. Dad sat in his chair holding the glass Virginia gave him, rolling it around and examining it like there were answers inside it.

Olive spent a lot of time sleeping, except when Hugh was over. Then they'd sit out back with their heads close together, whispering. She never spoke a cross or annoyed word to me, which, although nice, wasn't normal.

I drifted through the house from room to room, feeling like a ghost. I was used to being overlooked, but this was different. It was like everyone was in their own box and couldn't even see the people around them. If I were to scream or drop a bowl on the floor so it broke into a million pieces, I don't think anyone would notice or care. My biggest fear was it would always be like this.

A car pulled up outside our house and broke the silence. A car meant someone important had arrived. I listened to the doors open and shut, then heavy footsteps come up onto the porch. Mom stopped darning and folded her hands in her lap. Dad dashed down the last of his drink and tucked his glass under the chair.

The bell rang and I stayed where I was. So did Mom and Dad. All three of us waited for someone else to take action. The visitors knocked a second time. Olive walked past the living room with Hugh close behind her. Deep, muffled voices floated down the hall. Officer Kowalski walked into the room, followed by a stranger.

"Good afternoon, Connor, Helen, Rose," Officer Kowalski said, even nodding at me. "This here is Detective Victor Lapointe of the Sudbury OPP. He's been sent to take over the case, and I'll be assisting him."

I'd never seen a real detective. He was around the same height as Officer Kowalski, but he stood taller and seemed sturdier like someone that would be hard to knock over. His face was always serious. He didn't have the crinkles or lines of someone who laughed a lot, which seemed like a good thing in a detective. The one feature that stood out was a deep scar that tugged at the corner of his right eye, just a bit, and scooped around down his cheek like a backward letter C.

"Would it be all right if we had a seat?" Officer Kowalski asked, then moved to the chesterfield when no one answered.

Hugh and Olive stayed standing while the rest of us turned towards the two men. We waited to hear what the stranger would say.

The detective sat forward and rested his elbows on his knees. His eyes were grey, like the rocks of Creighton.

"Mr. and Mrs. Boyle, I want to express my condolences to each of you." His voice was smooth, like a radio announcer.

I couldn't take my eyes off this man who seemed so official. He was the one we'd been waiting for. Just like The Shadow, he'd catch the bad guy and give us the answers we were looking for.

He took out a notebook and began asking Mom and Dad questions about Virginia, mostly times and dates and things like that. He didn't stumble or wring his hands like everyone else did when they said Virginia's name. Our tragedy didn't make him uncomfortable.

"Have you ever caught a murderer?" I blurted out, which was not something I normally did around adults.

"Yes, I've solved every murder case I've had so far." He looked right at me when he spoke. "I know you've already spoken to Officer Kowalski about the day of the crime, but I'm going to need to talk to each of you separately." He looked around the room at each one of us, then stopped at Hugh.

"Are you a member of this family, son?"

Hugh swallowed hard and looked over at Olive before answering, "No, sir, just a friend."

The detective just raised his eyebrows.

"Hugh McLellan, sir. I go to school with Olive." He turned to Olive. "I should go. My parents will be expecting me."

He said goodnight to my parents, and Olive walked him to the door.

"Is there somewhere private I can conduct the interviews?" the detective asked.

Mom offered him the kitchen since it had a door. The first person he spoke to was Dad, then Mom, and then Olive. Each time someone came out of the kitchen, they looked worn-out, like they'd just climbed to the top of Tank Hill and back. Officer Kowalski tried to make small talk in between the long stretches of silence. He told us they'd go next door to June and Oscar's after they finished with us. The closer it came to my turn, the more my stomach gurgled.

"He wants to talk to you, Rose," Olive said when she came out of the kitchen. Her eyes were red, and she dabbed her nose with a hanky.

Mom came with me, and I clung to her hand, which I hadn't done since I was a little kid. The detective was looking down at his notebook when we walked in, and without looking up he pointed at the chair across from him.

"Take a seat, Rose," he said, remembering my name.

"I'll stay in case Rose needs some help. She's not good with details," Mom said and reached to pull out a chair. I shrank down in my seat.

"Actually, I'll need to speak to her alone. It's regular police procedure. Is that all right with you, Mrs. Boyle?"

Mom looked at me and then the detective. She looked like she wanted to say no, but I didn't think the detective was a man people often said no to.

"All right," Mom said, then she hissed at me, "Rose, sit up and answer the detective's questions."

I pushed myself up in my seat like the way we did when the principal came into the classroom.

"I'm going to ask you some questions, Rose, and I want you to tell me everything you remember, okay?"

I liked that he used the same voice to talk to me as he did to Mom. Some people used different voice when they spoke to kids.

"Okay." I nodded, determined to give good answers.

He started out by asking me all about that day. When I stopped to think, he didn't get impatient or annoyed. Sometimes he asked me the same question just a little bit differently, which helped me to remember things.

I thought I did a really good job until he asked me about when I found Virginia lying on the rocks. That's where things got jumbled in my brain. I couldn't recall who said what or who exactly was there or when all the people arrived. The only thing I could remember was all the sounds: yelling, crying and Maggie sobbing then whimpering like a puppy. It was the sounds from that day I'd never forget.

"I don't remember," I answered to his last question. "Sorry. I guess I should have paid more attention."

He leaned forward. "Rose, did your sister ever mention any one she didn't like or that she'd had an argument with?"

"No, Virginia was nice to everyone." I didn't count the time she was kind of rude to Mrs. Clarke the day everyone brought sweets. And I didn't think it was worth mentioning about the time she asked us to tell Eddie Szymanski she wasn't home. I didn't want the detective to think poorly about Virginia, but I did tell him what she said about Paulette Carmichael. "She told me when she was a teenager, Paulette Carmichael fudged her berry-picking numbers, but she did eventually forgive her. In fact, she wasn't even upset when she saw that Paulette had..." I slapped my hand over my mouth. I'd almost given away the secret.

The detective's eyebrows lifted. "Rose, can you finish what you were going to say?"

I shook my head.

"Rose, if you want me to catch the person who did this to your sister, I need to know everything."

"I can't. We made a pinky swear." I held up my pinky finger so he could see.

He leaned back in the chair and crossed his arms. "I see. You know, Rose, being able to keep a secret is really important in certain situations. In fact, in my job, I have to keep a lot of secrets, but there are circumstances where keeping a secret is the wrong thing to do. And I am pretty sure a pinky swear only counts when both parties are still alive. So, you wouldn't be breaking your promise by telling me now."

I relaxed into the chair. I didn't know that about pinky swears, but it made sense a detective would know about such things.

"I was just gonna say that Paulette's engagement ring, the one she got from Gregory Hansen, used to be Virginia's promise ring. She'd given it back to Gregory when they broke up, so she didn't care that Paulette now had it. She only made me keep it a secret because Paulette didn't know it was a second-hand ring and Virginia thought she might not be happy to find out."

The detective asked me to spell Paulette and Gregory's names, which I did as best I could. He asked a few questions about Virginia's life before she moved to Los Angeles, but I didn't know much. He also asked me who she visited here and what she felt about certain things, and I didn't know the answers to those questions either, which made me feel like a really bad sister. It was like I didn't even know Virginia, but I did. I knew her heart and that she loved me, but very little else I realized.

"Thanks, Rose. That's all I need right now." He closed his notebook.

"Can I ask you a question?"

"Alright."

"Why would anyone want to kill my sister? She was the nicest and prettiest girl ever. It doesn't make any sense."

"And I suggest you don't try to make sense of it. There are very few reasons that justify one person killing another," he said, sitting back.

"But there are some?" I asked.

He seemed surprised I asked, but he didn't hesitate. "War is one of the few times it's okay to kill another person, but even then, only in certain circumstances."

I wanted to ask him more about that, but his eyes had gone sort of empty, so instead I asked, "Do you think the bad guy is a monster?"

"Anyone who would kill your sister is going to be some kind of a monster, but the tricky part for us is he won't look like one on the outside."

SIXTEEN

VICTOR

I'd told the young girl, Rose, that murderers are monsters. That was mostly a lie, but it was the best way to explain it to a kid. In my experience, what made killers so frightening was they ended up being the grocer, the bank manager, or your neighbour.

In the case of Virginia Boyle, I added miner to that list, but unfortunately, no miner in particular. Gene and I struggled to come up with even the flimsiest motive for her killing. Who would hold a grudge for five years? She'd been in town just over a week, hardly enough time to make a mortal enemy, so it made sense that her murder would be linked to her past. That meant having to dig up some ancient history.

It didn't take me long to start appreciating having Gene by my side. He knew everyone in town: the troublemakers, the thieves, and the closet drinkers. He could name who knocked his wife and kids around, and who was just a plain old asshole. He had a dedication to his job I wish some of my fellow officers back in Sudbury shared.

My earlier conversations with the Boyle family revealed very little reason as to why Virginia had left Creighton Mine in the first place. She had no family or friends in Los Angeles, and all her parents would say was it was youthful folly and she left to see the world.

I expected we would get more information on her earlier life from her friends. So, our first interview outside the Boyle family was going to be Gregory Hansen. Little Rose had mentioned Virginia dated him before moving away, which made him as good a place to start as any.

Gene sat in the passenger's seat and directed me to mine shaft number four. I could have found it on my own as it jutted up from the middle of the town with homes all around it.

"So other than Hansen having dated Virginia Boyle, we have no reason to suspect him." Gene posed it as both a statement and a question.

"At this point, a jilted lover is as good a start as any," I pointed out.

"I guess."

The wheels ground to a stop, and we got out. I looked over at the gaping doorway to the open mine shaft. Not for all the tea in China could anyone have persuaded me to take that plunge into the darkness. Small spaces had always been a bit of a problem for me, even more so after the war.

"Gene, you take the lead on this," I told him as we headed for the administration building.

"You know, Detective, three years ago I was showing up here in coveralls myself, going into the pit with the other guys." He pointed towards the entrance. "Now I keep the peace, track down stolen goods, and convince drunks to go home and sleep it off. I don't want to mess this up. There's a lot at stake."

"I understand, but I'd like to be a fly on the wall for this one. All you need to do is ask him about his relationship with Virginia. He knows you and will probably be more comfortable opening up. Don't think of it as an interrogation; think of it as a conversation to see if he can help us out, okay?"

Gene nodded. "Yeah, okay, I think I can do that."

I followed him inside the building, which had a forgotten feel to it. Not a single picture hung on the walls, except an occasional safety poster, yellowed and curled at the edges. Stale smoke hung throughout. Gene stopped at an office with an opening but no door.

"Hansen, you got a minute?" He walked in before getting an answer. I followed.

Gregory Hansen sat behind a metal desk. I stopped in the doorway, unable to take another step in as I looked at the man inside. Gregory's blond hair was smoothed back, and his eyes were pale blue. Most people would describe his looks as collegiate, but all I saw was Germanic. It was a visceral response. I immediately found myself hating this man in front of me. I was taken aback when he spoke, as his voice was pure Northern Ontario, not sharp and guttural like the German soldiers I came across during the war.

I pulled my eyes away and surveyed the office, taking slow breaths. On the wall behind Hansen hung a framed *Certificate of Accounting*. I read each word on the diploma to refocus and bit hard on the inside of my cheek until I felt able to safely look at the man we'd come to see. Gregory Hansen's desk was organized with precision, and his name plate, G. Hansen, gleamed with a polished fervour. It was as pristine as the young man sitting there. Gene was already seated and making small talk, so I took a few stilted steps into the room but remained standing.

"What can I do for you, Gene?" Gregory asked.

"Greg, this is Detective Victor Lapointe from the Sudbury OPP. He's come to help us out with this messy business." Gene shook his head and made a tsk-ing sound. "Can you believe something like this could happen here?"

"I know. We're all pretty shaken up about it. Paulette's afraid to leave the house unless I'm with her. Do you have any suspects?" Hanson leaned forward with folded hands, making a steeple with his fingers.

Gene shook his head. "No, not a one yet. We're just following leads. I think we have to interview damn near everyone in town, which brings me and the detective to you."

For the first time, Gregory Hanson acknowledged my existence. He nodded perfunctorily then turned his attention back to Gene.

"I don't know how I could possibly shed any light on the situation. I haven't seen Virginia in years."

"No one has. That's what's making our job so difficult, but since you were a friend of hers in the past, we wanted to get your perspective."

Gregory relaxed slightly. "Sure. Ginny was a sweet girl when I knew her, but that was so long ago. We didn't keep in touch when she left, and I didn't catch up with her when she came back."

"Ginny? I haven't heard anyone call her that before," Gene said.

"Yeah, we all had nicknames in school. Edgar was Swifty and George was called Rat." Gregory smirked.

"Oh, what was yours?" Gene asked.

"Ashley." Gregory shook his head and laughed. "It was dumb. It's because Leslie Howard had blonde hair when he played Ashley in *Gone with the Wind*. It was a popular movie when we were in school."

"So how long were you and Virginia an item?" Gene asked.

"About five years. We were young when we started going steady, around fourteen, I think."

"Did any of the other guys ever make comments? Maybe they were a little jealous of your relationship?" Gene asked.

Gregory shrugged. "Sure, every guy was jealous. Ginny was a real looker, and you know, I'm the only one she ever went out with."

He grinned proudly like she was a prize he'd won at the fair.

"Really? And who broke up with who?" Gene asked, even though we knew Virginia had returned the ring to him.

"It was so long ago." Gregory rubbed his chin. "I think it was a mutual thing."

"And how serious would you have considered the relationship?"

"Not serious at all. We were young. I barely remember it," Gregory said.

109

I didn't take my eyes off him. The blond hair, the smooth lies. I knew I had to get back to an unbiased place. There was nothing in the case that pointed a finger at this man, but everything in me reacted like he was the one. It had definitely been the right decision to put Gene in charge, considering my reaction, but I sensed Gene was unsure where to go next.

"Can you tell us about when she left?" I jumped in, trying to keep my tone neutral. "Were you surprised, or did she tell you ahead of time about her plans?"

"God, that was so long ago. I can't remember." Gregory chuckled, but it came out thin and unsure. He had to look up as I was still standing. I allowed the silence to continue and thankfully Gene also stayed mute. "I guess we spoke about leaving Creighton, everyone does at that age, but I wouldn't say I was surprised she left. By that time, we had sort of gone our separate ways, so I don't think I even noticed she was gone until I began hearing around town that she'd left."

"How serious would you classify your relationship with Miss Boyle?"

Gregory glanced over at Gene as if he expected an ally, but the officer stayed silent.

"Ahh," he rubbed his head, messing his perfect hair, "I guess I'd classify it as tame. How serious can you be at that age? I was probably more interested in sports than boyfriend-girlfriend stuff." His voice inflected up at the end. "As I said, we were just kids, really."

"So, you weren't planning long term then? You know settle down after high school, live happily ever after…that kind of

110

thing?" Gene asked in a cheery neighbourly voice, which seemed to relax Gregory.

"Marriage?" His voice went up an octave. "No, no, no, that was the furthest thing from my mind at that time." He reached out and readjusted the name plate on his desk, keeping his eyes down. Everything in his manner hinted that he *had* given marriage some thought, and it was still a bone of contention for him.

"So, for a number of years you two were an item, pretty much all through high school, and then you broke up. She leaves town without telling you and returns five years later as the talk of the town. That had to sting a bit. I mean, you're still here, not married, working at the mine like everyone else, while she'd become a big deal." I liked to poke the bear a bit during interrogations. The best pieces of information often slipped out during periods of high emotion.

"She wasn't a big deal," he scoffed, "and I do have plans to leave Creighton. In a year or two I'll get moved to the Sudbury office, and after that, who knows where I'll go."

"I've seen pictures of her. She was a beautiful girl, and you must have been curious about her life. Did you two meet up, perhaps reminisce over old times?" I could sense Gene watching me.

Gregory sat still. He looked away from me and spoke down to his shoes. "No, I barely gave her a second thought. I'm engaged to Paulette Carmichael now, and Ginny is all in the past."

"So, you didn't see her when she returned?" Gene asked.

Gregory glanced up at him, then back down to his desk. "No, not really."

"Not really, or no?" Gene asked.

"Well, I saw her once at the diner, but only by coincidence. I was picking Paulette up after work."

"And you never got a chance to meet up alone with Virginia?"

"No, I just said so." He crossed his arms like a petulant child.

"Okay, fine." Gene held his hands up in front of him. "Just making sure in case anything pops up later during the investigation."

"Pops up? I don't know how that could happen. As I said, I didn't see her. Why? Has someone said something to you?"

Gene ignored the question and turned to me. "Detective, is there anything else you would like to ask Mr. Hansen?"

"Just one more thing. Where were you the day of the murder?" I stared pointedly at him.

"I was with Paulette most of the day. You can ask her," he shot out.

"Most?" I said.

"Yeah. She was getting everything ready to bake a bunch of pies. Her little brother was out picking with his friends and was bringing his haul to her. Paulette makes the best pies."

"And you were with her the whole time she was doing that," I pushed.

"Pretty much. At one point she realized she didn't have enough sugar and sent me to fetch some."

"When exactly was that?" I made a show of writing in my notebook. People got very particular about what they were saying when they knew you were keeping a record.

"I don't remember exactly. It was probably around noon," he said slowly.

"Noon, hmm. Okay, thanks. Oh, and what store did you buy the sugar from?"

"Valenti's." He swallowed.

I wrote it down, then flipped the notebook shut so it made a slapping sound that caused Gregory to flinch.

"Thanks, Mr. Hansen. Gene, are we good?" I looked over at the officer.

Gene smiled. "Yes, we are, Detective. Thanks for your cooperation, Greg. We'll be in touch."

"I guess you'll be needing to talk to everyone in town?" Gregory was sitting tall in his chair, arms folded on his desk like a primary school student waiting for the bell.

"Pretty much," Gene said.

"Have you had a chance to talk to Paulette yet? Just because I know she's at work today, in case you're looking for her."

"No, we haven't, but thanks for letting us know," Gene answered.

We'd barely cleared the doorway when I heard the rhythmic sound of a phone being dialled.

Gene shook his head. "That boy would be a terrible poker player. Every emotion he has just comes busting out of him. Makes me wonder if he'd ever be able to commit a crime and hide it."

Back outside the office, the fresh air helped clear my head. I couldn't imagine working a job where you spent eight to ten hours a day stuck inside, in one place. Gene chuckled beside me.

"That was kind of fun, watching him squirm. I never liked that kid."

"No? How come?" I asked.

"He's so full of himself. The girls call him Gregory Handsome. I wouldn't be surprised if he started that himself. There are plenty of fathers who steer their daughters out of Hansen's path."

"He's engaged now, as he liked to point out frequently," I said.

"From what I've heard, there are bets that he'll never marry her. He is more of a 'catch and release' kind of guy."

Gene stopped at the car, and his smile faded. A line of kids rode past the gate on their bikes, carrying an assortment of fishing poles and nets.

"He acts like they were passing acquaintances, but from what my wife told me, they were pretty serious, and it was a shock when they broke up. How long would a guy hang on to something like that?" Gene looked over at me.

I shrugged. "Some never get over it."

"But is it something a guy would kill over?"

"That's what we have to find out," I said, knowing it was definitely something men would kill over and the question we had to answer was if Gregory Hansen was such a man?

SEVENTEEN

VICTOR

The interview with Gregory was a dead end. In times like this, I missed the freedom I had during wartime. I'd honed my interrogation skills working with the French Resistance. My only job was to get results using whatever means possible. Unfortunately, the tactics I learned then weren't acceptable now, so I had to rely on old-fashioned detective work.

Since joining the Sudbury force, I'd worked on a number of murder cases – revenge, domestic, drunken brawls that got out of hand – but this was the first one that felt personal. It wasn't the situation, even as mysterious as it was, but the victim herself. Virginia Boyle brought up memories I wanted to keep buried. She had a strong resemblance to another woman whose body was also found in a wooded area. Except the woman, Margaux, her body had been in much worse condition. The signs were clear that her death had been painful and prolonged. This case brought those memories back and began haunting both my days and nights.

I did my best to shove the thoughts out of the way. Rehashing Margaux's death wasn't going to help me with this case. In fact, it would likely get in the way, mostly of my judgement, as my reaction to Gregory Hansen had proved.

I turned my mind back to that interview. We went in with nothing and came out with barely much more than that. None of Virginia Boyle's murder made sense, and if we didn't get a tip or break, I wasn't sure how we'd ever solve this case.

I pulled into town and realized how quickly the smokestack and other sights had become familiar to me. Instead of going straight to the station, I made a quick stop at the diner across the street. I'd learned Gene had a bit of a sweet tooth, so I picked up a couple of Danishes. I'd only made it a few steps outside the diner when I was confronted by two of the locals.

"Detective? We just had to rush over when we saw it was you. I'm Mrs. Little, and this here is Mrs. Chumsky."

Both ladies wore dresses more reminiscent of the previous decade, which I'd recognized as a common feature of Creighton. It explained why I always felt like I'd stepped back in time when I was here. Mrs. Little stood with hands on hips while Mrs. Chumsky's arms crossed over her chest. I recognized an interrogation stance when I saw it.

"Hello," I said and tipped my hat.

"Well, sir, I think I speak for the whole town when I say we've all slept a little more soundly this past week knowing a real detective is on the case," Mrs. Little said.

"It's been so upsetting, and shocking, and disturbing," Mrs. Chumsky jumped in.

"It is a tragedy, but Officer Kowalski and I are doing our best," I said, knowing not to promise something I might not be able to deliver.

Mrs. Little reached over and gripped my arm with impressive strength. "Who do you think did this terrible deed, Detective?" She leaned in so close that I was engulfed in a strong scent that was most likely a perfume, but I couldn't be sure. "You must have a list of suspects and clues by now?"

"It's still early in the investigation."

"If you want our opinion," Mrs. Chumsky slid a glance over to Mrs. Little, who nodded and pursed her lips, "we think you should take a good hard look at those single fellows that stay in the rooming houses. They're outsiders, and that's the only one who could have done this type of thing."

"Wait, what about the bootleggers, hmmm?" Mrs. Little said. "Alcohol can turn men into the devil."

"Thank you, ladies, I appreciate your insights and will share your thoughts with Officer Kowalski." I wanted to make it clear that Gene was an important part of the investigation. My reason wasn't altruistic. I was hoping the townspeople would reach out and bother him with their theories and tips more than me. "Now, if you will excuse me, I have a lot to do." I took a quick step sideways and moved around the women.

Other than a few shout outs of "Morning, Detective" and "Good day, Officer," I made it to the station without any more interruptions. I wasn't comfortable with this situation. An ability to blend in and not draw attention to myself was something I learned during the war and used it often in my detective work, but here anonymity was impossible.

Gene was already at his desk, spit-and-polished, ready to face the day, when I delivered his pastry.

"What are your thoughts on single men living in the rooming houses and bootleggers for suspects?" I asked.

Gene shook his head and chuckled. "I'm guessing you've got an earful from some helpful members of the public."

"Yeah, something like that," I answered.

"That didn't take long, eh? I've received a few myself. Everybody in town will have a theory, and they won't be shy about sharing it. Lily, my wife, she and I were just talking about that last night. She's worried anyone with a grudge on their neighbour or bad blood with someone else will race down to put them on the suspects list, like some kind of witch hunt."

"She's probably correct," I said.

"Lily also wanted me to invite you for dinner some evening. If your wife doesn't mind you staying late," Gene said.

"I'm not married."

"Damn, if I tell her that, she's going to want to send lunches for you too."

"That's really not necessary."

"I know it's not," Gene leaned back in his chair, "but for some reason women are convinced without them we're helpless. Funny how they think we're capable of going to war and taking care of ourselves in cases of life and death, but once we're home, we're like children." He took a bite of his pastry and, for a man who didn't carry any extra weight, he finished it in an impressive few bites. "Speaking of the war, were you overseas? I joined up with the 48th Highlanders. Spent most of my time in Italy, then ended up in Apeldoorn in the Netherlands. It was a nice way to end the war, liberating the town. How about you?"

It was a question I ran into on occasion because it was the one thing men could find a connection over, no matter their place in society. Over the years, the question was asked less frequently as people stopped looking to the past. My dilemma came when I signed the Secret War Acts contract. I was committed for life never to speak about my role.

"I did my part."

For some people, that explanation was enough, but others would continue to dig. Gene was thankfully the former. He nodded, then licked the frosting off his fingertips. "So, back to work then?"

I'd only ever worked with a partner when I was an officer back in Toronto. Here the OPP detectives were spread thin over a large territory, so I mostly worked alone. But for this case, I started to lean on Gene's knowledge of the town and its people. He proved to be a capable officer, despite his lack of experience with serious crimes.

"We're going to have to be extra careful with whatever we dig up. The killer is most likely someone in town, and we don't want any information leaked that might tip them off. That includes sharing with our closest confidants or wife." I looked at Gene pointedly.

He stretched, standing up. "I got it. Loose lips sink ships, but keeping secrets in Creighton may be tougher than solving the crime." He chuckled. "Here, secrets aren't something you keep; you just tell them in a low voice."

"Great," I responded. "So, who's next on our list to pay a visit?"

"Other than Gregory, Virginia's closest friends before she left were Paulette Carmichael, Lorelei Clarke, Edgar Pelletier, and George Brasseur. Only George moved to Saskatchewan a few years back."

"So that leaves three. What can you tell me about them?"

"Paulette, who you know is now Gregory's fiancée."

"Yeah, that's interesting. Okay, what about the others?"

"I had to rely on my wife for most of the background, as I've only been here thirteen years, which makes me an outsider." He smiled. "But Lily grew up here, only a few years older than Virginia. So, Edgar, otherwise known as Swifty in high school, dated Paulette, and Lorelei married Jefferson Clarke, the public-school vice-principal and high school PE teacher. It was a minor scandal because he used to be her teacher, but that died down quickly and now they're starting a family."

"Hmm, okay, that's a bit of a spider's web there. Hopefully it will lead to something substantial."

"Each of them have settled down somewhat and gone on with their lives. It makes no sense that any of them would have a reason to want to hurt Virginia Boyle."

"Well, you know the old saying, 'Who knows what evil lurks in the hearts of men? The Shadow knows'?"

"Eh, what's that?" Gene frowned.

"Nothing, just my guilty pleasure. It's a radio program called *The Shadow*. He always gets his man."

"Well, we could use a little of that Shadow here then."

"Yes, we could."

EIGHTEEN

ROSE

"Don't try to make sense of it." That's what Detective Lapointe had said about Virginia's murder. That's all I did, all day – think about why. Why would someone do this? How could someone be so mad at Virginia that they'd want to kill her? And then Mrs. Valenti told me and Maggie, "Don't think about it." How could I not?

Hugh was the only one whose advice kind of made sense. "I don't know why this happened, but sometimes bad things can remind you what's really important, like your family." And he might have been right because I didn't want to go to the Inco Club, to Tank Hill, or up on Slater's Rock to play. I wanted to stay close to home. It felt safe to be with my family right now.

But it was odd that no one spoke about Virginia. When someone did talk, it was about things like what time it was, was it raining, or would the milk be delivered today? It felt rude to ask someone what they were feeling. Even before this happened, our family wasn't one for talking about their emotions.

A few days earlier, I'd gone to some shops on George Street with June and Maggie, just for something to do. The people looked at us with pity and whispered behind their hands. We were now the centre of attention, which I used to wish for, but not this way.

One of the bad things about staying home so much was I did lots of thinking, like if I hadn't gone so far away to pick the stupid blueberries could I have saved Virginia? Or if I'd stayed closer to her, would I be dead too? If I was to die with Virginia, would we be together in Heaven, or would I become a ghost wandering over the barren hills forever?

It hurt so much to think about her. When I closed my eyes, I could see her face, alive and smiling, snapping pictures all the time. Mom moved Virginia's clothes up to the attic. I didn't like that because the attic was a place for spiders, mice, and forgotten things.

Mom asked Olive if she wanted any of Virginia's clothes, but Olive just shook her head and said, "No, I couldn't." That was a surprise considering how much Olive had gushed over Virginia's wardrobe.

I hid Virginia's camera under the bed to could keep it for myself. The only other thing Mom missed when packing up was Virginia's perfume. It stayed on top of the bureau and sometimes I'd take off the lid, with the two birds on top, and take a deep breath. I only did this to feel the hurt more, because if I didn't feel pain, then I didn't feel anything. It felt wrong not to ache all the time.

Sometimes I'd go over the conversation I had with the detective. He'd asked me lots of questions about Virginia that I couldn't answer and should have been able to.

As I sat on the back porch steps, trying to remember everything I could about Virginia, Angus came out the back door of June and Oscar's house. I didn't even know he was in Creighton. Him and Oscar got along well, so he'd often visit them before coming to our house when he came to town.

Angus walked over and sat down beside me but didn't say anything. He lit his cigarette and squinted out over the yard. I watched the smoke swirl out of his mouth and nostrils, then float away. His profile was sharp. I knew women thought him handsome, but to me he was a mystery to which I never gave much thought until now. Not long ago, Virginia was also like a stranger to me, but she ended up being one of my most favourite people ever. How is it my own brother and sister could be so unknown to me? Did they know or even care to learn about me either?

If the detective had asked me to describe Angus, all I could really say was he worked in the mines, like all the other men, and from what Mom said, he sometimes liked to drink too much, but that was really it.

There had been so many things I never got to ask Virginia. What was her favourite colour? Her favourite food? Was there someone in Los Angeles she loved? Now I'd never know, and as I looked at Angus, I realized if something happened to him, I'd have the same questions.

"Angus?"

"Hmmm." He didn't turn to look at me.

"What's your favourite colour?"

He thought for a second. "I don't know."

"What's your favourite food?"

He drew hard on the end of his cigarette, then tossed it into the dirt, slowly exhaling the last of the smoke. "I don't have a favourite food. What's with all the questions?" He turned to look at me.

We were sitting so close that for the first time I saw he had a chicken pox scar above his eyebrow. Why had I never noticed it before? I had one in almost the same spot. Without thinking, I reached out and touched it with my fingertip.

"Hey, what's up?" He leaned away.

"I have one too." I pointed at my own.

He turned away while I looked him over, trying to memorize things like the nicotine stains between his fingers and the comb lines in his slicked-back hair.

"Meatloaf," he said. "That's my favourite food."

"Mom's meatloaf? I like it too."

"Actually, I have a—" he paused, "a friend, and hers is even better than Mom's, but don't tell anyone I said that."

The biggest surprise of all was that Angus smiled, just a little bit.

"Who is she?" I asked.

"Just a friend of mine. When I visit her, she makes really great food. Sometimes it's things I've never heard of with fancy French names. One day, she wants to open her own restaurant, and it would be way better than the diner." His face softened as he spoke.

"Angus?"

"Yeah?"

125

"Do you miss Virginia?"

His lips pursed, and all the softness disappeared. He rubbed his hands together, and I saw his right knuckles all had fresh scabs on them. It startled me when he stood up quickly.

"I gotta go," he said.

"Go where?" I didn't want him to leave. I wanted him to stay and keep talking, to tell me more things I didn't know about him.

"Never mind where, just go inside."

"I don't wanna. I just came out here."

"Then just don't leave the yard," he snapped and pointed at me. "If I find out you've gone wandering, I'll take Mom's wooden spoon to you, you hear me? There's a killer around, and you'd be easy pickings."

Before I could say anything, he stomped off between the houses and disappeared. Angus had never barked at me before, but for some reason it didn't make me feel bad; it actually made me feel all warm inside.

NINETEEN

VICTOR

I knew I was being watched when I stepped out of my car in front of the Boyles' house. Across the street, curtains fluttered, and screen doors creaked as neighbours poked their heads out to catch a glimpse of my arrival.

It gave me some insight into how Virginia Boyle must have felt on her return. People gawking, eyes following you everywhere. The people who lived here had such an isolated existence, even the slightest whiff of new or different was cause either for celebration or suspicion. Virginia would have been the first; I was, for some, the second.

If Virginia was anything like me, being the centre of attention just for showing up may have been unwanted and uncomfortable. I found myself thinking about her more beyond the regular crime victim. A small-town girl who left for the big city, but no one described her as a girl who'd been in search of fame or adventure. Besides standing out for her beauty, I had the impression she wasn't flamboyant or an attention seeker. If that was true, then why did she leave Creighton? It wasn't a common thing to do. She could have married her sweetheart and lived the rest of her life within arms length of her family and everything she'd ever known. The other plausible motivation a young woman could have for leaving was to escape something, which was a theory I had no proof of.

I took a final drag on my cigarette, then crushed it under my heel, anxious to make some progress on this case. The Boyles' house looked similar to the others around it, except in one way: it was like their house had lost its breath. No curtains fluttered in the breeze; no voices carried out the front door. Not a bird or a bee settled on the flowers that fought their way up between the rocks. The Boyles didn't need to drape their home in black bunting to announce they were in mourning, like in the days of the Victorians. Tragedy flowed from their home and spilled onto the street.

I was surprised when the young boy, Mikey, showed up at the station to fetch me, saying his grandma wanted to speak to us. Gene and I were in desperate need of a break, and I hoped Helen Boyle was going to give us one. Since Gene was out dealing with a shed break-in across town, I came on my own. When I got to the door, Helen Boyle was already waiting for me.

"Your grandson said you wanted to talk to me?"

Without inviting me in, she turned and disappeared into the darkness of the house. I let myself in and followed her to the front room. I took a seat directly across from her. She fidgeted, straightened her dress, and readjusted the pillow beside her. I waited as patiently as I could for her to open the conversation.

"The day you came to talk to us all, you asked me why Virginia left Creighton in the first place."

I nodded trying not to show any excitement or anticipation.

"What I told you was mostly true. I have no idea why she chose Los Angeles to move to, and it did happen very quickly. One day she told me she had saved some money working at the drug store and was leaving. I never asked her why, because I thought it was a good idea. She wasn't happy here."

"Was there any particular reason she wasn't happy?"

"How should I know, Detective?" She sniffed. "I had a husband, children, grandchildren, a house to keep; it would be impossible to do all that and keep track of everyone's moods and thoughts."

I leaned back and folded my arms.

"Virginia had become sullen and kept to herself most of the time anyway. I just assumed she'd grow out of it someday."

"Do you think it had to do with her breakup with Gregory Hansen?" I felt like I was pulling teeth and becoming frustrated. She was the one who summoned me.

"They broke up about a year before she left, but he still came around often. He was always trying to win her back."

I was tempted to go over and shake her. Whatever she had to tell me, she was very reluctant to say it.

"So do you think Gregory Hansen had something to do with Virginia's death?"

She looked at me like I had two heads.

"Gregory Hansen? Why would you think that? He was over the moon for her. No, what I called you here for was…there was something about Virginia." Her jaw clenched as if she was trying to keep her mouth from opening.

"What about Virginia?" I prompted.

"It's probably nothing. I didn't even want to bring it up, but Mr. Boyle insisted. He reads too many of those *True Detective* magazines and thinks everything is a clue, but before I tell you, I need you to promise that what I say won't leave this room. That no one will ever know about it." She pierced me with a look I was sure kept her family in line, but I'd come across more formidable women than Helen Boyle.

"Mrs. Boyle, I can't make that promise. If what you tell me helps catch Virginia's killer, it may come out in the trial. But if you don't tell me, we may never stop this person." Since I still needed the information, I softened my approach slightly. "But I will do my best."

She narrowed her eyes at me, struggling with whether to continue. I sorely hoped her need for justice would overcome her reluctance to share whatever skeletons were in the Boyle family closet. I'd run into this before; people would convince themselves, since their loved one was dead, nothing good could come from rehashing the past. I desperately hoped this wouldn't be the case.

"Virginia was a good girl," she stated. "What happened wasn't her fault and whoever did it coerced or tricked her into it. Of that, I am sure." Mrs. Boyle dared me to disagree with her potent stare.

"Into what?" I prodded.

"When she was fifteen, she became pregnant." She dropped her head and I waited. "And it wasn't by Gregory Hansen, who was her boyfriend at the time. That much she said. If it had been, he would have married her right away."

"Then who was it?" I itched to take out my notebook but didn't want to spook her into silence.

"I don't know. I tried to get her to tell me. She had never been defiant before, but whenever I asked her about it, she'd just close up. Since there was no father for her to marry, we did what we thought best. If anyone found out, her reputation would have been ruined. But not just hers—the whole family's. So, we told everyone I was pregnant, and because of my age, I needed to go to Toronto for special care and that Virginia was coming to help me."

"What happened to the baby?" I asked, even though having done the rough math in my head, I had a pretty good idea of what the answer would be.

"It's Rose," she confirmed.

"Does she know?" I asked.

"What good would that do anyone?" She looked at me like I was simple.

"Do you have any suspicions about who the father could be?"

"No, not at all, and Rose looks like our side of the family, so I never could figure it out."

"Can you tell me a little bit about what was going on with Virginia just before you found out about the baby? Who was she hanging out with then? Did her demeanor change?"

"If I felt there was something not right going on, Detective, I would have stepped right in," she said defensively.

"I'm sure you would have, Mrs. Boyle, but it might help if you could remember anything about the months before."

"There was nothing. She always had the same circle of friends.

I'd seen real tragedy and things much more worthy of the label of shame in my life, but it was all about perspective. Small-town life had a way of making your entire world small, which magnified molehills into mountains. So, for Mrs. Boyle, an unwed, pregnant daughter was a tragedy of epic proportions.

"I've only told you this because Connor thought it might help your work," she said.

"And you don't?"

"It's been nine years. We've hid the shame, never rocked the boat. I would think the father would know we had as much reason to keep this quiet as he did, so what would be the use of killing Virginia? She wasn't a threat."

It always amazed me how much people could rationalize what wasn't rational. Murder was rarely well thought out and never about common sense, but people often tried to find logic where there wasn't any.

"Perhaps whoever did this still felt she was a threat."

Mrs. Boyle sniffed and frowned. "Well, that's all I needed to tell you." She stood up, making it clear our conversation was over. I got up and thanked her for her time.

On the drive back to the station, I felt a buzz of adrenaline. Finally, something to go on, and even with the few details Mrs. Boyle had shared, it gave us a plausible suspect and our next step was figuring out who that suspect was. Either someone had seduced her or forced her, and whichever one it was, a fifteen-year-old girl would be easy pickings. But for once, the fact that everyone in town knew everyone else's business could play in our favour. Now all that had to be done was pry open nine-year-old memories.

TWENTY

ROSE

Nine days since Virginia was taken away. I kept track because Hugh told me it would get better with time, and it hadn't so far.

I sat between our house and June and Oscar's. The sun was hot, and I preferred the cool of the shade here. I was more comfortable in the shadows anyway. Maggie had gone with June and Mikey to the barbershop. June said he needed a haircut for the funeral. They invited me to go, but I didn't want to be stared at anymore, and ever since that day we found Virginia, Maggie rarely left June's side.

I stayed hidden in the shadows, able to see what was happening in the Dardanelles without anyone being able to see me. There were other kids playing games while their moms did regular things like hang out the laundry. I heard some people laughing a few yards over, and I wanted to cover my ears to block it out. How could they be happy when a black cloud hung over everything?

I sniffed my wrist, and tears came to my eyes. I'd put on a dab of Virginia's perfume that morning. I was back sleeping in my bedroom with Olive, but even that was different. She didn't steal the blankets or get mad at me for moving around too much. It wasn't like I was invisible but more like she couldn't see anything outside of herself. I preferred the old mean Olive. This new Olive sometimes shook the bed in the middle of the night when she cried.

I heard the car before I saw it. The detective drove a regular car, not a police car, but it was nicer than most of the pickup trucks and older cars I was used to seeing around town.

He got out of and looked around. Mrs. Little poked her head out the front door of her house across the street. He stood still for a moment to finish his cigarette. He was a watcher, like me. I stayed still in the shadows and waited for his footsteps to go up and into our house. When the front door banged shut, I slipped around back. The only reason the detective would come to our house was if he had news, and I wanted to know what it was. Our screen door squeaked and banged like all the others, but I knew how to open it just enough to slip through before the hinges would give me away.

I had as much right as anyone to know what was going on with the case, even if the grown-ups didn't think so. Mom used to say if *I didn't call your name it isn't your business*, but this *was* my business. Virginia and I were closer than sisters; we'd become like best friends, and I was the one who found her, so I had just as much right to know what the detective had come for.

I tiptoed in, relieved that the kitchen door was open enough so I could eavesdrop on the two of them. I laid on my belly and scooched forward. I had to stay down because it was possible to see into the kitchen a bit from the front room. The safest listening spot was under the table. I'd done this before. I tucked my legs underneath me and rested my chin in my hands. By the time I got settled, I'd missed some of what had been said. Thankfully, the detective had a deep voice that I could hear clear as a bell.

"Do you think it had to do with her breakup with Gregory Hansen?" he asked.

Gregory Hansen? Was he a suspect? Why would he want to hurt Virginia when he had a new girlfriend?

"Gregory Hansen? Why would you think that? He was over the moon for her. No, what I called you here for was...there was something about Virginia." I recognized that tone in Mom's voice. The one that made people listen.

"What about Virginia?" the detective asked the same question I had in my mind.

Mom's voice dropped so I couldn't hear what she said. I scootched forward a bit more and caught the detective saying something about not being able to promise.

"When she was fifteen," Mom paused like she was unsure of herself and that was not normal, "she got pregnant, and it wasn't by Gregory Hansen, who was her boyfriend at the time. That much she said. If it had been, he would have married her right away."

My ears stopped listening while my brain spun in circles. Virginia was a mom? How could that be, and where was her baby? So many questions bounced about. Had she left the baby in Los Angeles? Or did something bad happen to it, like my brother Francis? Maybe it got sick and died. I had to make myself stop thinking or I'd never catch the rest of what they were saying.

"What happened to the baby?" the detective asked.

"It's Rose."

"Does she know?"

"What good would that do anyone?"

I shook my head, and my first thought was, why did she name her baby the same as me? Then I remembered that would have been some time ago. Maybe I was named after her baby, because if Virginia was fifteen when she got pregnant, then… I counted slowly, using my fingers: seven, eight, nine. Virginia's baby would be about nine years old, just like me… just like me.

Even lying flat, I thought I might fall over. My head spun. I needed to get out of the house. I couldn't stay there one more minute.

Slowly, I backed out from under the table, unable to focus on the conversation anymore. I caught a few snippets. "It's been nine years. We've hid the shame, never rocked the boat… Perhaps whoever did this still felt she was a threat". Once free of the table, I silently slipped out the same way I'd come in.

Outside, I ran as fast as I could to nowhere in particular. Just up and away from my house. None of it made any sense. Running kept my mind busy, so I didn't have to think hard. I kept going until my legs wouldn't go any farther and the air hurt my lungs. I stopped in a small area with spindly trees. A spot that was far away from my house and the town below. A place where the blueberry bushes grew undisturbed with plump fruit that no one wanted to pick because these berries would be cursed.

I fell back onto the flat stones. Thin, wispy trees swayed lightly in the breeze. It was private here the way I thought a cemetery would feel like. Would a part of Virginia still be here? At that moment, she was the person I needed most in the world.

"Is it true, Virginia?" I asked out loud and looked up to the sky, hoping she'd hear me. "Are you really my mom?" But I didn't ask out loud the biggest questions I wanted answered: Why? Why didn't she take me with her? Why did she leave me behind?"

Mom's words bounded around my mind: "We hid the shame."

I was the shame.

My chin and bottom lip trembled, and big fat tears spilled out of the far corners of my eyes, rolling down the side of my head. It hurt so bad inside me. Everyone lied to me, even Virginia.

What was wrong with me that made Virginia not want to be my mom? Did my mom – or, I guess, my grandma – did she ever love me? How could you love a kid you were ashamed of? A kid who was a lie.

There were too many questions I didn't have answers for, but I knew I'd never ask them of anyone because I was too afraid the answers might hurt even more.

Virginia dying was awful, but this hurt almost as much. I loved my sister so much that a part of me died with her, and now I'd found out it was my own mother who'd been killed. I never got to say, "I love you, Mom." I'd never be held in her arms, knowing it was my mom holding me.

There were so many "never going to happens" that my head stopped thinking while my stomach tightened up. I rolled over and threw up into the dirt. My throat burned, my nose and eyes ran with tears and snot, and I didn't care, not about me, not about anything. When I retched for the last time, my arms that had been holding me up collapsed. I stayed there and hugged my knees to my chest.

There were no more tears. I felt empty of everything that had been me. My name hadn't changed, but I was not the Rose Boyle I was that morning. I didn't know who I was now or where I belonged, if anywhere. Everyone in my family had either lied to me or been lied to like I was. All I could think of was how much I hated them, all of them, even Maggie and Mikey because they knew who they were, where they belonged.

And Virginia…it was so unfair that I couldn't yell or scream at her. I had no one. No mother and no idea who my father was, but I was so angry with him too.

I lay there with hate flowing through me, and it made me feel just a little bit better. My anger made me warm, like a little flame had started that would become a great big fire. It was all I had now, so I would make it mine: anger and hate. I wanted to get back at everyone who made my life a lie.

I put my head down on the rock, the same rock where Virginia last laid hers, and I ran my hand over the fading stain. I don't know how long I stayed there, exhausted by the thought that I was nobody's child.

TWENTY-ONE

ROSE

"Rose, what do you suppose happens when you die?" Maggie asked.

"You should know better than me. You go to church all the time," I snapped.

It was the type of question Maggie and I had asked each other before, imagining what Heaven would be like. Would we live in fancy houses? Would there be cars, or could we just fly everywhere? But I didn't want to think about it because I knew Heaven was for good people.

Could you still be good if you told a lie? A really big one? Are secrets a kind of lie? I didn't mean little secrets, but the big one that maybe should be told. And now that I was keeping a really big secret, did that make me a bad person?

Only two days ago, I'd been someone else. Now I wasn't sure where I fit into my family. My mom wasn't my mom. Olive was really my aunt, not my sister. For once it made sense that Maggie and I were cousins. Except I couldn't say it out loud or let anyone know that I knew.

Just thinking about it was exhausting, and even though I knew it wasn't my fault I was born a shame, I was one anyway. Maggie for sure didn't know about Virginia being my mom, but did Olive or June? What about Angus?

"They tell us you go to Heaven if you're good and follow the sacraments, but Virginia wasn't Catholic. Still, I think she would get in, don't you?" Maggie's voice cut into my thoughts.

June converted to Catholicism when she married Oscar, but the rest of our family were still part of the United Church in town, even though we rarely went.

"Of course, she would. It's not just Catholics that go to Heaven." Even though I was still mad at Virginia, the thought of her not going to Heaven or anyone questioning it made the hair on the back of my neck stand up. I gripped the locket around my neck. The one I'd worn every day since Virginia gave it to me.

"I know when you're dead, you shouldn't mind, but I don't want to be buried in the ground. It sounds scary," Maggie said.

"Well, you will be just like everyone else." I noticed one of the buttons on my top didn't match the others. I wore a faded yellow blouse that carried the shape of everyone else who'd worn it before me. Mom…or Grandma — it was so mixed up — had picked out my clothes for today.

She'd also picked out what Virginia was to be buried in. She chose the red rose dress, which was all wrong. Virginia was happiest in her work pants, the ones with a lot of pockets to keep her camera things in, and her pale orange blouse. That's what she usually wore when she went picture taking.

141

"Are you almost ready? Mom wants us all in the living room now." Olive came into the room. She looked at me and cocked her head to the side with a frown.

"What?" I looked at myself, then at her navy-blue dress, short white gloves, and matching belt.

She pursed her lips, then pushed past me to the closet. She came out with a burgundy blouse and shoved the hanger at me.

"Here, it's a bit small on me, so it shouldn't be too bad." She crossed her arms and waited.

I quickly slipped into the top. There were small blue flowers on it, but the darker colour felt more fitting for a funeral. I tucked it into my skirt so no one would be able to tell it was a bit too big.

Olive stepped in front of me and ran her hands gently along my shoulders. She smoothed out the creases and flattened down the collar. I could smell her perfume; she was also wearing Virginia's L'Air du Temp.

"That's better," she said. "Let's go."

My whole family was gathered in the living room wearing the best clothes they owned, and Virginia had been right: Mom did find an occasion to wear her hat with the feather. The black netting hid Mom's red-rimmed eyes, and even though it was fancier than the old-fashioned black dress she had on, it was a good match. I didn't want to think about how hard it must have been for her to put it on. After the funeral, the hat would be returned to its box, put on a shelf at the back of the closet, and forgotten, like a body in the ground.

June organized everything and instructed us where to go and when. She'd been managing everything since the tragedy. She'd do our laundry, make meals, clean up after, and host the visitors who dropped by. Mom spent a lot of time in bed with a headache.

Our whole family walked together to the church. We'd never done that before. Car rides were arranged for each of us to get to the cemetery after the service. Everyone in town would come to the church, but only some people had cars, so there'd be fewer at the cemetery. Hugh's parents were taking Olive, Maggie, and me with them.

For the first time, I truly understood what people meant when they said someone had the weight of the world on their shoulders. I felt like that as we walked towards the church. I had even thought about not going, saying I had a sick stomach. It wouldn't have been much of a lie, since my stomach had been topsy-turvy for days, but I changed my mind when I saw Dad come down in his suit. He gripped the banister, stepping carefully as if he just might shatter. I decided that if he could bear it, I could too.

A large crowd was already gathered outside the church when we arrived. A group of women hustled over and surrounded Mom with quiet words, hugs, and tears. They seemed to know what to do and say. Although I was still angry at Mom, I was glad those women were there to hold her up.

I followed my family up the stairs of the United Church. Sometimes I went to Sunday school here when I had nothing else to do. The crowd waited for us to go first. There were kids from my school, some with their families and others standing together in small groups. My face felt warm, and I wished they'd stop staring at us and whispering. Maggie slipped her hand into mine, and we held onto each other tightly.

We were led to the front pew. I always thought you had to be special to sit up front and secretly envied the people who were honoured with those spots. Now I'd trade seats with anyone for a chance to sit in the very back.

Once everyone was seated, Reverend Joyce appeared in his black robes. He was a cheery man who always had a silly joke for us kids, but today his smile crinkles were missing. He looked more serious, like Father Mancini, the Catholic priest.

Reverend Joyce talked about God's will and having faith. I stopped paying attention. He mentioned Virginia's name a few times, but I didn't feel her in the service. There was no talk of her smile, how she could tease Olive and not make her angry, and how she wanted to work for *Life Magazine*.

The minister spoke about a Virginia I didn't know. A teenager who sang in the choir. The stories he told didn't bring to mind my Virginia who came from a magical land far away and made me feel special and loved. Of course, he didn't mention her three greatest sins; giving me away, leaving me to go to Los Angeles, and then dying. Three times she had left me, but I loved her more than I hated what she did.

The doors at the back of the church stayed open, but it didn't help. The heat bugs buzzed outside, and all around me people were using the program with Virginia's smiling face on it to fan themselves.

Maggie's eyes fluttered a few times until she slumped against June. All the adults, including Olive, sat ramrod-straight, listening to the pastor's sermon about God's plan and a better place.

Olive elbowed me. I hadn't noticed everyone stand up. There was only the sound of pews creaking, feet shuffling, and people clearing their throats. Someone put their hand in the small of my back and lightly pushed along to the end of the pew.

We followed the wooden coffin out of the church. Dad, Angus, Oscar, Hugh, Mr. Valenti, and Mr. Brodie, Dad's friend from work, carried the coffin out the door and into the hearse. When they finished, they each pulled out a hanky and wiped the sweat from their foreheads.

People milled about and talked quietly. Some men in dark suits came to shake Dad's hand. They must have been from Inco, because there wouldn't be any other reason for strangers to come. Maggie took my hand, and I followed her behind a rusty truck.

"I don't want anymore hugs, Rose." Maggie sat down on a rock. "Everyone is so sticky."

"There sure are a lot of people here," I said.

"Yeah, it looks like the whole town came."

Maggie moved over, and I sat down.

I hadn't paid attention while the Pastor was speaking and my mind wandered, as it usually did to Virginia, and all the unanswered questions. The kind that sometimes made it hard to sleep.

"Maggie, if everyone in town is here, then that means whoever killed Virginia must be here too," I said. She looked at

145

me with eyes as wide as saucers. That's when I realized how hidden we were from the rest of the crowd. "Maybe we should go back."

She nodded and we'd just stood up when Gregory Hansen stomped around the side of the truck. He looked as startled as we were.

"Oh, hey, girls," he said. The sun behind him put his face in shadow. "I'm really sorry about your sister." His words came out jerky.

"Thank you." Maggie and I answered automatically.

Gregory ran his hand over his eyes and through his hair, which made it stand up at the front. He sucked in a sharp breath.

"You know, if she hadn't come back, none of this would have happened." He kicked at the dirt. "Actually, if she hadn't left in the first place, and we got married, like we were supposed to, she'd still be alive." It took me a second to realize his eyes were damp. "Uhhh." He wiped them angrily and ran his jacket cuff under his runny nose, the way a kid would. "Why do you women always bring these things on yourself?"

I shrugged, not knowing what to say. Maggie stayed quiet too. All I could think of was when I overheard the detective ask Mom, "So do you think Gregory Hansen had something to do with Virginia's death?"

Could he be the one? As quickly as he had appeared, he turned and stomped off, talking angrily to himself.

The detective had told me you couldn't tell a killer by looking at them, but with his tear-stained face, angry eyes, and accusations, I could almost believe he could be the one.

TWENTY-TWO

ROSE

Maggie and I went back to find the rest of our family. It felt better being close to them. Soon after, Hugh came and collected us to go to the cemetery. Most people headed to the Inco club to set up for the luncheon. The few who were going to the cemetery piled into their cars and trucks, packing as many people as they could get in. Olive was already in the back seat of the McLellan's Packard, dabbing at her reddened nose with her hankie.

Maggie and I slid in beside her while Hugh took a seat up front between his parents. We easily could have fit another one or two people in the back. Mr. McLellan pulled out and followed the solemn line of cars out of Creighton onto the highway. He drove very seriously with both hands firmly gripping the wheel.

Mrs. McLellan's hair was pulled tight into a twist in the back. I could see a net and a dozen or so bobby pins threaded throughout her hair. There wasn't a single flyaway. As we drove in silence, I saw Hugh's jaw had a few rough areas where it looked like he'd shaved.

"So, Olive, will you stay working at the pharmacy, or do you have other plans when you finish school?" Mrs. McLellan turned her head slightly to look back at us.

Olive gripped her hands together so tightly, the small pearl button pulled, looking close to popping off. "I haven't really given it much thought, Mrs. McLellan. I was supposed to move to Los Angeles with Virginia, so now…I'm not sure. I guess I still could. After all, Virginia was able to do it, so there's no reason I can't." She shrugged and stayed focused on her hands.

This was the first I'd heard Olive mention leaving. I assumed, after everything that happened, she'd stay in Creighton Mine. Now Hugh turned around as well. It was obvious from the look on his face that he was as surprised as me by the news.

"What do you mean? You're only sixteen. You can't leave Creighton all by yourself. You have no idea what happens in the big city. Isn't that right, Mother?" Hugh's words tumbled out.

Mrs. McLellan used that smile people do when they think you're being simple. "That's right, dear. Olive, you wouldn't last a minute in the big city by yourself."

I could tell Olive was getting annoyed. She hated being told what to do, but Mom had drilled good manners into us, so she kept her eyes cast down. "I could learn, just like Virginia did." Her voice was tight.

"But wasn't she…like…twenty when she left?" Hugh said.

"Hush, Hugh." His mother's voice never changed, like a kindergarten teacher speaking to her pupils. "Now, Olive, after everything your poor mother has been through, don't you think it would be rather selfish of you to leave her now? She just lost

149

one daughter. How do you think she would cope if something were to happen to you, hmm?"

"I guess so," Olive said.

Mrs. McLellan smiled with tight lips then turned back to face the road. The rest of the drive was spent in uncomfortable silence. The cemetery was far down the highway. We passed Meatbird Lake. Maggie pointed as we went by an area under construction. It was the new town of Lively that Inco was building. They said the new houses would have indoor plumbing, heating throughout, and basements. Eventually we turned off the highway and drove under a metal arch that read *Waters Cemetery*. My stomach dropped.

"We're here." Mr. McLellan spoke up for the first time.

When we stepped from the car, a strong wind swept in. I closed my eyes against the fine pieces of dirt that pelted us.

"My goodness," Mrs. McLellan gasped, grabbing her hat.

Clouds swept in quickly and darkened the sky, like someone had just tossed a quilt over the sun. It wouldn't be long before the rain started.

I'd never seen so many vehicles at one time. People in their best funeral outfits climbed out and walked in small groups to the gravesite, glancing nervously up at the sky. I instantly recognized Gregory gripping Paulette Carmichael's elbow tightly. She dabbed at her eyes, while his face was hard as stone. I darted around Olive and Hugh who were going slowly because her heels kept sinking into the ground.

Maggie and I reached the crowd that was already there and pushed our way to the front where the rest of our family was. I looked down by my feet and saw the gaping hole. It was dark, and cool air drifted up, causing goosebumps on my legs. The soil smelled heavy and wet like the mud pies we'd make after it rained. I saw something move through the dirt, some kind of bug that scurried, not liking that it had been disturbed.

Everything about this was wrong. It felt final in a way it hadn't before. In my mind, Virginia was just somewhere else. Seeing the coffin there, beside the hole, I now pictured her laid out like Snow White: beautiful, perfect, and still. Only there wouldn't be a prince to bring her back.

I almost said "Mama" out loud, but instead whispered it under my breath. Two large hands fell heavy onto my shoulders. It was Angus holding me in place. He didn't know it, but he was keeping me from falling into the pit or running away.

Reverend Joyce stepped up and began reciting a prayer. A flash of sheet lightning caused a few people in the crowd to gasp. The wind picked up. It whipped strands of hair in front of my face. It felt right that it should rain and thunder. That the whole world would mourn with us. Putting Virginia into the ground felt too big for it just to matter to us. She deserved more. Rain fell onto hats, bare heads, and into the hole, collecting into a puddle and making a splashing sound. Beside me, June cried while Dad cleared his throat over and over.

Just like in the church, none of what the Reverend said comforted me at all. Virginia was dead. I clenched my fists because all I could think about was how there was someone out there, or maybe even here at the graveside, who'd killed her. That person would get to wake up in the morning, and eat their breakfast, and listen to the radio, and do whatever they wanted. It was so unfair. It felt like there were screams bouncing around my insides, so I bit my lip to keep it all in.

Finally, Reverend Joyce closed his book. The people around me bowed their heads and folded their hands for a prayer. Angus dropped his hands away from my shoulders, and as soon as I heard his deep voice mumble the prayer, I slipped away. I couldn't stay and watch Virginia go into the damp ground. I moved through the crowd unnoticed, brushing against them like a ghost.

The air was cooler away from the damp, sweaty spectators. The droning of the prayer faded as I walked farther away. Some of the tombstones stood proud and polished while others were tilted with inscriptions too faded to make out. As the rain darkened the stone, the names become easier to read. I walked to the far side of the cemetery, as far away as I could get. There I saw the carvings of cherubs with dates from birth to death that were closer together. I did the math in my head: twelve years old, three years old, one only a few months. I picked up my step and let my eyes roam over the names of the children.

Grace, Jonathon, Sofia, Mikael, and then I found it. It was a flat stone; the kind that seemed to grow out of the ground. A moss-covered angel with tiny wings was carved in the top corner. Its hand reached out towards the name. *Francis James Boyle, Jan. 29, 1931,* was all it said.

Here was my brother…no, I corrected myself, my uncle. He'd always been just a name. A faded baby picture in my parents' bedroom. Standing next to his grave, he became real to me, and

I felt the loss for the first time. How many more of my family would end up here too early? When would my time come? My breath caught, like my lungs stopped working. I didn't want to become a faded name on a gravestone.

Francis Boyle, forever two years old, and now his sister, Virginia, would join him. It was so wrong, both of them gone before they got to live a full life. Francis taken by sickness or the hand of God, while Virginia was taken by the hands of someone evil. Someone had purposefully put her here, and they shouldn't get away with it. Virginia, my mama, deserved so much better.

I stepped away from where the cherubs lay and walked slowly back towards the other mourners. Water dropped from the ends of my braids, and I shivered through my damp clothes.

That's when I saw him, a few rows back from the crowd, standing as still as the stone angel beside him. It was Detective Lapointe. He wore a dark suit with his hands clasped behind him. The only movement was the smallest turn of his head as, little by little, he scanned the crowd.

TWENTY-THREE

VICTOR

"What kind of name is Swifty?" I asked Gene as we made our way up to the front door of a house that had little love. "Was he a fast runner?"

"No, he could swipe candy and be out of the store before anyone knew what happened."

I knocked on the screen door, which made it fall partially towards me. The top hinge was attached to the house but not the door.

"Yeah, I'm coming," a voice bellowed from within. A tall man appeared. He looked like Jimmy Stewart if he'd never made it to Hollywood, lived a hard life, and got old before his time.

"Gene? What brings you here?" A poorly rolled cigarette hung unlit from his mouth, but his demeanour softened when he saw the officer.

"Hi, Edgar, can we bend your ear for a couple minutes? We've got some questions and thought you might be able to help us," Gene said.

Edgar looked me over and didn't try to hide the fact that he didn't like what he saw. I was used to that. About two thirds of the people I met through my work were unhappy to see me. I was either bringing bad news or coming to arrest them. The rest looked at me like some kind of saviour who was going to solve all their problems, which never happened.

"Yeah, I guess come on through."

I let Gene go first. As my eyes adjusted to the darkness, I noticed the house had a similar layout to the Boyles', but in comparison, theirs was fancy. We passed a living room with a lopsided chesterfield missing a leg. A small child with a dirty face, and wearing only a diaper, stared at us as we passed.

"Take a seat." Edgar pointed to a couple mismatched chairs when we entered the kitchen.

"Hey, Darla." Gene spoke to a woman with her back to us and a small baby on her hip.

She didn't turn around, only grunted a greeting as she washed dishes impressively with one hand while the other held the child. This one smaller, but just as grimy as the one in the front room.

Edgar lit his cigarette and leaned back in his chair. "So, this is about Virginia Boyle, I 'spose?"

"Yeah, it is, and this is Detective Victor Lapointe from the Sudbury OPP."

"I guessed as much."

"I didn't see you at the funeral," Gene added.

Edgar leaned forward. "I was working. The mine doesn't stop, even for murder."

A bang came from the other room, followed by a piercing cry.

"Darla, go take care of that."

155

The woman turned, and although she couldn't have been more than twenty-five, she looked like youth had left her some time before.

"Did you see Virginia Boyle when she was here?" I asked. Frustrated with the lack of progress, I'd become impatient to start getting answers and clues.

"I saw her outside the shops one day, but I didn't speak to her."

"How come? Weren't you good friends when you were younger?" Gene asked.

"Yeah," Edgar scoffed, "and that was a long time ago. We're not friends now." He said "friends" like it was a dirty word.

"That's what we want to talk to you about. The time you were *friends*." I punctuated the word as well.

"Can you tell us your recollections of Virginia and Gregory Hansen's relationship back then?" Gene said.

Edgar snorted and looked out a grimy window. "The golden couple. Not much to say. Virginia was nice enough. Her and Gregory mostly called the shots in our small group. They decided whether we'd go to the Rio for a movie or the Inco club to the dance. The rest of us fell in line like a row of ducklings."

"Who was the rest of you?" I asked.

He glanced at me, then began rolling a new cigarette even though he still had a full one on the go. "There was me, Paulette, Rat, and Lorelei for the most part."

"Were you all in couples?" I asked.

"Uh-huh. Back then Paulette and I were together. Rat and Lorelei dated, broke up on a monthly basis, and then they'd get back together again."

"What about Virginia and Gregory? Did they ever break up and get back together?" Gene asked.

"Nope. The one-time Virginia called it quits was the only time, and no matter how much he begged she never took him back." Edgar grinned slightly at this.

Interviews and interrogations were my specialty and the part I enjoyed most. It was like a cat-and-mouse game pitting intelligence and intuition against people's reticence. But I struggled with how to ask him about Virginia without letting on about the pregnancy.

"Outside of school, what kind of interests or activities did Virginia take part in?" I asked.

"What do you mean?"

"When she wasn't hanging out with you, what was she doing?"

"Shit, I don't know. Ask the girls. They'd remember that stuff better than me."

"Edgar, can you tell us a bit more about when Gregory and Virginia broke up? Like how Gregory took it." Gene asked.

Edgar leaned back and smiled. "Oh, yeah, that I remember. Greg was wrecked. He moped around like a lost puppy. He kept chasing after Virginia, begging her to take him back. The guy had no dignity."

"I get the impression you and Gregory are no longer good friends," I said.

"No, we're not."

"Can you tell us what happened?" Gene prodded.

Edgar's eyes hardened. "Gregory was always a bit of a bastard, but Virginia kept him in check. Once they broke up, he showed his true colours. Since he was miserable and unhappy, he was going to make everyone around him the same. He'd pick on people, treat them like shit, and he made it his goal to ruin everyone else's relationships." He took a long pull on his cigarette. His fingers were nicotine-stained and cracked.

"How exactly did he do that?" Gene asked.

"He'd tell Lorelei that Rat said something about her, which he didn't, and then he'd tell Rat he saw Lorelei flirting with some other guy or the gym teacher, just crap like that. They were easy pickings, but then he started messing with me and Paulette. Eventually she broke up with me, thinking she'd go steady with Gregory, but he was still sniffing after Virginia."

"They're together now, though," I added.

"Yeah, but that didn't happen for a few years. He dated a couple other girls in between. Like those other girls, he'll dump Paulette at some point and move on to ruin someone else's life. Trust me, he'll never marry Paulette. Everyone knows that but her."

"Do you think Gregory would still be carrying a torch for Virginia?" I asked.

Edgar looked at me intently with bloodshot eyes. "Detective, are you asking me if I think Gregory is the kind of guy who'd kill a girl years later for breaking his heart?"

"Well, is he?" I asked.

Edgar's smile was more like a grimace. "I don't think Gregory has much of a backbone or likes to get his hands dirty, but to be honest, I've never seen a guy take a breakup as hard as he did. It wasn't just like she broke his heart; it was like she took his whole life away. He used to talk about when they get married and move away and crap like that. After she left him, he never talked like that much."

"Did he ever mention getting back at her or anything like that?" I asked.

Edgar rubbed his face and leaned back in his chair. "Listen, I don't like Gregory; in fact, I can't stand him and would love to punch him in his smug face, but I can't quite bring myself to point a finger at him and say, yeah, he'd kill Virginia. I'll leave that to you fellas. Once we graduated high school and Paulette and I broke up, we hung out with different crowds. I don't know much about him now and haven't spoken directly to him in years."

"Well, thanks, Edgar, we really appreciate your help," I said and rose from my seat. Gene followed while Edgar stayed seated, deep in thought.

"Detective," Edgar said as we turned to leave. "I hope you catch whoever the bastard is that did this. Virginia didn't deserve what happened to her."

TWENTY-FOUR

ROSE

It had been fifteen days since Virginia was taken away, six days since I learned she was really my mom, and four days since we put her into the ground. I didn't have anything else to do but count days.

Maggie sat beside me on the front steps. Olive leaned against the railing while Hugh stood close by, kicking stones. Everyone was making their kids stay close to home, including us. Although Olive was older, she also kept nearby. If she did leave, it was usually only if Hugh was by her side.

"Hey, Rose?" Maggie said.

"Yeah?"

"Mikey told me that Lefty Koskinen told him that everyone is saying it was a hermit that did it and that he lives in a cave not far from here."

"Really?" This was news to me. "Has anyone seen him, for real?"

"Mikey said that Lefty said that some hunters told someone that they'd seen him, and he only wore animal skins and was really dirty," Maggie said.

"It wasn't a hermit, a witch, or any of the other stupid things people are saying," Olive snapped. She stood up and crossed her arms with a look halfway between angry and sad. "It was a monster, a monster of a man. A horrible, cruel killer that doesn't deserve to live."

Hugh walked over and put a hand on her shoulder. "Hey, Olive, it's okay. The girls are just trying to make sense of this." He turned to us. "You know, girls, there are going to be a lot of wild stories you should just ignore. Let the police do their job. My father is pretty sure it was a drifter because no one in Creighton would do such a thing."

"Look, here comes Maybelle." Maggie jumped up and knocked my shoulder getting past me.

The Valentis' grocery wagon plodded down the road, pulled by Maybelle, a horse who who had been delivering groceries since before Olive was born. Maybelle had walked the same route so many times that I heard one time Mr. Valenti got her hitched up and stepped away for a minute, and when he returned Maybelle was gone. She was already walking the route all on her own.

The wagon stopped in front of our house, but Mr. Valenti wasn't driving. It was Nick, his son, who was in Olive and Hugh's grade. Maggie grabbed the horse's bridle and kissed Maybelle's nose as soon as they stopped. The horse shook her head like she was trying to get rid of an annoying fly.

"Hey, Nick, how come you're doing the deliveries and not your dad?" I asked when I saw him.

"He hurt his back lifting bags of flour, but what does he expect? He's over forty." Nick jumped down easily, undid the back of the wagon, and shoved a bag of flour to the side. It was almost the size of Maggie, but he pushed it like it weighed nothing. Olive walked over and leaned against the wagon.

"Hey, Olive." Nick was one of the popular kids. He was a star pitcher and good-looking. He took Olive on a date to a school dance at the beginning of the year.

"I got your family's groceries, and my mom sent over a pie she made too." He reached into the back and pulled out a blueberry pie. It made my stomach turn just looking at it. I never wanted to eat another blueberry again.

"Oh, thanks." Olive took the pie without looking down at it. "So, will you be playing in the game this weekend?"

"Yeah, and I can't wait to throw against the Frood team. I know we're gonna beat them this time. Oh, hey, you probably didn't hear I'm going to be in tomorrow's issue of the *Inco Triangle*. Eddie Szymanski took my picture and interviewed me. He said I might even be on the front page."

"Virginia was supposed to be in the *Triangle* too," I blurted out.

Everyone turned to look at me like I'd said a swear word or something bad.

"Well, she is. Eddie interviewed her and took lots of pictures. I was there with her," I said.

"That was before, Rose...everything is different now," Olive said through clenched teeth.

"I'm real sorry about your sister, Olive," Nick said and put his hand on her shoulder.

"Thanks, Nick." Olive looked up at him with a sad smile.

"I only saw her the one time, but she was a real looker," he said.

"Yes, she was beautiful," Olive said softly.

I climbed into the back of the wagon to look for our groceries, since Nick didn't seem in any hurry to get them.

"Did she stop by your parents' store?" Olive asked.

I found a box with a receipt that had our name on it. There were eggs, sugar, lard, and some vegetables. I tugged and pulled it towards the open end of the wagon.

"No, it was after baseball practice one day. I was on the path behind Summerhill. I saw Gregory Hansen talking to a pretty woman I'd never seen before, so I knew it had to be her." He shrugged.

I pushed our grocery box to the end of the wagon with all my strength. "What was Virginia doing with Gregory?" I asked.

"I don't know." Nick shrugged. "They were just talking, I guess." He leaned over, grabbed the box from me, and swung it over to one side as if it weighed no more than a stack of sheets. Then he looked off, squinting. "Actually, she was shaking her finger at him like she was giving him a real talking-to. Then she left and Gregory just kind of stood there staring at his feet. It felt kinda awkward, you know, so I didn't say hi or anything, just kept going."

I wondered what Gregory did to make Virginia mad at him?

"I can take that." Hugh stepped up and pointed at the box Nick was holding. "I'm sure there's a lot of people waiting for their deliveries, and Mrs. Boyle will probably need this for our dinner tonight."

Nick straightened up and held out the box. "It's pretty heavy, Hugh. Are you sure you can handle it?" He grinned and let it go so it would drop it into Hugh's arms.

"Nope, I'm good," Hugh said and caught the box easily, slinging it up under one arm the same way Nick had been holding it. Both Olive and Nick looked surprised. I sort of was too, because I never thought of Hugh as being as strong as someone like Nick.

"Are you coming to the game on Saturday?" Nick asked, turning back to Olive.

"Maybe, we'll see."

Nick leaned in closer. "If you're up for it Friday night, a few of us are going to Slater's Rock. It's my first time as the opening pitcher for the game, so I'm going to prove myself, and it would be great if you could be there to cheer me on."

Olive bit her bottom lip and glanced over at Hugh, who didn't say anything. "Maybe. It might be good for us to get out of the house and do something fun. Thanks."

Nick glanced over at Hugh, then back to Olive. "Great, see you then."

"Oh, and thank your mom for the pie, please," Olive said and went inside with Hugh following close behind.

I jumped out of the back of the wagon. Nick climbed up into the seat and turned to me.

"So, your sister and Hugh, are they…" But he didn't finish his thought; he just squinted and looked at our house like something puzzled him.

"Are they what?" I asked.

"Never mind," he said, then made a clicking noise with his tongue and slapped the reins against Maybelle's behind. I yanked Maggie away from the horse so she didn't get stepped on.

I couldn't stop thinking about what Nick had told us about Virginia being mad at Gregory for something. It made me think of my favourite crime fighter. What would The Shadow make of this? He'd most likely use his hypnosis to get Gregory to confess to the crime, if he did it. Since I couldn't do that, instead I decided to tell the detective. He'd know if it was an important clue or not.

TWENTY-FIVE

VICTOR

"Is this normal?" Gene asked and put down his copy of the *Inco Triangle* he'd been reading. The monthly magazine covered the three mining towns, Creighton Mine, Frood, and Copper Cliff, with company news and feel-good stories about the towns. Gene had already informed me there wouldn't be any mention of the murder, even though it was all anyone was talking about.

I was used to the media hanging around and reporting the facts wrong when it came to murder cases. It was nice not dealing with any of that here. Gene told me the Sudbury paper was here the first day but hadn't been back since. I guessed there were juicer crimes to cover in the city and it wasn't worth the drive to Creighton

"Is what normal?" I leaned back in my chair, glad to have my thoughts interrupted. There were only so many times I could go over our interviews with Edgar 'Swifty' Pelletier and Gregory Hansen. I was looking forward to talking to Virginia's girlfriends; I hoped they'd have better memories than Edgar had.

"The amount of time it's taking to solve this crime. We don't have any clues or real leads, and it's been sixteen days since that poor girl was murdered." Gene shoved the *Triangle* off his desk into the wastepaper basket.

"There is no normal in a murder investigation. If you rush it, chances are you might miss something important. Then again, if you take too long, the trail can go cold," I shrugged.

"So, damned if we do, damned if we don't?"

"Yeah, something like that." I sympathized with Gene. The movies always made murder investigations look so dangerous and exciting, when the reality was we sat around a lot or talked to the same people over and over until something shook loose.

A small shadow fell across the door. I looked up to see Rose Boyle standing on the threshold with wide eyes as they moved over the entire room.

"Whoa. I've never been inside here before," she said.

"Come on in, Rose. We won't bite." Gene gestured to the young girl to enter, which she did, slowly and with reverence.

The word that came to mind when I looked at the kid was "ragamuffin." Her hair was tied back, but pieces had come loose that hung in her eyes. There was a patch on the hem of her dress, and her feet were bare. She didn't look neglected; I'd seen enough kids like that to know the difference. She was more like someone who was most comfortable outside. It reminded me of what my own mother would say to my father after I returned from a day out with my friends: "A dirty child is a happy child."

"Do your parents know you're here?" Gene asked, as she moved deeper into the station.

Rose glanced over at him, then away. "No one was home. My mom is over at June's house, so I couldn't tell her I was coming here."

"Rose, June lives in the house right beside yours. If you walked all the way here, you could have walked a few steps to tell your mom where you were going." Gene gave her a look halfway between amusement and disappointment.

"Yes, sir." She hung her head.

"It's not safe to be wandering around by yourself, you know that," Gene said.

His comment deflated her some. "I stayed on the roads the whole way here, honest."

"Are you here because you have some information for us?" I jumped in, hoping my guess was correct.

"I'm not sure, maybe." She shrugged.

"All right, take a seat then." I grabbed a pad of paper and pen.

Rose slid into the chair opposite me. Gene came over and perched on the corner of the desk.

"Well, I'm not sure. It might not be anything." She tucked her hands under her thighs.

"Tell us what you know, and we'll decide if it's useful or not," I said.

"It's okay, take your time, sweetie." He patted her shoulder.

She took a deep breath and let it all out in a rush. "Nick Valenti was delivering groceries, since his dad threw his back out because he's old. Nick was telling Olive about practising for baseball, and I was listening in, like Lamont Cranston does, you know, The Shadow. It's how he learns things. I've always been really good at listening in and not being seen—"

"Rose…" I snapped my fingers to get her attention. "I'm growing old here. What did you come here to tell us?"

Gene frowned at me over his shoulder, but it worked. Rose took a deep breath, which slowed her down.

"Nick says he saw Virginia and Gregory Hansen talking on the path. He said she looked mad at him and shook her finger," which she demonstrated by shaking her finger at me, "then Virginia stomped off." She finished and looked back and forth between me and Gene, then shrugged. "And that's it."

Gene whistled low and looked over at me. This time his eyes were wide.

"Is that helpful at all?" she asked.

I slapped my palm on the desk and couldn't keep in a chuckle. This was something, all right, and at that point in the investigation, it was desperately needed.

"Yeah, Rose, that's helpful," I told her.

Her cheeks reddened, and she sat up a bit straighter.

"Rose, did Nick say if he heard what they were talking about?" I leaned across the desk towards her.

"No, just that after Virginia left, Gregory just stared at his shoes." Her voice went up at the end like it was an odd thing for a man to do.

Gene and I looked at each other, excited about having something new to sink our teeth into, but not wanting to talk in front of Rose.

So many thoughts ran through my mind. Virginia and Gregory had fought a few days before her murder, and he lied to us about seeing her. It wasn't a confession, but sometimes a handful of circumstantial circumstances were as powerful as one piece of evidence.

But it was also important to play the devil's advocate so we didn't get stuck on one idea. So, what if they ran into each other on a path? They may have had sharp words for one another; it isn't uncommon for exes not to get along. We needed more.

"So does this mean Gregory is maybe the one?" Rose asked.

I looked at the young girl sitting across from me. She reminded me of some of the young French kids I worked with during the war. The Resistance wasn't shy about using children when needed. They could slip in and out of places without being noticed and the Germans, thankfully, often ignored and underestimated them.

I had no doubt Rose would have been one of those kids. She was an observer and was the kind of kid who didn't get things just handed to her. It was obvious she hadn't been coddled or overprotected. And during the interview with her, she'd kept her emotions in check, even though it was clear she loved her sister. So, was I underestimating her too? She sat still without fidgeting under my direct gaze.

"Rose, tell me about the day Virginia was killed." I ignored her previous question.

She frowned and scrunched her nose. "I already did. What else do you want to know?"

"What did you and her talk about that day? Can you remember?"

"I remember everything she ever told me," Rose said. "I asked if I could visit her in Los Angeles. She said yes, but she also said she would start coming home for visits a lot more often. Then she told me, when I got older, she was going to take me to live with her, but I couldn't say anything because she thought it would make, umm, my mom sad, but I didn't think it would make her sad at all."

I caught it in that one hesitation before she mentioned her mom. She knew. Helen Boyle didn't want Rose to know the truth about her real parentage, but somehow Rose had found out and kept it to herself. So, Rose Boyle could learn secrets and keep them to herself.

"Tell me about everything from the moment you found Virginia lying there."

Rose wiggled back in the chair as if she needed a moment to collect her thoughts. She repeated the same details she had when we spoke in her kitchen.

"That's all I can remember because, after we left the spot, my brain went all fuzzy. The only thing I can recall is Maggie kept tugging on my shirt because I wouldn't hold her hand."

"Why wouldn't you?" I asked.

"I couldn't because I was holding Virginia's camera really tight and didn't want to drop it." She said as if it made all the sense in the world.

"Wait," I cocked my head, "Virginia had a camera with her that day?"

"Well, yeah, she never went anywhere without her camera. Didn't you know that?"

"I knew she liked to take pictures, but no one said anything about her having her camera that day, including you." I pointed my finger at her, and she had the decency to shrink back a bit.

"Oh, didn't I?" Her voice had gotten smaller.

"Where is the camera now, Rose?" Gene asked in that fatherly voice of his.

"At home. Under my bed." Her dark eyes darted back and forth between me and Gene.

"We need that camera, Rose," I said.

She didn't answer right away as she chewed on her bottom lip. "The camera is real important to me," she said, squinting at the two of us.

"We need to see the pictures that are on the camera. Do you remember her taking pictures that day?" I asked.

"Sure, she took lots of pictures of us and just, you know, all around us." A thought popped into her head that caused her to sit up straight. "Are you going to get the pictures developed? You know the drug store does that. Olive told us about it at dinner one night. They send them to Sudbury, and then they come back in a couple weeks. If you do that, can I have the pictures when you're done with them?"

"Any of the pictures we don't need for the investigation, I promise, when this is over, you can have them all," I told her.

"For free?" she negotiated.

"Yes, for free," I said.

"Then it's a deal." She held out a grimy hand for both Gene and I to shake.

TWENTY-SIX

ROSE

When I closed my eyes, it felt like I was flying. I'd never sat in the front seat of a car before, and the detective let me stick my head out the window. We pushed through the air, making our own wind, and for the first time in weeks, it didn't feel like I was being held down by heavy rocks. All too soon, the car pulled up in front of my house.

"I'll wait here," the detective said, pointing at me, "and remember your promise."

"Yes, sir."

After the detective and Officer Kowalski found out about Virginia's camera, they really wanted to see her pictures in case she'd taken a picture of something that could help their case. The detective said it was a real long shot, but that you never knew what they could learn from her photographs.

Officer Kowalski suggested getting Eddie Szymanski to develop the pictures for us. He said Eddie had a dark room in his house where he developed his photos for the *Inco Triangle,* and it would be faster than taking them to Sudbury.

Officer Kowalski went to talk to Nick Valenti. He wanted to ask Nick about when he saw Virginia and Gregory together. I offered to show the detective where Eddie lived. They only agreed as long as my mom said it was okay.

I ran into the house and grabbed Virginia's camera from under my bed, where I'd wrapped it up in a pillowcase along with a few of her rolls of film.

Next door, Mom and June sat at the kitchen table, drinking tea. It was quiet, as if no one had spoken in some time. Maggie was there too, playing with the paper dolls. I'd lent them to her a few days ago because I didn't feel ready to play with them.

"Hey, Rose," June said. "Maggie, scooch over so Rose can play with you."

"I can't," I barked, not meaning to sound rude. Mom looked up at me for the first time. "Can I go with the detective to Eddie Szymanski's? He needs someone to show him where it is. He's out front." I pointed in the direction of our house.

Mom sat up and looked annoyed. "What are you talking about, Rose? Why would the detective come here for your help? There are plenty of people who can show him where to go."

I'd already decided not to tell her about my trip to the station.

"He stopped by to get Virginia's camera and asked me if I could help him." I crossed my fingers that she wouldn't go out and talk to him. Sometimes if I talked really fast, she'd get annoyed and just shoo me away. It was a trick I'd used before.

"Wait, why do you have Virginia's camera, Rose?" June asked.

"I brought it back with me the night of…well, you know. I told Mom I'd keep it in my room. Remember, Mom, when I told you about it?" I had never lied right to my mom's face before, but things were different now, and she seemed even less interested in what I did than before. Besides, she'd lied to me my whole life, so I didn't feel much guilt about doing it to her.

"Maybe…oh I don't know, Rose, just don't get in the detective's way, and have him bring you straight back after. No wandering the streets alone. You hear me?"

"Can I go too?" Maggie jumped out of her chair. "I want to go with Rose."

"No, Maggie. The detective doesn't want a bunch of kids around. He'll probably make Rose stay in the car the whole time. You stay here," Mom said.

I mouthed "sorry" to Maggie, even though I was secretly glad. I'd tell her all about it when I got home because Maggie always listened when I talked to her, just like Virginia used to.

Before anyone had a chance to change their mind, I ran out the back door and around to the front. The detective was leaning against his car, staring up at the sky like he was looking for something up there.

We got back and I put the pillowcase between us. I directed him to drive along French Street, down Summerhill, and I pointed out where he could pull over at the end of Joffree Street where Eddie lived.

"Which house is his?" the detective asked as we got out of the car.

"It's over there," I pointed down the street, "but you can't take a car there, so we gotta walk."

Joffree was one of those streets you couldn't take cars on. Where there should be a road, instead there were giant rocks and boulders, easy enough to walk on foot but no good for cars.

He made a little snort then reached his hand out to me. "Here, I'll take that."

I slowly handed him the pillowcase.

"Don't worry, I'll get it back to you when we're done with it," he said.

I stopped and faced him, holding out my one hand and crooking my little finger towards him. "Pinky swear?"

He frowned at me. "Rose, I swear on my detective's badge. How is that?"

"Can I see it?" I asked.

He sighed but reached into his back pocket and pulled out what looked like a leather wallet. With a flick of his wrist, it opened and displayed a silver badge in the shape of a shield. I wanted so badly to reach out and touch it, but wasn't sure it that was against the law.

"Is that good enough for you?" he asked.

I nodded and he flicked it shut with a satisfying slap. "Can we go now?"

I led him to the end of Joffree Street, where Eddie lived with his mom. His dad had died a few years earlier, so it was just the two of them. He had an older sister, but she married a miner from Copper Cliff and moved away.

"This is it." I pointed at the house in front of us.

I'd never been inside before, but I knew where pretty much everyone in town lived. The house looked like it was in sore need of a handyman. The porch was more than sloping—it looked like it could collapse at any time. I might have been able to use the stairs, but I was pretty sure the detective would crash right through them, so I led him around the back.

I was surprised to see a room had been added on and whoever built it didn't do a very good job. The right side was a bit higher than the left, and you could tell it was all found material, since nothing matched. The weirdest thing of all was there wasn't a single window.

The house looked kind of rundown, but the garden had all kinds of pretty flowers planted in straight lines. There were white ones, yellow and purple ones, and when you got close you could smell them, like perfume, except underneath it all was another smell that reminded me of science class, like something chemical.

"Can I help you?"

Mrs. Szymanski had come around the corner and held a garden tool in each hand like she was ready for battle.

"How do you do, ma'am? I'm Detective Victor Lapointe of the OPP, and this is Rose Boyle. We're looking for Eddie Szymanski. Would that be your son?"

"Eddie's my boy. What do you want him for?" She was plump in a droopy way, like her house.

"I have some film here I was hoping he could develop for me." He held out the pillowcase for her to see. Her shoulders loosened up, and she put her tools into her oversized apron pockets.

She looked over, stared at me for a minute, and then nodded. I understood it was her way of acknowledging me and my family's tragedy. Some people aren't comfortable with saying things out loud. June's husband, Oscar, was quiet that way. I'd gotten pretty good at knowing what they meant without having to hear the words. I nodded back.

"He's inside sleeping. Come on, I'll get him for you." She went in through the back door. I followed the detective. As soon as we stepped into the darkened hallway, she pointed at us and snapped, "Wait here."

The chemical smell was much stronger inside. I pinched my nose closed. As soon Mrs. Szymanski left, the detective pushed open the door beside us. I wasn't sure what to do. She'd told us to stay here, and she didn't seem like a lady to disobey, but I wanted to stay close by the detective. My curiosity beat out my manners.

The room was sparsely furnished, with a wooden table in the middle, and a stained laundry tub in the corner. He pulled a string, and a faint light pushed through the shadows from a single bulb. More strings criss-crossed the low ceiling. Some were empty, and others had photographs clothes-pinned like small stiff pieces of laundry.

This must be where Eddie developed his pictures for the paper. Virginia had told me about the dark room at the studio where she worked.

I walked over to look at a line of pictures. I recognized the girl's softball team. There were faraway photos of the team playing and close-ups of the girls posing in their uniforms holding baseball bats.

The strong chemical smell started to give me a headache. The sound of metal scraping made me jump. The detective had squatted down and was going through an opened file cabinet drawer. He grabbed a few folders and brought them over to the table, under the light bulb.

I stepped over and peeked past his elbow, watching him flip through handfuls of photographs. There were nature shots, close-ups of blueberry bushes and rocks, people swimming at Meatbird Lake, and other pictures of mine shafts and buildings. Some of them were from Creighton and a few I recognized from the other Inco towns, Frood and Copper Cliff. As the detective looked through them, a picture of a woman caught my eye, and I grabbed his arm. Even though it was from behind and a bit of a distance away, I recognized her immediately.

"Hey, that's Virginia." I poked my finger at the photograph.

"Hmm," was all he said.

He shuffled the rest in his hand, and there was a dozen more, all of them of Virginia in different places around town, walking along a path, a glimpse of her half cut off by a house, and a few of her standing on top of a rock. The back of my neck prickled.

The pictures were nice enough, but there was something about them that made me feel a little uneasy. Not because Virginia was no longer with us, but it was the way she looked in some of them, like he'd caught her at a moment that should have been private. All except the last one. In it she stood against the side of a building I recognized as the diner. Her body was pointed towards the camera, but her face was looking down beside her. Even from the side you could see how happy she was.

She was looking at me, but I was looking at the camera, and I was smiling too; a big, goofy grin that showed where my bottom tooth was missing. Other than my school picture, there weren't many photos of me. Sometimes, on special occasions, Oscar would bring out his camera to take pictures, mostly of Maggie or Mikey, but I'd slip in when I could.

I'd never seen myself look so happy. The picture started to go all blurry, and I had to sniff hard to keep my nose from running.

The detective picked up an envelope from the table and opened it. Dozens more photographs of different sizes spilled out. I recognized a lot of the women and girls, but the ones I didn't know must have been from the other towns. A few of the pictures were posed with them smiling for the camera, but most were like Virginia's: from behind, far away, or bent over. There was even one taken through a window.

"Hey. that's Lorelei Clarke," I said and pointed at the woman in the window.

"Is it now?"

"Oh, hey, Detective." Eddie stood in the doorway. He glanced down and saw the pictures spread out on the table, and his smile disappeared. He went still, like he was holding his breath.

"Sorry to wake you," the detective said. Eddie's hair poked out on one side in what my dad called bed-head. "I hope you don't mind us looking at some of your pictures."

"No, yeah, sure. There's so many, I don't even know what I have anymore. I was up late developing those pictures," he said, pointing at the baseball pictures hanging up. "Mother said you needed some help with something."

"Yes, I was hoping you could help us out and develop the film from this camera." The detective pulled Virginia's camera from the pillowcase and put it on the table.

Eddie limped over and picked the camera up. "A Rolleicord, and a nice one too." He turned it over slowly in his hand, but his eyes kept flicking back to the pictures spread out in front of us.

"It's Virginia Boyle's camera," the detective said. "She had it on her the day she was killed, and I was hoping to get the film developed. You know, just in case there was something of interest on the film."

Eddie looked up at the detective, surprised. "Yeah, sure, I can develop what's here and get the prints to you," he said eagerly.

The detective reached over, took the camera from Eddie, then held it out for me to take without taking his eyes off Eddie.

"Except we've got a bit of a problem now, don't we, Eddie?"

"D–do we?" Eddie stammered.

"Would you like to explain these pictures of Miss Boyle and these other women?" The detective pointed at the collection.

"Sure, yeah, um, well, I was doing a story on Virginia Boyle for the paper. She agreed to it. Isn't that right, Rose? You were there." He rubbed his withered leg as if it were causing him pain.

I stayed quiet, holding the camera to my chest. The detective held up the picture of Lorelei Clarke taken through her window. "And did you get permission to take this picture?"

"Hmmm." He squinted and leaned in like he didn't recognize it. "No, I just —" Then he stopped talking like he'd forgotten what he was going to say.

The detective scooped up all the pictures, put them back into the envelope, including the ones of Virginia, and tucked them under his arm.

"What say you come for a drive down to the station? I'd like Officer Kowalski to join us for a discussion." He took a step towards Eddie, who next to the detective, looked like a kid.

"Come on, Rose."

I grabbed the pillowcase and followed behind, carrying the camera and film. When we stepped outside, we all stopped for a moment and squinted after being in the dark. I lifted my hand up to shield my eyes.

"I thought you were doing picture stuff. Where are you going?" Mrs. Szymanski appeared beside us with a trowel pointed at the detective.

"To the station," I blurted out.

"Why? What did you do, Eddie?"

"I didn't do anything, Mother. The detective just wants my help with some stuff." Eddie flashed a look over at Detective Lapointe, whose face didn't show any emotion.

"What use would you be?" she said and brushed her hands down her apron, leaving streaks of dirt.

"It's just…never mind. We gotta go." He turned, leaving a long trail in the dirt where his one foot dragged behind him.

"How about you?" she said to the detective. "Are you gonna tell me how a cripple like him is gonna help with a real police investigation? Unless you think he's a suspect." She wheezed heavily, which I realised was laughter. I glanced over at Eddie, who was standing beside the car ready to leave.

"It's photography stuff," the detective said, then turned away. "Rose, you get in the front. Eddie, the back."

We each went where we were told. No one spoke on the ride to my house, but when we pulled up to the front, the detective turned to Eddie. "Wait here. You're not going to give me any trouble, are you?"

"No, sir."

"Good. Come on, Rose."

I followed him out of the car.

"I'm going to have to take the camera and film back. I'll take them with me to Sudbury and get them developed there."

I wasn't happy they'd be going so far away.

"Is Eddie in trouble or something?" I asked.

"I just want to talk with him. See what he knows."

"Can I have that one picture from the drawer? The one Eddie took of me and Virginia?" I wanted it more than anything I had ever asked for.

He looked away and made a sucking sound with his teeth. "Sorry, Rose, but it's not mine to give away, and right now it could be evidence."

I stared down at my feet, feeling like I might cry again.

"I tell you what," he said. "When all this is over, if possible, I will do my best to get it for you, okay?"

"Okay," I mumbled.

"Also, I need you to do me a favour, Rose," he said, and I looked up at him. "I know you are the kind of person who can keep a secret. Not just little secrets, but big ones too. The kind that would feel better if you could let them out and tell someone, but you don't. So, I need you to promise you won't tell anyone…and I mean *anyone* what you saw and heard at Eddie's today, okay?"

I nodded. It was true; I could keep the most important secrets of all.

The detective squinted at me as if he was trying to see inside my head to make sure I was telling the truth. Maybe he did have mind powers like The Shadow. Then he shook his head and mumbled to himself, "This is crazy," and he held out his hand with all his fingers tucked away except his pinky finger. "Pinky swear?"

I took a deep breath and performed the ritual. "Pinky swear," I said in the most serious voice I could.

"Good," he said and then left with Eddie Szymanski still hunched down in the back seat of the car.

TWENTY-SEVEN

VICTOR

I should have left the kid in the car when we went to Eddie Szymanski's, but I never expected to come across what I did. Still, I was confident she'd keep the secret. She may not even have caught what those pictures meant.

Gene was at the station when we arrived. I was interested to hear what the Valenti boy might have had to say, but this came first. I tossed the envelope to Gene, which he caught and opened up. He began shuffling through the pictures. The farther along he got, the more creased his forehead became, until he reached the last one, dropping it onto his desk.

He looked up and shook his head, "Oh, Eddie."

I grabbed a chair and pointed at it. "Sit." Eddie lowered himself into it, keeping his bum leg straight.

"Would you like to explain these to us?" Gene said.

"There's nothing to say, really. They're just random pictures from different events around town. I have a lot of photographs that never make it into the *Triangle*. I keep them just in case I need them for something later on…" Eddie trailed off without conviction.

"Really? You think this picture of – well, it's hard to tell, but I'd guess that's Paulette Carmichael – is something you might put in the *Triangle* someday?" Gene held out a picture of a woman from behind, bending over.

Eddie didn't answer.

"Or how about this one, and this one, and this one, and all these?" Gene fanned out the dozen or so photographs of Virginia Boyle.

"I was doing a story on her and needed pictures. She said I could take her picture."

"Then why wasn't she looking at the camera in any of these, and this one," he pointed at one with a branch partially obscuring the picture, "it looks like you're hiding in a bush?"

"It's a style of photography called candid shots where the subject doesn't know they're having their picture taken. It makes for a more natural shot. Photographers do it all the time."

"Candid, you say? To me it looks a lot more like lurking." I held out a particularly disturbing one of a woman in her bathing suit, only her head was cut off in the picture and the focus was on her torso.

"And why so many of Virginia Boyle?" Gene asked. "It seems like there are more of her than anyone else, and yet she was only here a short time."

"And she was the only one who was murdered," I added.

Eddie's head snapped up. "You can't think I had anything to do with that? Come on, Officer Kowalski, you know me. I would never hurt Virginia. She was lovely." His voice softened when he said her name.

"Really? Tell me about your relationship with Virginia Boyle, Eddie." Gene grabbed a chair and sat across from him.

"Well," Eddie leaned forward, "we had a lot in common. The day I interviewed her, we talked about photography for like half an hour. She shared a lot about her hobbies and personal life with me."

Gene looked over his shoulder at me, eyebrows raised. I jumped in.

"What kind of things did she say about her personal life, Eddie?"

His eyes lit up. "Well, she didn't have a boyfriend back in Los Angeles, and she talked about real things, not make-up and clothes and other silly things like most girls. She's smart and talented. Did you know she was doing a retrospective on life in a mining town? I bet you didn't know that about her." He leaned back with a smug smile on his face, like he just shared the greatest secret of all.

"Eddie, where were you when Virginia was murdered?" Gene asked gently, but Eddie still flinched at the words.

"Oh, I was working. Every year the editor wants pictures of the first day of picking season," he said.

"Were you here in Creighton or one of the other towns?" Gene asked.

"Here. I was going to go to Copper Cliff, and if there was still time, Frood, but with everything that happened, I never got there," Eddie said and stared at his feet.

"Then what did you do for the rest of the day?" I asked.

He glanced up at me, then looked away quickly, and we let the silence draw out.

He rubbed his eyes then began speaking. "When I first heard the commotion going on, I went to see what was happening."

"Sorry," I interrupted, "so where were you that you could hear what was going on?"

"I had just come down from Tank Hill and was near Albion's Pond. There were some young kids picking around there, which always makes for good pictures. Wholesome is the goal, according to my editor."

"You could hear what was going on all the way down by Albion's Pond?" Gene asked, as I tried to picture the geography in my head but wasn't clear on the distances.

"There were a lot of voices and yelling coming from the Dardanelles, where the Boyles live, just above Albion's Pond," he explained, looking at me, "so I went to see what was going on. When I got up there, a lot of people had come out of their houses. All I knew was there had been an accident up the hill past Robert Street, but no one really knew what was happening. I headed up there and eventually got the story from some women who were coming down."

"Well, that was lucky you were so close when she was found," I said and watched his reaction.

"Nothing lucky about it," he murmured.

"Eddie, did you ever ask Virginia out on a date or anything?" Gene asked.

Eddie rubbed at his left hand hard, like he was massaging a cramp. "Not a date, but we were going to meet up and talk

189

photography and stuff, but we never got a chance." He looked at me, then glanced away quickly.

It was just a hunch, but I doubted Virginia was of the same mind about them getting together.

"Why did your mom ask if you'd done something?" I asked.

"In case it wasn't obvious, my mother doesn't think much of me."

"Why is that?"

"You'd have to ask her, but if I was to hazard a guess, it started just after I caught polio. She thinks I'm weak for catching it because no one else in Creighton did."

"It is odd that you were the only one." I knew polio usually showed up and spread.

"I didn't catch it here. We were visiting family out in Nova Scotia, but she's embarrassed that no one here has caught it and says it's because the kids in Creighton are made of sturdier stuff."

"That doesn't make any sense," I said, and he just shrugged.

"As my dad used to say, that's female logic for you. Listen, I didn't do anything wrong, and I would never have hurt Virginia Boyle. She was like an angel." He smiled in a way that made me feel a little uneasy.

"If we had to check on your whereabouts the day of her murder, can you remember who the kids were you were taking pictures of?" Gene asked.

"Hmmm, now that you mention it, I don't quite remember. You know how hard it is to keep track of which kids belong to who." He shrugged at Gene.

"Do you have the photographs? That would tell us who it was, and then we can check with them and get you all cleared." Gene smiled back at him.

"I'll have to look around for them. As you can guess that day was kind of a blur, and I don't remember where I might have put them. I'll look, and as soon as I find and develop those pictures, I'll get them right to you. I'm sure they're on a roll somewhere."

"That would be great if you could find those pictures, Eddie, and get them to us real soon. Detective?" Gene turned to me.

"That's all for now, Eddie. We need those pictures."

"Yes, sir." He turned and grabbed the back of the chair to steady himself as he stood up.

"And from now on, Eddie," I said, "stop taking pictures of women without their knowledge, or soon you'll be facing an angry husband or boyfriend, and things will go very bad for you. Now, can you get yourself home, or do you need a drive?" I asked.

"I may be a cripple, but I'm not an invalid," he said, sounding more defiant than petulant. "Can I get my pictures back?" He pointed at the stack in Gene's hands.

"No, Eddie, we'll be keeping them, just in case." Gene used his best father voice and head tilt.

Eddie glanced longingly one more time at the photographs and then limped out of the station.

"Well, what do you think?" I asked Gene once we were alone.

"It seems like a bit of a coincidence that he was so close to the scene of the crime, and these pictures are quite off-putting. I'm just glad there wasn't any in here of my wife, or I'm not sure how impartial I would have been able to stay." He chuckled and moved back to his desk.

I made a mental note to dispose of the picture of Mrs. Kowalski I'd removed from the envelope and tucked away into the glove compartment of my car.

TWENTY-EIGHT

ROSE

How could a bunch of pictures of people from around town be evidence? That's what the detective had said about Eddie's photographs. I'd listened to enough episodes of *The Shadow* to know evidence was a gun or a letter.

I pulled on a clean top from the closet. The whole family, except Dad, were going to the Inco Club tonight. June thought we needed to get out of the house, and although Mom said no at first, June kept at her until she agreed.

I wasn't really in the mood either, which wasn't normal. The Inco Club was one of my favourite places in Creighton. The mining company built the club for the employees and their families. There were all kinds of things for us to do there. You could bowl or play badminton, hang out in the lounge, or dance to songs on the jukebox. It was where special events were held, like variety shows and our yearly Christmas party. Although I didn't feel much like going, the thought of being left behind was worse, so I tagged along.

When we reached the club everyone, split up; June and Mom went to the bridge room, Olive and Hugh went to find their friends, and Mikey and Joey took off to watch the baseball practice out in the field by the club.

Maggie and I went to the bowling alley. We usually played on a team together, but I didn't feel up to it and plopped down at the far end of the bench to watch.

Maggie threw a spare. It was nice to see her smile. I know she was sad about Virginia, but it wasn't the same for her as it was for me. Seeing all those photographs that Eddie had of Virginia had made it so I couldn't stop thinking of her. The picture of her smiling, of her walking the hills, or standing still on a rock, looking away from the camera, they all kept shuffling through my mind like flipping through a picture book.

I was used to being sad, but I began to feel other things too. I'd pretend she was alive, and she and I would sit together up on Slater's Rock that looked over the town. I'd get a chance to tell her how wrong it was of her to go away and leave me behind. In these conversations, she'd always say how sorry she was and that she'd never leave me again.

The clanking of pins falling over and the clunk of balls hitting against one another annoyed me. There were too many noises, and too many people laughing and carrying on like the worst thing ever didn't just happen.

I left the bowling alley without telling Maggie. I couldn't stay another minute. Down the hall, I stopped at the card room and peeked in. Cigarette smoke and perfume mixed together and hung in the air above the heads of the women, seated at tables of four. Everyone talked and laughed, except the table in the corner.

Mom and June sat across from Mrs. Valenti and Mrs. Chomsky. Mom stared at her cards until June nudged her to take a turn. A look passed between Mrs. Valenti and Mrs. Chomsky. It was a look filled with pity, which Mom would have hated if she saw.

I probably would have been better off if I'd stayed at home with Dad. We could have sat together quietly in the living room. Him sipping from his El Mocambo glass and sighing really loudly. I drifted through the club without stopping to look in the lounge, where I knew Olive, Hugh, and the other teenagers would be stretched out on the couches gossiping, flirting, and trying to act older than they really were.

The squeak of sneakers from the gymnasium signalled a game of badminton. I knew I shouldn't leave the club, but I needed to get away from all the activity and the people acting like life could just go on. I needed to breathe some fresh air.

I slipped out the side door and leaned against the brick wall, wondering if I'd always feel like a ghost drifting around living people. It was the secret that made me different. I should have brought a sweater with me, like June suggested. I wrapped my arms around myself and wondered if Virginia also felt cold down in the dark, wet ground.

As I walked slowly along the side of the building, I dragged my hand against the rough brick, letting it scrape the skin on my palm. Sometimes I purposely did things that hurt. I'd pluck some hairs from my head, pinch myself, or dig my nails into my arm. At church, they'd talked about offering up your suffering to God. That's what it felt like. I could prove that I loved Virginia more than anyone else because I hurt more and wouldn't let myself be happy. Sometimes I pictured her looking down at me, and she'd feel really bad because it was her and Mom's lie that made me the saddest girl in Creighton.

When I got near the corner of the building, I heard voices. They were grownups, so I stopped, not wanting to interrupt.

"Why don't you just go back inside? I already told you I don't want to talk to you."

The woman's voice sounded snooty.

"You're being ridiculous, Paulette. We both know there is no way you are going to break up with me."

I recognized Gregory Hansen's voice.

"I already did," Paulette said.

"Come on, sweetie. Why don't we go back to your place? We can talk about this and…"

"No, stop it. I've wasted enough time with you. Everyone our age is married. Lorelei is about to have a kid, Swifty has two, and I'm still waiting on you to set a wedding date."

"I will, Paulette. I promise."

"I'm not an idiot. It wasn't a coincidence that you wanted to postpone wedding planning just before Virginia came back. If she was still alive, you'd be putting me off and chasing after her right now."

"Then I guess it worked out nicely for you that someone killed her."

I slapped my hands over my mouth to hide the squeak I made. That was an awful thing for Gregory to say.

"What's that supposed to mean?" Every word sounded like she bit it off and spit it out.

"You've always been jealous of Ginny. Everyone knows that."

"And you're pathetic. Everyone knows that. She dumped you, and you kept chasing after her, begging her to come back. Kind of like you're doing to me right now." It sounded like she was holding back a laugh.

Gregory snorted. "You think you can compare to Virginia Boyle? Ginny was a hundred times the woman you are."

"Well, that sounds a bit like an infatuation." Paulette's voice was tight. "And I'm sure the police would be very interested in finding out how much you enjoy choking women. That it's kind of your thing."

"You better keep your mouth shut, Paulette. It might not look good on you if the police knew how you threw yourself at me, even when I was still with Ginny. You've always been jealous of her and wanted her out of the picture, eh?"

"You're crazy. No one would believe you, Gregory," she hissed.

"Really? I'm a college graduate and a respected Inco employee, and not a grubby miner. An actual office worker. What are you? A diner waitress? A floozy?"

"Stop it, you're hurting me, Gregory! Let go of me!"

I peeked around the corner but stayed in the shadows. Paulette took a few steps backwards, rubbing her wrists.

"I'm not afraid of you, Gregory. Besides, I could tell the police how I sent you for sugar the day Virginia was killed, and you were gone over an hour. It doesn't take an hour to fetch a bag of sugar."

Gregory took several steps towards Paulette, but she moved quickly, keeping her distance from him.

"Be careful, Paulette. I can turn this whole town against you. You're practically a spinster waitress and no one will believe you broke up with me. I can make it so every guy in town sees you as damaged goods. You might want to think good and hard about what you start blabbing about." He pointed at her, then stormed off.

Paulette stood and watched him leave with her chin high, but as soon as he was gone, she shrunk down and her shoulders began to tremble. She was crying. It felt uncomfortable to watch what I knew wasn't meant for me to see, so I backed away quietly.

I made my way back inside the club. No one had noticed I was gone, and for the rest of the evening, I sat in the bowling alley and pretended to cheer Maggie on. I waved and smiled every time she threw a strike or a spare, but in my head, I kept going over what I heard outside.

Paulette wasn't ever a good friend to Virginia, but could jealousy make someone a killer? Gregory liked to choke women Paulette said. I didn't understand what she meant by that. And now there was Eddie, who the detective felt had done something wrong. I wondered if it was as hard for the detective to make sense of all this as it was for me. All I kept thinking was, what would The Shadow do?

TWENTY-NINE

VICTOR

We walked up a wooden staircase on the outside of the building. Paulette Carmichael lived in an apartment above a dress shop. It was her day off from the diner, and Gene had arranged for us to talk with her. The door opened immediately to our knock.

"Hello, Paulette. I'm sorry, did we catch you on your way out?" Gene asked, sounding a little unsure. Paulette wore a dress with more cleavage than normal for daytime and a full face of makeup with a sparkly clip in her hair.

"No, not at all. I was expecting you gentlemen. Come in."

We were ushered into a bright kitchen, clean and compact. The smell of apples and cinnamon wafted up from the counter, where a pie sat cooling.

"Shall we go into the front room?" she asked.

She led us into her sitting room decorated with an abundance of frills and flowers. The front windows let in a nice breeze, the sound of voices, and the occasional vehicle from the street. She directed Gene to a worn chair and took a seat rather close beside me on the chesterfield.

"I just made an apple pie. I love to bake, Detective." She looked at me and smiled proudly. "As soon as it cools, I'll serve you both a slice. I hope you have a sweet tooth, because I've actually won awards for my pies. Isn't that right, Officer Kowalski?" She spoke to him while she looked at me.

Gene seemed surprised about this news but recovered quickly. "Ah, yes, now that you mention it, I seem to remember."

Her smile deepened, showing off a smear of red lipstick on her front teeth.

"We were hoping you might be able to answer a few questions we have about Virginia Boyle, since you two were friends growing up." I wanted to get right into the interview.

"Oh, of course, Detective. I'll do anything I can to help catch the person who did this to our poor Virginia. And to be honest, I haven't been able to sleep much at all since it all happened. I don't feel safe as a single woman sleeping alone at night."

I made a move as if I were getting comfortable and used it to slide farther away from her.

"I'm sure you'll feel better once you and Gregory tie the knot and you're not alone anymore," Gene said.

"Oh, Officer." She laughed, turning to him. "Haven't you heard? I decided Gregory and I weren't a good fit after all." She looked back at me. "I'm single now."

"We hadn't heard that. I'm sorry," I said, taking out my notebook as a sign to get down to business. "Do you remember back when you were about fifteen?"

"Of course, I remember. It wasn't that long ago." She leaned over and slapped me playfully on the arm. I could see Gene holding back. He found this funny.

"Great," I said. "You and Virginia were close friends?"

"Oh, yes, and Lorelei. Us girls would talk about boys, school, share secrets, you know the way girls do at that age."

"Great. Do you remember after Gregory and Virginia had been a couple for a bit, did she share any problems they were having or talk about, I don't know, maybe being interested in anyone else?"

"No, Gregory was the best-looking guy in our grade, really the school. Virginia would have been crazy to be interested in anyone else."

"Outside of school, what kind of things was she into, specifically the year you were all fifteen?"

"Why are you asking about something so long ago? What could that have to do with her murder?"

"We are just trying to cover everything. You know get a full picture of who she was growing up. It's standard police work," Gene jumped in.

"Oh, okay, well, let's see. Our group, we had most of our classes together. Outside of school we hung out a lot, went to the movies, the Inco Club, swimming at Meatbird Lake, sneaking up to Tank Hill, or just hanging out at different spots like Slater's Rock and such. Geez, I don't know, the guys played baseball. Virginia and I were on the basketball team together. Lorelei was no good at sports, so she just watched. Our grade ten year we won the championship. It was the first year Jefferson Clarke taught at our school, and he coached us. Ever since he came, the girl's basketball team started winning more of their games. He was such a great coach, and it didn't hurt that he was young and handsome. He was an outsider, so I'm not going to lie – we were all a little smitten with him. It's still kind of hard to believe Lorelei ended up marrying him."

"Why is that?"

"I don't think he even knew she existed when she was in school. He was one of those teachers who had his favourites, and the girls on the team were definitely his favourites. He taught history as well as coached different sports teams. In our history class, Virginia and I, and I'm pretty sure some of the other girls on the team, well, he always marked our assignments and tests pretty easy. I'm embarrassed to say I got a much better mark that year than I deserved. The next year I had Mrs. Brown for history and my parents couldn't figure out why my marks went way down."

"Do you remember what Virginia was like that year? What I mean was, did she act differently or share anything going on in her life?"

"I remember that fall being really surprised, and to be honest, pretty mad at her for not wanting to be on the basketball team after we'd won the previous year, but then I found out about her mom and how Virginia had to go to Toronto with her. Something about her mom having trouble because of her age, so they had to go away to have the baby. I was kind of jealous that she got to go to Toronto, but when she came back, I realized it must not have been much fun and probably kind of scary because she was a lot quieter after that."

"Did she ever talk about it?"

"No, but that was kind of when she and Gregory started having problems."

"Can you tell us about that?"

"I think she had more responsibility at home with the new baby, and then she got a job at the drug store, so she didn't have as much time as before to just hang out. To be honest, she wasn't as much fun as she had been before."

"And that caused problems between her and Gregory?"

"Well, sure. When you're a couple, you're supposed to spend time together. Put the other person first, wouldn't you say?" She directed the question at me.

"Can you think back really hard if she ever mentioned anyone else she may have been interested in?" Gene interjected.

"No, I already told you she never mentioned any boys. In fact, it was almost odd how little interest she took in men. Even after she and Gregory broke up, I don't think she ever went out with anyone else. Then again, we weren't hanging out as much, kind of grew apart, as often happens."

"Were you surprised when she left?"

"Well, yeah, wasn't everyone? Very few people leave Creighton, and if they do, it's usually a man leaving for a job or a woman because she got married. But to just up and take off to Hollywood, well, it didn't really make any sense. Gregory used to talk a lot about leaving, how he and Virginia planned to go to Sudbury after graduation, but that was just Gregory talk. I don't recall Virginia ever talking about that. So, when she left, a lot of people thought it was pretty reckless of her, especially to go off to a big city all the way to the United States. We thought for sure she'd be back in no time, but we were wrong. I couldn't figure out what would keep her there."

I could think of a hundred things, but Paulette had probably been no farther than Sudbury in her whole life, so she'd have no idea what she was missing.

"Paulette, can you think of any person or any reason why someone here would have wanted to harm Virginia?" I asked.

We stayed silent and waited. She chewed her bottom lip, then slowly began to shake her head back and forth.

"Sorry, I can't think of anyone. I have no idea why someone would have wanted to kill Virginia. Maybe she rubbed someone the wrong way. You have to admit, all the hoopla about her return was a bit much, and the men in town were all agog, as if they'd never seen a pretty girl before. If I were to guess, she may have turned down the wrong man and he didn't take it well." She stood up quickly. "The pie should be ready. Would you gentlemen like a cup of tea and a slice?"

"Thank you, Miss Carmichael, but we can't stay. We have more interviews to conduct," I said quickly, but before we left, I needed to address the elephant in the room.

"What about Gregory? You know him best. Is he capable of something like this?"

She opened her hands, palms up, as if she was about to give a blessing. "How can we ever know what another person is really capable of?"

THIRTY

VICTOR

I lied to Paulette Carmichael. We didn't have any other interviews, but I did have an engagement. Gene's wife, Lily, had invited me for dinner and it had been too long since I'd had a real home-cooked meal. The drive back and forth between Creighton and Sudbury most days had me throwing together eggs and toast or heating up a can of beans for dinner.

I leaned back in my chair, hoping the top button of my trousers didn't pop loose. "That is the best meal I've had in years," I said in all honesty.

Lily Kowalski waved her hand at me. "Oh, it was nothing special, Detective, but I'm glad you enjoyed it." She sat down next to Gene.

"Everyone settled?" Gene asked.

"It took two stories, but I did it." She took a sip of her glass of sherry. "They were still so excited about having a visitor for dinner."

Gene and Lily's two daughters were six and seven, as they had proclaimed during the lively dinner conversation. They were well behaved but chatty. Gene had warned me, a stranger for dinner was a big deal, and the girls would be extra talkative.

They had interrogated me on what Toronto was like and then regaled me with stories of catching frogs in Albion's Pond, skating in the winter at the outdoor rink, and going swimming at Meatbird Lake down the highway.

After putting the girls to bed, Lily joined Gene and I in the living room. The Kowalski family was everything I pictured a middle-class Canadian family to be. The home was tidy, the furniture worn in places but sturdy with plenty of use still in them. The modern touches hadn't reached Creighton yet, but Mrs. Kowalski's taste leaned more towards current fashion than the patchwork remnants of the prior decades I'd noticed in most of the homes I'd visited.

"You know, you are welcome for dinner anytime," Gene said, yawning with his post-meal lethargy. As much as Lily downplayed this as a regular meal, I knew when guests came women brought out their best to impress. Taking it all in, I was reminded of a time, before the war, when I had thought this would be my life. Back when I was engaged to be married and expected a traditional life, but war has a way of changing priorities and messing up plans.

Like a lot of young men, I informally proposed to Alice when I signed up, never expecting I would be sent to Camp X. It was the combination of my police training and fluency in French, thanks to summers with my grandmother in Montreal, that got me recruited to train in the areas of sabotage, recruitment, interrogation, and other useful skills.

I took well to the training, but the downside was, due to the secret nature of my work, and getting dropped behind enemy lines in France, sending letters home was impossible. After two years, Alice had enough and found a more stable soldier in the infantry to marry. I couldn't blame her.

"So, Gene tells me you're from Toronto. What brought you to Sudbury?" Lily picked up the questioning where her daughters left off.

Before I could answer, the phone from the hallway rang, interrupting the conversation, which I sent up a silent thanks for. It was hard to explain what drove me to leave Toronto for the North when I wasn't quite sure myself. After the war, the city no longer felt like home. Things had changed. Most likely it was me who'd changed. Gene rose from his seat and headed out to answer the phone in the hall.

"I wish we hadn't gotten that phone line put in. We managed perfectly fine without one for years." She took a sharp swallow of her drink.

"When did you get it?" I asked.

"As soon as he took the police job, Inco sent one of their men over to hook it up. They didn't even ask us. Apparently, all the officers have to have one. Most of the time I don't mind, but sometimes, especially at night, the ringing startles me. It's such a jarring sound." She shook her head and smiled. Her eyes were small and squinty, which gave her a jolly look, like she was always on the verge of laughing. "I was glad when Gene got out of the mines. It's dangerous work. We've had accidents where men were killed or maimed, but those that don't still aren't lucky. Most end up with breathing and other health problems. So, when he became an officer, I thought I didn't have to worry anymore. Until the tragedy in Copper Cliff, just over a year ago now."

"The police officer who got shot?" I said.

"Yes, you know about it?"

"It was in all the papers, probably right across the country." I didn't mention that I'd been at the funeral as an official representative of the Ontario Provincial Police.

"Gene knew Martin Lovett. They did some training sessions together. It was so tragic and unnecessary. He was minding his own business, eating a bowl of soup, when that crazy man just walked into the hotel and shot him. Martin never had a chance to even get out of his chair. And then the coward went off and killed himself, so there wasn't even a sense of justice or a chance for someone to ask him why he did it."

There it was again. That need to know why. People always wanted to know, as if that would somehow deaden the pain of their loss, but it didn't. In fact, it usually just magnified the senselessness of the death.

"He was married, Martin was, with a wife and children. Now when Gene is at work and the phone rings, I practically jump out of my skin. I want to just let it ring and not answer it in case it's bad news."

Gene came back into the room. "There's been an accident over at Slater's Rock. Nick Valenti got injured. Sounds like kids fooling around, but the doctor asked if I would come by. You know, put the fear of God in them." He chuckled. "It's a big part of my job description. I'm really sorry to run out like this. Not very good manners, I'm afraid. Go ahead and finish your drink."

"Do you mind if I tag along?" I said and drained the Scotch left in my glass.

"I don't mind at all." He leaned over and placed a kiss on his wife's forehead. "I shouldn't be long."

"Thanks again for the meal, Mrs. Kowalski," I said.

"Anytime, Detective, and call me Lily." She coaxed out a smile, but I could tell her mind was still on Martin Lovett. She grappled with the same fears every woman who called a police officer "husband" had since the beginning of the profession.

We pulled up outside a pretty two-storey home. It had a fresher look, as if it recently had a paint job. Fresh flowers grew in baskets on the porch. The house was on Wavell Street in an area referred to as Snob Hill, because it was where the shift bosses and other more affluent members of the community lived. Apparently, the doctor was one of them. There was a car parked half-on and half-off the doctor's front lawn with the passenger's-side back door wide open.

"Whose car is that, Gene?" With so few in town, I knew he'd have an answer.

"The McLellan's."

Gene knocked once on the front door, then walked in without waiting for an answer. Lights blazed throughout, and numerous voices came from the back of the house. We passed a tastefully furnished living room. With a quick glance, I could tell by the book on a side table and the smouldering cigar in the ashtray that the doctor had been enjoying a relaxing evening before the interruption. A tall, broad-shouldered, middle-aged woman strode around the corner, shaking her head and muttering to herself.

"Barbara," Gene said.

"Oh, Gene, hello. Dear me." She patted her hair and came forward. "And you must be Detective Lapointe?" She reached out to shake my hand. Her grip was strong and efficient. "I don't think any crime has been committed here other than poor judgement and mistaken belief in one's own invincibility."

"Where is the doctor?"

"In the back bedroom. The house isn't set up as a surgery, so we put the Valenti boy in there. His father should be here soon. I called over to the Inco Club. It's bowling night, don't you know."

"We'll just pop in and see if we can be of any help," Gene said.

"I'm sure Ernest would appreciate that. Maybe you can get those kids to go home. They're more of a hindrance than a help. With all the drama and the way they're carrying on, you'd think the boy had been shot by gangsters." She shook her head.

"Well, when Mr. Valenti gets here, they may wish they had. That man's temper is infamous," Gene explained for my benefit.

"Lord have mercy on all of us then. I'm off to fetch some bandages."

She scurried off while I followed Gene down the hallway.

We entered a chaotic scene. Five teenagers crowded around the doorway, the girls sniffling and the boys talking over each other.

"Okay, everyone, step back and keep it down," Gene announced.

Like the Red Sea, the group parted and ceased talking.

"Thanks for coming, Gene," the doctor said from his place beside the patient. Nick Valenti was ghostly pale and sweaty. Sitting on the opposite side of the bed, holding Nick's hand, was Olive Boyle.

"Young Mr. Valenti here seemed to think he was like that Superman we hear on the radio. He tried to scale Slater's Rock, in the dark, no less. Now he's suffering from a dislocated shoulder and a broken arm, which will mean the end of his baseball career, at least this year," the doctor announced.

The statement caused a collective gasp from the teens and an even louder moan from the patient. Gene turned to the group huddled around the doorway.

"Jeff, I expected better from you." A young, freckled boy, tall but gangly, hung his head. "What will your parents say? I have no doubt we will all hear about this in your father's sermon on Sunday. Now, someone, please tell us what happened," Gene said.

"A lot of the boys do it," Olive Boyle spoke up from the bed, "just before a big game." She lifted her chin proudly, like she was defending a sacred ancient ritual.

"Like a test of stupidity?" Gene said.

"I checked the rope myself." Nick spoke through clenched teeth. "I don't know what happened."

"He was almost at the top when the rope snapped and he fell," a short, stocky boy said and shivered, as if he was reliving the moment.

"We thought he was dead." A girl in braids spoke before burying her face in her hands. The pastor's son consoled her with an awkward pat on the shoulder.

"Hugh got his parents' car and carried Nick to it, then we brought him here." The other girl spoke up for the first time. "Hugh's the real hero."

I observed Hugh's face go several shades of red.

Gene sighed, pinching the bridge of his nose. "Well, there weren't any laws broken, but each one of you will be answering to your parents." He pointed at them. "And the rest of the town, when they find out they have lost their star pitcher."

It was then that the true horror of their actions sank in. I watched the emotions, from guilt and sadness to outright fear, play across their faces.

"I suggest each of you make your way home immediately. Jeff, make sure Cheryl gets home safely. You kids stay together, you hear me?" Gene snapped the last words, prompting the group to scramble into action, bumping into one another in their haste to escape. All except Olive.

"I'm going to stay. Nick needs a friend by his side." She lifted her chin defiantly.

"Oh, no you're not," the doctor said. "'I'm going to have to snap that shoulder back into place, and once the screaming starts, you'll likely pass out and just be in the way. Hugh, will you make sure she gets home?"

212

"Yes, sir."

"It's all right. I'm staying at Cheryl's tonight. I'll walk with them. Goodnight, Hugh. See you tomorrow." She left with the group.

"I better get my parents' car home," Hugh said and headed for the door. I followed him out.

"Hugh?"

"Yes, sir?"

"Can I ask you a few questions?"

He glanced at the car as if he would rather be in it. "Umm, okay."

"You know the Boyle family pretty well."

"I guess so."

"How are they managing with everything going on?"

"Okay, I suppose."

"Did you know Virginia well?"

"Not really."

It was like pulling teeth. I had to change up my tactics.

"What has Olive told you about her sister, about what happened, and what the family thinks about who could have done this?"

He thought hard, like he was getting ready for an oral test. "Olive thought Virginia was the bee's knees. She really liked her clothes and said how she wanted to be as sophisticated as Virginia, but Olive is already the most stylish girl in school. There is no one like her."

"What about who killed Virginia? Does the family ever speak about it?"

"No, sir, they are as stumped as the rest of us." He shrugged.

"Have you heard any rumours or anything you could share with me? Any little bit could help."

"Well," he looked around as if making sure no one was nearby to eavesdrop, "I have heard about a hermit who lives somewhere between here and Dogpatch. I don't know where, and no one has really seen him, but there's talk it could be him."

I mentally shook my head. We'd heard all the wild conjecture of hermits, woodsmen, and drifters passing through. No one wanted to contemplate the real truth that their neighbour was most likely a murderer.

"Well, thanks, for your help, Hugh. You better get going."

"Yes, sir." He scurried down the steps and jumped into the car.

Gene came out on the porch. "See, for a small town we have a lot of excitement." He laughed.

"At least this will give people something to talk about other than the murder," I said. "I'm guessing within a few days the story will be blown into mythic proportions."

"You catch on quick, Detective. I think I'll head up to Slater's Rock tomorrow morning before the crowds show up. I want to remove the rope so the other numbskulls in town don't get any bright ideas."

"I'll join you. I'm curious to see what this infamous rock is all about."

THIRTY-ONE

VICTOR

It was early, and the dew still clung to everything, which made the rocks slippery. Gene stepped lightly from rock to rock, his feet landing solidly each time. He moved like he was walking on a flat wooden floor, whereas I flailed and cursed more than I normally did early in the morning. Halfway up, Gene stopped and turned around.

"You wanna wait at the bottom, Detective? I wouldn't want to have to carry you to Doc's for a broken bone."

"Don't worry about me. I've been in tougher situations than this. Just because you people here are part mountain goat doesn't mean I can't do it," I said, then slipped inelegantly.

When we reached the top of Slater's Rock, I was sweating, and my knee was screaming at me. I was relieved to be on flat ground where I could catch my breath and not worry about breaking my neck. Gene crouched down beside a large boulder. A sturdy rope looped around it, with a short tail trailing off.

"Detective?"

His voice held a note of warning that got my attention. I bent over to see what he was pointing at. The ends of the rope were not frayed, as one would expect from a break. It was severed, cleanly.

"Here." Gene pointed to the rock beneath it, where I could see a series of multiple thin grooves, white and chalky against the dark grey rock. "Those were made by a knife. Goddamn it." He stood up, kicking loose stones towards the edge.

I followed him and looked over the edge to the ground.

"That kid is lucky he didn't die," Gene said.

"Yeah, considering someone wanted him to."

"What the hell? It doesn't make any sense." Gene crossed his arms and stared at the ground. "Could it be a prank gone wrong? I can't imagine any of those kids trying to kill Nick Valenti. They're all good kids. I've never had any trouble with a single one of them, but they were up here when it happened, damn it. Don't we have enough on our plates without this as well?"

We both turned at the sound of voices coming up the hill. A group of boys spilled into sight. I recognized Jeff, one of the boys from last night, as well as Mikey McFaye, Virginia Boyle's nephew. The group came to a silent standstill when they caught sight of us.

"Boys." Gene's greeting held a note of warning.

"Hi, sorry, we were…" Jeff trailed off.

"I'm actually glad you're here, Jeff. We have a few questions for you." I waved Jeff over to where we were standing and lowered my voice. "We need you to tell us exactly what happened last night, and don't skip anything."

The boy swallowed several times under my gaze. "Well," his voice cracked, which he tried to cover up with a cough, "so we were all standing here…" he pointed to the edge of the rock, "looking over at Nick. I had a flashlight that I kept on him so we could see what he was doing."

"Were you all here at the edge the whole time, or did anyone in the group wander off or leave?" I asked.

Jeff scrunched up his face as if the thought took extreme effort. "No, at least I don't think so. We were all just grouped together, laughing and talking."

"Did you hear or see anyone else come up the hill?" Gene asked.

"I didn't hear anything, but the girls were pretty giggly, and it was pitch black last night. Without my flashlight, we wouldn't have been able to see our own feet."

"So, someone else could have been up here, just a few feet from you, and you wouldn't have known it?" I said.

"I guess so. Why? Are we in trouble or something? At least more trouble than we already are? My parents are making me work at Valenti's store until Nick gets better. My mom is really sore at me."

"As she should be," Gene said. "Nick could have died last night. Then how would you have felt?"

Jeff stared at his feet, answering with silence.

"Are you sure you didn't see or hear anyone else up here? Any noises out of the ordinary?" I pushed.

"No, sir, I really didn't."

"Fine." Gene sighed. "Get going, and I don't want to hear about you doing any more tours up here. In fact, I want all you boys to stay off this rock for a while. You hear me?" He raised his voice so the rest of the gang could hear. A few muted *yes, sirs* made their way back. Gene and I both turned and looked back over the edge of the rock. I wondered if the Valenti boy would ever realize how close he came to being a fatality.

"Hey, Officer Kowalski, did you notice this rope looks like it's been cut?" Jeff's voice made Gene and I spin around to see the young man with his finger pointed at the end of the rope.

I looked at Gene, knowing my face mirrored the same "goddammit" look he wore. "Jeff, is there any chance I can depend on you and the boys here to keep this a secret for a while?"

"Oh, you bet, Officer Kowalski. You can count on us. Scout's honour." He held his hands up in the familiar three-finger salute. Jeff left with the other boys, leaping effortlessly down the steep rocks.

"Any chance the boys will keep their promise of secrecy?" I asked Gene.

"None whatsoever." Gene shook his head, heading over to the large boulder to remove the evidence.

THIRTY-TWO

ROSE

It was a surprise when June announced we'd be having a birthday lunch for Olive. She was turning sixteen, but our family didn't really make a fuss over people's birthdays. If you needed something, Mom would order it and say it was for your birthday. I'd gotten underwear, socks, and shoes at different times. The gifts wouldn't arrive on your birthday, and they weren't wrapped, but were called a gift anyway.

This was just another example of how Olive got everything she wanted. I thought it was wrong to even celebrate a birthday right now, but June insisted we needed something fun to take our minds off our troubles.

I took my usual seat and looked around the table. We'd all changed so much. Each of us wore our sadness differently. Olive was more still, which I hated to admit made her look more mature. Mom looked lost, like everyday tasks were a puzzle to be solved. June was forever making lists and doing tasks, even ones that didn't need doing, like sweeping half a dozen times a day. Mikey didn't want to be at home. June said Joey's family was going to think they had another kid, since he was over there so much. Even Maggie had changed. She no longer bounced and giggled like she used to.

Hugh and Joey joined us for lunch and the cake that would come after. When we finished eating our toasted tomato sandwiches and potato salad, June brought out a two-layered cake with strawberry frosting. Although Olive turned sixteen, there were only four candles of all different sizes, a sign that June had put the lunch together at the last minute.

Everyone began to sing "Happy Birthday." June overpowered us all, doing her best to make it sound less gloomy. Although he sang softly, Hugh, like June, tried to make the best of the moment. He also was the only one with a gift; a small box wrapped in brown paper.

It showed how much he'd become a part of the family that it would have seemed weird if he wasn't there. Before, Hugh was like Olive's shadow, always following behind her. Now he was more like a smokestack, sturdy and dependable. The strength Olive leaned on. I saw how he'd changed, too; he looked less like a scrawny kid, as Dad called him. It was like the food he ate actually stuck to his bones now. If his face filled out a bit more, it might help his nose look smaller.

"The cake is delicious, Mrs. McFaye."

"Thank you, Hugh," June answered. "So, have you had a chance to visit Nick Valenti, see how he's doing?"

Hugh stopped with his fork halfway up to his mouth. "No, ma'am. I keep meaning to, but Mother is keeping me close to home."

"Did you get in a lot of trouble, Hugh?" Joey leaned in.

220

"Well, my parents were…disappointed in me." He half smiled at Olive, who reached over and patted his hand. "And I'm pretty disappointed in myself. I don't know what we were thinking, letting Nick take such a risk."

"Hopefully that knocked some sense into you kids. He could have been killed." Mom spoke up for the first time.

Everyone looked down at their plates.

"Did you hear anything? I heard there were giant footsteps found around the rock where the rope was cut," Joey said.

"Is that true?" I asked and pictured a large-footed man slicing through the rope.

"You know, I might have heard something," Hugh said, "but then again, we were all watching Nick and calling out, encouraging him and stuff like that." He shrugged. "I really wish I had seen something, then maybe I could have caught whoever did it because, well, you know…" He looked around the table at us.

"It could be the same person," I said.

"Yeah, that's what people are saying," Hugh said.

"Well, I'm just glad everyone is all right and we get a chance to celebrate Olive's birthday today," June jumped in. "After all, sixteen is a pretty big deal."

"I am an adult now. So many things you can do at sixteen. I can get a driver's licence." Olive regained a little of her sparkle when she spoke.

"To drive what?" Mikey scoffed.

"That's not the point. It means they think you're responsible enough to drive, get married, finish school. Lots of things."

I saw Hugh's ears flush beet-red when she mentioned marriage.

"Well, since we are talking about being a grown-up, I think now's a good time to tell you all…" Olive looked at Mom, who turned her head away with the faraway look I was becoming familiar with. Olive sighed and put down her fork. "I'm moving to Toronto."

She spoke so softly I thought I misheard her. The table went silent, and there were a lot of puzzled looks as we all waited to hear more.

"I'm going to stay with Aunt Addy. She's got a spare room, and she's excited to have me," Olive explained.

"Aunt Addy?" June turned to my mom. "But we barely know her."

"She's your father's sister, and it's true we haven't kept in touch much, but family is family, and she's already agreed to keep an eye on Olive and help her get a job." Mom sounded like she'd practiced this answer.

"After everything that has happened to this family, how can you let her go?" June asked, which was the same thing I was thinking. Olive and I were never close, and there'd been times I'd wished she'd disappear, but not anymore. It already felt like our family had lost a limb. How could we lose another part of us?

Mom's back stiffened. "It was coming to Creighton that killed Virginia, not leaving. She was happy in Los Angeles. She told me enough times, and now it's Olive's turn to be happy. Maybe leaving Creighton is the best way I can protect my children."

She tossed her napkin onto her half-eaten plate and walked out. June's questions had annoyed her, but it was more than that. I saw fear on her face. Too much had happened: first to Virginia, then Nick Valenti, and it had everyone wondering what might happen next.

The kitchen became quiet. June stood up, cleared away the plates, then without a word, left out the back door and went back to her house.

"You're really leaving, Olive?" Mikey looked confused. "Why would you want to live in a big city, all by yourself, without any of us? Won't you miss all the great stuff here? Meatbird Lake, the water tower, the Rio, and berry picking in the summer?"

"I never want to pick another damn blueberry." She banged her palm against the table, rattling the dishes.

"Olive, why didn't you tell me?" Hugh's voice wavered between hurt and anger.

"I just did, silly," she said and reached out, putting her hand over his, which he snatched away.

"But Toronto?" His voice was thick. "I can understand Sudbury, that would be okay, but Toronto? You might as well be going to the other side of the world."

"I have to go," she said.

"No, you don't. You can't run away from sadness. In Toronto, you'll still be sad, but you'll be lonely too." He was right. How could she leave her family after all that had happened?

"I was hoping at least you would understand, Hugh." I'd never heard Olive plead before.

Hugh stood up slowly, like an old man whose body ached in every joint. "I thought you'd changed. That you were finally growing up a bit, but you're still the selfish girl you've always been." He picked up his plate, put it into the sink, and then walked out the back door.

The air in the room felt frosty. I'd never heard Hugh speak to Olive or anyone like that. The world had turned upside down.

"Trust me, he'll be back tomorrow. If there's one thing I am sure of, it's Hugh." Olive's voice trembled.

She reached over and picked up the wrapped box Hugh left behind. She opened it up, and sitting inside were two hair combs, each with a strand of pearls along the top.

"Oh my," was all Olive said.

THIRTY-THREE

VICTOR

Do you know why war is simple? Because there's no guesswork as to who the bad guys were. They were easy to find. They'd strut around the French villages with eagle emblems and swastikas on their chest and caps like malevolent peacocks. My only motivation at that time was to kill them before they killed me, and there were no rules about how to accomplish that goal. I had free rein for extracting information and was encouraged to eliminate anyone who got in my way.

Although those tactics were efficient, they had a lingering effect on me. In fact, no matter how hard I tried to close the door on the war years, the memories were as vivid as the moments I lived them, often reappearing at the most unwelcome moments, such as when I was walking through town to conduct an interview.

When I thought about the case, I pictured Virginia Boyle, and when I thought of her, it always took me to the face of another dark-haired beauty. One I'd tried very hard to bury.

Margeaux was as beautiful as Virginia but with a hardness the Boyle girl didn't possess, at least from the stories I'd heard and the pictures I'd seen of her. Then again, she hadn't been exposed to the atrocities Margeaux had in seeing the Germans take over her country.

Still, similar to Virginia, Margeaux's body had been left sprawled out on the ground, but instead of lying amongst the blueberry bushes, she was flung outside a French manor that had been commandeered as a Gestapo prison and place of interrogation.

The difference in that case is I knew who had killed Margeaux. I knew his name and his face, with its strong jaw, blond hair, and blue eyes, but he had been unreachable. There was nothing I could do to get back at him. I had a mission to complete, and a personal vendetta would have compromised that.

Now I was here, worlds away, with the same burning desire for vengeance, only without any idea who to take action against. This case had me chasing shadows, and nothing made sense. What possible motive could there be to kill a young woman home for a visit and attempt to kill a teenage boy showing off for his friends? And that was assuming the two cases were linked. We had no proof; it was just a hunch.

One way or another, I was determined to bring Virginia's killer to justice. Something I was unable to do for Margeaux.

Gene had been called away to a shed fire he suspected had something to do with a bootlegger. Creighton was a dry town, but there was no way to keep a population of miners sober, no matter what the law.

I'd be conducting the last interview of Virginia's inner circle of friends on my own. I hoped Lorelei Clarke could provide something more helpful than the previous interviewees. We needed a break.

I was able to walk to the Clarke's home in a few short minutes. I found the house easily from Gene's description of a well-tended garden. Roses bloomed from bushes out front, and the porch steps were sturdy with a freshly painted appearance. I knocked on the screen door, and a voice carried from the back of the house.

"I'm coming."

It took longer than expected, but when I saw Mrs. Clarke shuffling slowly down the hall, I realized why. She was a petite lady, which made her large belly even more prominent. I opened the door and let myself in to save her having to complete the walk. Every step looked like an effort for her.

"Mrs. Clarke, how do you do? I'm Detective Lapointe."

"Yes, of course, I've been expecting you. Please come in." She escorted me to the front room, where a pot of tea and cookies were set out.

"I thought Officer Kowalski would be joining us." She gingerly lowered herself to a chair with a small grimace.

I sat on the chesterfield opposite her. The room was spotless, with everything in its place.

"He got called away. A shed fire over near Dogpatch."

Her laugh was breathy. "Sounds like someone's still may have overheated."

"That's exactly what Gene said."

If asked, I would describe Mrs. Clarke as cute as opposed to pretty. She had small features that made her look younger than her age, and her teeth were a bit too large for her face, so when she smiled all you saw were pearly whites.

"I take it the bootleggers are an open secret in town."

She waved her hand. "Oh, yes. Most of them are just regular men in town making a bit of money on the side. They go to Sudbury, load up, and sell booze from their living rooms or have a little still but don't cause any problems. But like in a classroom, there's always one or two problem children who don't play nice with others."

"Spoken like a true teacher."

"Well, yes, I was." There was a strong emphasis on the past tense.

"You miss teaching?"

"I do. I really enjoyed being at the front of the class, teaching something new and seeing in the kids' faces the moment they got it…you know? My favourite subject was mathematics, and I worked very hard to help all my kids pass at some level."

"Will you go back?"

"No, I don't think so. We plan on having a few children, so Jefferson says I'll be needed at home. And speaking of Jefferson, sorry he couldn't be here. He had to go to Sudbury to pick up the crib I ordered. We didn't want to wait any longer, just in case." She patted her belly.

"Yes, I guess not. Do you mind if we get started?"

"No, please. Oh, and help yourself to tea and cookies. I made them myself."

"Thank you, I will when we finish up." I learned to always take some of what a woman offered if she made it herself and these were enticing. The smell of warm chocolate filled the house.

"I'd like to ask you about Virginia back when you were teenagers, around the age of fifteen. In the time before she went away to Toronto with her mother."

She frowned but didn't say anything.

"Can you tell me about what was going on in your lives? In Virginia's life at that time?" Once again, I cursed the vagueness I needed to employ. If you wanted good answers, you needed to ask very specific questions, but I was finding it hard to do so and not to give away the situation of Virginia and the baby. It was obvious Mrs. Clarke was confused too, by the look she gave me.

"I'm sorry, Detective, can you be a bit clearer? I'm not sure what exactly you're looking for."

"I'm sorry I can't be more specific at this time. We're following a thread that may be nothing. Maybe if you could just tell me what you and your friends were doing at that time, we'll go from there."

"Well, we were in school, and we'd hang out together afterwards. Our little group were all in couples. Virginia and Gregory, Paulette and Swifty, and me and George, who we called Rat at that time." She shook her head and chuckled.

"Paulette told me she and Virginia were on the basketball team, but you weren't."

"True, I was too short and not athletically inclined."

"I was also told that the year Virginia and Paulette were on the team, Virginia was getting some extra help in school because she was having some trouble in one of her classes." Mrs. Boyle had told me this.

Mrs. Clarke's eyes opened wide. "Who said that? No, Virginia was a really good student. Not a genius or anything, but very diligent. Teachers reward that, I can tell you. I know because she and I used to compete for the highest mark. Sometimes I got it and sometimes she did, depending on the class, so I know she never failed or even came close. I'm thinking it was Paulette who told you Virginia was having trouble in school?"

"Why do you say that?"

"Paulette has always been jealous of Virginia. They were friends, but there was a lot of competition between them. Virginia and Gregory were the unspoken leaders of our group. Virginia had a way of drawing people's attention without trying. She was very pretty, but it was more than that. Do you know what I mean, Detective? Some people just draw you in."

A film played in my mind of Margeaux lying in a pile of hay, looking up at me with her captivating smile. I blinked hard. "Yes, I know what you mean."

"Well, that was Virginia, but Paulette, she was the opposite. She pushed people away because she tried too hard to be like Virginia, but you can't force that. As soon as it became clear Virginia and Gregory were having problems in their relationship, Paulette moved right in, offering to be a shoulder to cry on for Gregory and making snide comments about Virginia. She wasn't very subtle."

"Did it work?"

"Not at first. Gregory was so head over heels in love with Virginia. Everyone was convinced they'd get married. It wasn't until she left that Paulette was finally able to get his attention. Just between you and I, Detective, his feelings for Paulette are nothing like they were for Virginia. That much is obvious."

"You must have been happy to see her when she returned."

A crease appeared between her eyes, and she took a moment to answer.

"I was looking forward to seeing her, and I did. The day after she arrived, everyone dropped in to her parents' place. A little homecoming party, but you know, people change. It had been five years, and our lives had moved on."

I wanted more. "Can you tell me what was different about her?"

"She seemed much more sophisticated than the rest of us, of course. I wondered what she must have thought of us after living in Los Angeles. She also, I don't know, you'll have to excuse me, I am much more sensitive than normal. It's the pregnancy. It makes women emotional in ways they wouldn't normally be."

She wiped lightly at the corner of her eyes that had become moist.

"Of course, take your time."

"Well, I felt… I'm probably overreacting, but she wasn't as kind as I remember."

"Can you tell me exactly what makes you say that?"

"I'll have to give you a bit of background first. You see, when Jefferson and I got married, it caused some gossip because I had been his student, and we have a bit of an age difference. It's a small-town thing that people probably wouldn't bat an eye at in other places. Anyway, it's all over now. People see we are in love, and we've settled into our traditional family life.

"But when Virginia found out who I married, she didn't seem happy. In fact, she made a comment about our age difference and then gave me the cold shoulder the rest of the time. It hurt my feelings because I thought, as a woman who was living her own independent life in a big city, she would be more open than the people here, but I was wrong. She seemed just as judgemental."

"She was in your husband's class, and he coached her in basketball. Could there be some reason she didn't like him?"

"None that I can think of. Like the rest of us, she used to giggle over the handsome young teacher when he first came to our school," she blushed, "And she was really happy that, because of his coaching, their team won almost every game."

I could feel my pulse pick up as my mind started to connect dots.

"What does your husband think of Virginia? Her coming home, from what I gathered, was pretty big news in town. I'm sure you two must have discussed it."

"He never mentioned her, but when I told him how excited I was about her coming back, all he asked was how long she'd be staying and when she was leaving. I think he was worried the excitement wasn't good for my condition. Men can be so overprotective." She shrugged.

"Yes, we certainly can be." I reached out for a cookie and popped it into my mouth. "So, Mrs. Clarke, when did you say your husband would be home?"

THIRTY-FOUR

ROSE

"I win." Maggie scooped the marbles out of the hole we'd dug in the ground.

She'd won my favourite orange cat's eye off me, but I didn't have the energy to care, which was why she won in the first place. I wasn't paying attention.

"Maggie, bath time!" June called out the back door. "Rose, go back inside. It'll be dark soon."

"Okay," I said, slowly picked up the few marbles I had left, and put them in my pocket. I bent over and dusted off my knees, waiting until Maggie went inside and the door shut behind her.

I didn't want to go inside. Olive was in our bedroom. She'd been there all day, ever since Hugh walked out from her birthday lunch. I knew Mom and Dad would be in the living room, not talking or doing anything, just lost somewhere in their own heads. It was too hard to breathe in there.

I wanted to talk about Virginia, to bring her back to life with words. I wanted to hear stories about her from when I was little. Stories that might explain what she was like, that might help me understand why she'd done what she did, but that wasn't how it worked in our family. They tried to forget Virginia the same way they did with Francis. She'd end up a dusty photograph tucked behind the lamp on Mom's bedside table.

I walked away from our house not caring if I got in trouble or not. That was one of the things that had changed for me. Now that I knew Virginia didn't want me and Mom said I was "a shame," it felt like I wasn't really a part of the family anymore. Even surrounded by them, I still felt separate. Sometimes I wanted to blurt out everything I knew. I'd try to think of things to say to hurt their feelings just as mine were, but it was like there was a lock on my mouth, and I could only scream in my head.

I didn't plan it, but my feet took me up the hill. There was a newly worn path, which meant it had become a popular place to visit and also meant I might not be alone when I got up there.

It took longer than I expected, because my body felt heavy, like I had twice the amount of gravity pushing down on me. I'd been tired a lot lately too. I guess being sad did that to you.

I reached the small cluster of trees, and everything looked the same as last time. It would have made more sense if the trees had died and the blueberry bushes had shrivelled up. Then it would really look like a place where someone's life had ended.

The rocks were mostly flat, which made it comfortable for us to sit that day when we ate our lunch of cheese sandwiches. The boys had eaten quickly then left, not wanting to waste time sitting around. Maggie and I stayed a little longer, eating some of the blueberries we'd picked.

As we were heading out to pick again, Virginia called out to us, "You girls be careful out there, okay? Just holler for me if you need anything."

"We will," we answered, but I didn't say goodbye or tell her to be careful. My last words to my real mom were "we will." So stupid, so nothing. I sat down on the smoothest rock on the ground and pulled my knees up under my chin.

The blue streaks in the sky deepened along with the pink. The colours of a summer sunset were the prettiest. The air felt heavy, and I heard a rumble. It sounded far away, like a train in the distance. Then the sky lit up. Sheet lightning brightened the sky like the flash of a photographer's bulb, and it hit me then that Virginia would never see anything like this again.

So much had been taken from me. My Virginia, who made me feel special, and always noticed when I was around. All my plans for the future, getting out of Creighton, moving to Los Angeles, and living forever with Virginia. And then when I found out I was a mistake of Virginia's, the person I thought I was, that was taken away too.

It felt like there were two people inside me. One who was terribly sad and the other who got really angry at times. Sometimes, like the rest of the family, I thought it might be best to just forget. To push everything down inside me and never let it out. Other times I'd feel an energy inside me like I should be doing something, but I had no idea what.

Should I try to track down Virginia's killer? But how was a kid to do that? Or was it my job to keep her memory alive, even though speaking her name out loud seemed like the wrong thing to do?

Then I realized the problem was me. I was a coward. I was afraid to stand up for what I wanted. I was afraid to use my voice. So many times, I complained about being invisible, but it was like a blanket that kept me safe.

I wasn't brave like Virginia was. She was fire, burning her own way through the world. How many other girls were going to be famous photographers? I'd never heard of any. The only thing for a girl here was to marry a miner.

Was this what would happen to me? I couldn't even imagine someone falling in love with me enough to want to marry me. I wasn't beautiful, like Olive or Virginia, and not sunny and fun like Maggie. I was just me. So, then what? Would I be a spinster who sat in the corner of the room, darning socks, and being ignored by everyone around her, like in the movies?

Why wasn't there a bit of Virginia in me? Something passed from mother to child? Couldn't I become brave, strong, or just different from other girls? Maybe I could be a photographer or something like that and make my way out of Creighton myself. I couldn't imagine my family would miss me much, maybe just Maggie.

I closed my eyes and listened to the sounds around me. A whippoorwill called out. Behind my lids, I could still see the lightning flash, and it made me flinch. A fat drop of water hit my cheek and rolled down, followed by a few more. I didn't mind at all and stayed still, like I was glued to the rock beneath me.

"Virginia," I whispered, wishing so hard for her to hear me. I wanted her ghost to show up. I wouldn't even be scared. I'd tell her I loved her and missed her.

But no ghost appeared, and my heart didn't get any messages. She wasn't there. I opened my eyes and was surprised at how quickly the sky had gone dark. Looking down the hill, I could no longer tell the difference between the rock and the moss that grew in between. Only the occasional flash from the sky gave me a glimpse of my surroundings.

The rain became heavier, and I considered getting up. Behind me, I heard something rustle. Maybe a squirrel or mole running through the underbrush. I turned around but couldn't distinguish any shapes or movement.

A twig snapped, meaning something heavier, perhaps a deer. The hairs on my arms stood up because bears were always a concern, even though they mostly avoided people. It could have been a moose. I waited for another sound, but there was none.

The feeling that something was still there continued, and my stomach did a flip-flop. Something didn't feel right. What if Virginia's killer really was a hermit who lived in the woods and he'd come back to this spot and been here all along? Or what if someone had followed me up here? I would have seen them on the path…unless they'd used the back way. The rocks were much larger and harder to climb for someone my size, since you had to jump from one boulder to the next, but a grown man could do it easily.

I stood up slowly, trying to act natural. I'd heard that dogs and other animals could smell fear. I wasn't sure about bears but didn't want to take any chances. Behind me, there was a rustle and more cracking sounds. The thing in the trees wasn't even trying to stay quiet anymore.

I looked over my shoulder, and within the edge of the trees, I made out the dark outline of a person – a man – completely in shadow. Why didn't he speak? He must know who I was if he was from town. If I could see his face, I'd know who he was too. Was that why he stayed hidden?

I took a few slow steps backward, keeping my eye on him and feeling him watching me closely. The moment he crouched, like a runner getting ready for a race, I turned and threw myself forward, flying down the hill. Footsteps pounded behind me.

A flash lit up my way. I didn't turn to see who it was; I just ran. My bare feet were able to grip the wet rocks. From the grunts behind me, I could tell his shoes were making him slip.

I grew up on these rocks. I'd taken this path more times than I could count. Without really thinking about it, my feet sought out the small patches of spongy moss. I leapt without caring if I fell, just counting each step closer to the bottom and home.

I prayed the lightning would hold off long enough for me to make it to safety. The rain came heavier, and between it and the buzzing in my ears, I couldn't hear him anymore, but I knew he was still there. I sensed his movement behind me.

Then my toe caught a crack in the rock and wedged in while the rest of my body kept going forward. A hand brushed over my hair, trying to grab at it, but he'd been travelling as fast as me, so he kept going forward and went right past me.

I fell hard without feeling the scrapes that peeled the skin from my knees. He fell too, somersaulting a few times before coming to a stop.

I scrambled up, ignoring the pain in my toes and my knees and took off. I went wide to keep out of his reach. It didn't take him long to push himself back to his feet and continue the chase.

Up ahead was the glow of the one streetlight we had in the Dardanelles. I thanked my lucky stars it was on this night. Sometimes teenagers would throw rocks and break the bulbs so they could make out under the lamp, but my guardian angel must have been looking after me. I whispered to her, "Virginia, save me," over and over as I got closer. When my feet hit the flat surface of the road, I knew he was gone. I turned around as lightning sparked across the sky, making the ground look like it was daylight, but there was no one for me to see.

My legs started to shake, and now that I began to feel, the cold crept into me. My breath came in gasps, and pain pulsed from my knees where I knew the rain was washing away the blood that kept coming.

I limped into my backyard, but instead of going inside, I made a beeline for the outhouse. I went in, sat down, and locked the door. I tried to make sense of what just happened. Who had that been, and why were they after me? Was it just because I was there, or were they after me on purpose?

I couldn't decide if I should tell Mom and Dad. They would ground me and never let me leave the house again. I didn't want to face being stuck forever in our house of sadness.

What about the detective? He would want to know, and I trusted him, but I couldn't tell Officer Kowalski. He was too much like the other grown-ups and would tell my parents for sure. He meant well, but the detective was different. I liked that about him. The back screen door creaked.

"Rose? Where are you?" My mom's voice came out annoyed, not worried.

"Here! Just finishing up," I yelled back.

"Hurry up," she called, letting the back door bang shut.

I stepped outside and let the rain drench me to wash away any signs of my fall. The only good thing about my parents' sadness was they paid even less attention to me than usual. Mom didn't even turn around when I came into the kitchen. She put the kettle on the stove, then stood with her back to me, just waiting for it to boil.

"Try not to drip all over the floor," she said without looking around. "I told your father you were fine."

I went into the back room where we kept the iodine and old rags and made my way to my bedroom to fix up my knees and get into dry pyjamas. Olive was already in bed, reading a book. She looked over at me, and her expression never changed, even when she saw my bloody scratches and cuts. She never said a word and went back to reading her story. That was when I realized it was sometimes a good thing to be invisible.

THIRTY-FIVE

VICTOR

Ever since my interview with Lorelei Clarke, I'd itched to get Jefferson face-to-face and ask him some very pointed questions. When Mrs. Boyle told me Virginia had been getting extra work at school, I didn't give it much thought, but Lorelei was adamant Virginia didn't struggle with her marks. Since Jefferson was the only male teacher and with Paulette's admission that he gave special treatment to the girl's basketball team, I was curious how far that special treatment went. Unfortunately, Lorelei went into labour the day after we spoke, so it took almost a week to set up a meeting with Jefferson.

"Gene, how many schools has Jefferson worked at again?" I asked.

"Not including Creighton, there were three schools in five years."

"That's a lot of jumping around."

"I've only been able to speak to one principal. No one answered at the other schools. They're all closed for the summer, so I'll have to dig a bit more to track down the other two. The one I did speak to is the principal from a school in Barrie. A small town outside Toronto."

"Sure, I know Barrie. What did they have to say about him?"

Gene rubbed the back of his neck. "Well, not much, but it was more like what she didn't say that seemed suspicious."

"Oh, how so?"

"When I asked why Jefferson left the job after such a short time, the principal said it was a mutual parting. I tried to press her." He looked at his notes. "She told me Jefferson had been a popular teacher, well-liked by the students, and she had no complaints about the quality of his classroom instruction."

"But…?" I leaned in.

"That's it. I said her, 'Well, you must have been disappointed to lose a teacher like that.' She said, 'Sometimes it's best for everyone when a teacher moves on.' I was getting a little frustrated by all the vague answers, so I came out and asked if he had ever behaved in any way that would be considered improper towards a female student."

"And what did she say?"

"'I cannot comment on something I never saw, but as a principal it is my duty to ensure harmony amongst my students and staff, and sometimes it only takes one person to disrupt that. I found Mr. Clarke just wasn't the best fit for our school community,'" Gene said in a snooty, high-pitched voice. "Then she said she had to go and hung up. What do you make of that?"

"Pretty vague. I agree that what she didn't say is the interesting part. It sounds like she's trying to sweep something under the rug, make him someone else's problem. Maybe we can get Mr. Clarke to be more forthcoming."

"It boggles my mind to think one of our teachers could take advantage of a young girl like that. And to think I always liked the guy." Gene shook his head.

"Well, all we have right now is a suspicion. Let's not jump to any conclusions until we talk with him." Although, inside, I wasn't taking my own advice. With so few leads, the slimmest sliver of one had me leaping from one conclusion to the next.

We still had Gregory Hansen. Before Nick Valenti's fall, Gene had talked to the boy about seeing Gregory and Virginia together, but the details Rose Boyle gave us were apparently accurate. Nick didn't have much else to add.

Then there was Eddie Szymaski and his peeping Tom photographs. Both Gene and I struggled with the idea that Eddie could physically overcome Virginia. He was slight, but if he caught her off guard and had rage on his side, it was possible. I'd seen it before.

A knock at the door interrupted my brooding. When a smiling head popped around the corner and said, "Hiya, gentlemen," I could only guess this was our 11:00 a.m. interview subject.

"Come on in, Jefferson," Gene called out.

Jefferson Clarke had the air of an ex-athlete, still physically fit, with just a little softening around the edges and the kind of arrogance that comes from being handsome and athletic at a young age. Even after their looks and abilities are gone, men like that continue to see themselves in the past tense. Gene made the introductions. He gripped my hand firmly, which I returned with equal force.

"Will this take long, Detective? My wife is at home with our new baby. I shouldn't leave her too long," Jefferson said, as we led him to our new interrogation room.

"It's hard to say, Mr. Clarke. It all depends…" I let the sentence hang, allowing his imagination to fill in the rest.

Gene directed him to a lone chair on one side of the table while we sat opposite him.

"I can't imagine why you wanted to talk to me. I don't know anything about Virginia Boyle or what happened to her. Other than maybe teaching her, which I can't quite recall if I did or not," Jefferson offered.

I proceeded as if I hadn't heard him.

"Well, Mr. Clarke, I guess things must be pretty busy at your house with the new baby and all. So that would make you a father of two girls then, would it?"

"Two? No, this is my first child." He crossed his legs and arms at the same time, contracting inwards.

I looked in my folder as if checking for the culprit of the mistaken information, when in actuality, the only thing inside were some expense reports I needed to get to my chief before the next payday.

"Sorry, my mistake, not sure where that came from. Anyway, we appreciate you stopping by. Creighton Mine is a small town, but when you have to interview almost everyone for a murder investigation, it seems to grow in size."

"I guess it would."

"Just routine, you understand, Mr. Clarke," I said.

"Yes, of course, and you can call me Jeff." He settled back in his chair.

"Okay, Jeff, so the day of Virginia Boyle's murder, you were where?"

"I was at the school."

"School's out. What were you doing there?"

"Cleaning my office. Getting rid of all the accumulated junk from the previous year." He smiled as if it was some kind of joke.

"Did anyone see you there?"

He frowned. "No. I have a key. I like to go when I know I'll be alone so I can get things done."

"I see." I jotted down a few notes.

"What does that mean? *I see.*" He looked over at Gene, who didn't react or answer, something I'd instructed him to do.

"Nothing, nothing at all. So, Jeff, how well did you know Miss Boyle?" I paused. "Outside of school."

"Hmmm." He looked down, fiddling with his watch. "No better than any other ex-pupils. Mostly just what I heard about her from town talk, like she lives in Los Angeles, that sort of thing."

"From the pictures I've seen, she was a pretty girl."

"Maybe. I hadn't really noticed." He continued looking down.

"I'm sorry, am I keeping you from something?"

"No, it's just my wife and the baby. She may need me soon."

"I'm sure she will be fine. Women are eminently capable when it comes to babies. We men just get in the way." I smiled.

"I guess, but still she may need me to pick up some milk...or something. Do you have many more questions? I really don't know what else I can tell you."

"How long have you taught here in Creighton?"

"About nine years, which makes me a newcomer. Isn't that right, Gene?" He laughed but lost his friendly buddy look when Gene failed to respond.

"Where were you before that?"

"In Barrie, at the Worsley Street School."

"How long were you there?" I fired at him, not wanting him to have time to think in between the questions.

"Oh, a few years." He looked up into the corner of the room.

"A few? Like two? That's not very long. So, what made you leave to come all the way up here? Doesn't really seem like a step up the employment ladder."

"I was just looking for a change. I like fishing. There's lots of good lakes up here."

"So, you wouldn't mind if we called the principal from Worsley, would you?" I wasn't ready to let him know how little we had from his last place of employment.

"No, I guess not. I can get you the numbers. I must have them at home somewhere, but it's been a long time. I doubt any of the old staff are still there."

"Thanks, I'd appreciate that. You know we spoke to your wife last week?"

Jefferson swallowed audibly. "Yes, she told me."

"Now, your wife, she was one of your students, wasn't she?"

"Yes, but that was a long time ago. She graduated over seven years ago."

"And how long have you been married?"

"About two years."

I held up my fingers and counted. "So, a few years after she graduated as your student, she became your wife?"

Jefferson nodded slowly.

"Do you prefer younger women, Mr. Clarke?"

"My wife is an adult. She's almost twenty-five years old."

"And you're what? Thirty-six? If I was to call this school in Barrie, there wouldn't happen to have been any issues with you and a female student, would there?"

Jefferson sputtered, squirming in his chair, "No."

"Did you ever find yourself taking notice of Virginia Boyle when she was your student? Maybe around fifteen years old." I leaned forward, getting closer to Jefferson.

"No, of course not." His voice squeaked.

"C'mon, Jeff, she was exceptionally pretty. Small-town girl, impressionable, easily manipulated." I grinned wolfishly.

"No, I never touched her."

"I never asked if you touched her."

"Well, you implied it." He folded his arms, trying to look offended. "Gene?"

Gene stayed quiet but I could see his shoulders and jaw were tense. Our other interviews had been less aggressive and more to Gene's style, but Jefferson needed a heavier hand. I tapped the table to get Jefferson's attention back.

"I didn't imply anything, but since you mentioned it…"

"Listen, I never touched her. I don't know who you've been talking to, but I am a respected member of this community. A happily married man with a child. I barely knew Ginny Boyle."

I sat upright and looked at Gene, who had also come to attention. "Ginny?"

"Yeah?" Jefferson looked confused.

"You called her Ginny," I prodded.

"So?"

"I've never heard anyone call her that except her mother and her ex-boyfriend. Why would you use a nickname for someone you barely knew?"

A red, mottled pattern began moving up his neck into his cheeks. "I–it's just, I must have heard someone call her that. It's a typical short form for Virginia. I'm sure I heard Lorelei call her that. Listen, I don't like what you are insinuating. Am I free to go?"

During our interviews, neither Lorelei, Paulette, or Swifty had ever referred to Virginia as Ginny.

"Of course. You're not under arrest, if that's what you're asking." I sat back slowly.

Jefferson Clarke stood up, squaring his shoulders. "Obviously someone is misleading you, trying to ruin my reputation, although I can't think why. I am a vice-principal, a happily married man, and I have a daughter who needs me."

"So did Virginia Boyle. Did you know that?" I hadn't planned on disclosing this information, but with Jefferson about to walk out the door, it struck me that this was right time.

Jefferson Clarke blinked rapidly, turned, and walked out.

249

"Did you see that?" I turned to Gene, whose eyes were wide as saucers.

"Son of a bitch." Gene whistled. "He knew."

THIRTY-SIX

VICTOR

It had been four days since we'd interviewed Jefferson Clarke, and I kept imagining what kind of information I could have extracted if I'd been allowed free reign. The interrogation skills I'd developed during the war were much more effective than what I was allowed to employ as a police detective. Perhaps if Gene hadn't been present, I might have pulled a few tricks out of my bag and been able to move this case further along, but as it was, we were at least fairly convinced Jefferson Clarke was aware Virginia had a baby. This moved him to the top of a very short suspect list.

The Creighton case wasn't my only one, but it did take up the bulk of my time, especially with the driving back and forth between Sudbury and Creighton every day. Thankfully, my other cases were mostly routine: a few robberies, a couple assaults, and a missing person case that just kept dragging on.

I pulled into my usual parking spot behind the station but didn't go inside. Gene wasn't there. He had a meeting at the Inco offices with his bosses, who were no doubt looking for progress on the case. I was happy not to be involved in that meeting. The company didn't pay my wages, so I didn't have to answer to them, and I'd already been interrogated by my own boss when I dropped in to catch up on some paperwork.

I strolled down George Street, keeping to the boardwalks. After living in Toronto with its wide, paved sidewalks, this felt like something out of a Wild West movie. The raised wooden planks were put there for function, not style. As far as function went, I'd seen a few young boys crawl underneath and lie flat, presumably to peek up the women's skirts as they passed by. When you live in a small town, I guess you find adventure where you can.

As I went by the barber shop, I saw Nick Valenti through the large window. He was sitting in a chair against the wall, waiting his turn with his arm across his chest in a sling. It had only been a little over a month since I was assigned this case, and already I recognized a lot of the population by sight and dozens by name.

This day I wanted to avoid as many of them as possible. Everyone had the same question: "How close are you to catching this person?" It was the same question I asked myself. I'd never worked on a case with less to go on. The only suspects we had were based on old or tenuous relationships to Virginia, and there was zero evidence to tie any of them to the murder. Even Jefferson Clarke, if he was the father of Rose Boyle, it didn't automatically make him a killer.

The facts of the case just didn't add up. It couldn't have been a planned murder, since even Virginia didn't know where she would be berry picking that day.

I turned onto Joffree Street, the rocky road Eddie Szymaski lived on. There was no sign of life as I passed his place. It looked as run-down as I remembered. I stopped at the corner of Albert and Joffree, and from there I could see number twelve, Jefferson Clarke's neat and tidy house. The white picket fence gave it a picture of quaint domesticity. The front door opened, and the sound of a baby wailing came from inside. Clarke stepped out and lifted a match halfway up to the cigarette in his mouth until he caught sight of me. I smiled and waved. Even from a distance, I could see him square his shoulders and drop his arms to his side, fists curled. A fighter's stance. He snatched the cigarette from his mouth and went back in the house, slamming the door behind him.

I continued my walk. I didn't have a destination in mind, just a need to stretch my legs and thoughts. I found a well-worn path between two homes and followed it. One of the houses had a backyard that was a hive of activity. A toddler, runny-nosed and whining, clung to the skirt of a woman hanging laundry. Two young girls, about five and six, were arguing and tugging a doll back and forth between them at the far end of the yard. Not far from the girls, by the outhouse, a man expertly wrestled a large bucket of human waste towards a wagon. His skin was tanned and leathery, giving evidence that he was at least middle-aged, but he lifted his load like a much younger man.

I'd used my share of outhouses, when necessary, but for most of my life I was blessed with indoor plumbing, and this was the first time I'd witnessed how the system worked.

"That man is strong as an ox," the woman hanging laundry said with a strong French accent, "but I've always wondered if he's lost his sense of smell after all this time."

"I would hope so," I answered. "Who is he?" I was surprised I hadn't seen him before.

"Odert Heikki. He's one of the honeymen."

To me "honeyman" was almost a cruel name for someone who carted human excrement, but it had a nicer ring than any other alternative.

"I'm Detective Lapointe from Sudbury."

"Oui, I know who you are." She was thin and angular. She'd be pretty if she filled out her sharp edges.

"Of course. So, what do you think about all this business, about Virginia Boyle and all?" I liked open-ended questions to get people talking.

She sighed heavily. "I feel so bad for the Boyle family. They're good people, and it just doesn't make any sense, you know." She stopped her work and placed her hands on her hips. "Men can be cruel to women, but they usually do it for a reason, don't they?" she shrugged. "Either they lose their temper or want what a woman doesn't want to give them, but to just kill a young woman and leave her lying there, like an old deer carcass… it doesn't make sense. What does he get by doing that?"

"That's what we're trying to find out, Mrs….?"

"Boucher, Romy Boucher."

"Did you know Virginia well?"

"I'm a few years older than her, but I knew her like I do everyone in town, since there's very few people in Creighton who weren't born here. And that's another thing that puzzles me: why did she leave in the first place? If you're a boy, you get a job at the mine, and as a girl, especially a pretty one, you get a husband with a job. What more does a person need? To my mind, the only reason to leave is if you were running away from something." She shrugged. "I don't have any proof of that, but it just makes sense. Don't you think, Detective?"

I nodded in agreement, which was a lie. Living in a small town my whole life wouldn't have appealed to me, but I guess if you'd never been anywhere else and had nothing to compare it to, life here probably made sense.

"Thank you for your time, Mrs. Boucher. It really helps to get other people's view on things. Good day."

She went back to her chores and her family. I continued past a few more yards and out into an open area with the usual barren view. The ground inclined sharply. Up at the top of the hill stood the town's water tank.

I found a flat surface and took a seat so I could open the large envelope I'd been carrying around. A collection of photographs spilled out into my lap. They'd been developed from Virginia Boyle's film. She was a prolific photographer, as the pile attested, and although not any kind of an expert, I could tell she had been good.

The black-and-white pictures were striking and told a story. She was able to make the town of Creighton come to life and make the people seem interesting. There were only three pictures of her. One was a self-portrait taken by facing a mirror in what looked like a bedroom. Virginia appeared uncomfortable being her own subject.

The other two were tilted on an angle and slightly off centre. I'd guess it was Rose or one of the other kids who took them. In both pictures, Virginia was laughing with pure joy and beauty. I couldn't stop staring at her and wondering why someone would want to snuff out that much life.

The pictures that interested me most were from the day she was killed. The subjects were of the two girls, Maggie and Rose, off in the distance picking berries or landscape shots and a few close-ups of the berries on plants. It made my mouth water just looking at them. To my bitter disappointment, there was no picture that gave any hint of who killed her that day. Not that I'd really expected to find one.

Besides the envelope, I'd also brought a few older Sudbury newspapers. I hadn't had a chance to read them, and they'd been collecting on my desk at work. I opened one from the day after the murder. The story's headline read: "Hollywood Beauty Strangled on Creighton Rocks."

Police seek killer after woman's body found in the bush by blueberry pickers

The former Creighton Mine resident, 25-year-old Virginia Boyle, was taking a break from her glamorous life in Los Angeles, California, to visit her family when the shocking murder took place. On Saturday, July 7th, she was picking berries with her siblings. No one saw or heard anything until her younger sister and a group of women, also out picking, stumbled upon the gruesome scene.

"It was awful," one of the woman who claimed to have found her told this reporter. "At first, I thought she was sleeping, but then I noticed the spilled berries and her clothes were stained all down the front with juice. You never expect something like this to happen here."

For most residents, this is the first murder in recent memory, and their quiet, close-knit mining town has been shaken by the fear that a murderer is loose amongst them.

"She and I were the best of friends growing up." A teary Paulette Carmichael tried to make sense of the brutal slaying. "Who would want to kill Virginia? She was such a kind girl."

With no clues and no suspects, police are stumped. A young woman alone in the woods becomes the first murder victim in Creighton Mine for over a decade. Until someone is caught, this small town will be famous only for the brutal slaying of an innocent beauty. The question on everyone's mind is will this twisted killer stop at just one victim, or has Creighton Mine become the target of a madman?

The article contained all the hyperbole and scaremongering I'd seen time and again when it came to reporting on murders. I could picture Paulette wanting to share her story. She liked to be the centre of attention. The other woman, who wasn't identified, echoed the refrain I heard every time a crime happened in a small town: "You never expect something like that to happen here."

What was it that made small towns think they were immune to bad things happening? There are nasty people everywhere. The witness didn't have much else to say except what I'd heard from Rose and a few others about the spilled berries, like that was almost as big a tragedy as Virginia Boyle's death.

A cool breeze came by and threatened to snatch away the photographs sitting on the rock beside me. I returned them to the envelope. A number of the pictures were of the Boyle family and I'd planned on returning them when the case was finally closed.

On the walk back to the station, I kept going over in my mind what Virginia's last minutes must have been like. It was the same scene I'd replayed hundreds of times before, but this time something from the article nagged at me: "Her clothes were stained all down the front with juice."

I stopped to picture how that would have happened. The witness was specific that the whole front of her blouse was stained, and I'd seen the clothing myself on my first day in Creighton. It would have taken a lot of berries to make such a mess, possibly a whole basket.

Rose had found Virginia lying on her back, so Virginia didn't fall onto the berries. She had to have been holding them, and when she was attacked, they were squished between her and the killer.

That's it! I thought. It wouldn't have been just Virginia's clothes but her killer's as well. His shirt would also be covered with a large blue stain.

I picked up my pace to get back to the station. It was another long shot, but I'd resigned myself to the fact that some cases could only be solved by luck and chance. This just might be one of those.

THIRTY-SEVEN

ROSE

Maggie and I were dirty, tired, and I felt almost happy, or at least not too sad. Ever since I was chased down the hill, I'd stayed close to home. I hadn't told anyone about what happened. Keeping secrets had become a regular part of my life now. It was easier to stay quiet than explain my jumbled thoughts and feelings to anyone else. For almost two weeks, Maggie had kept me company. We played every game, done every puzzle and listened to everything on the radio from *The Shadow* to even the news, and we were both starting to get grumpy. Even June was complaining about us being underfoot.

When a few of Maggie's friends stopped by to see if we wanted to play, Maggie jumped at the chance. I didn't want to go, but June practically pushed me out the door saying I needed some sunlight or I would wither away.

"That was fun," I said and spat on my hands, which didn't clean the dirt off, only smeared it.

"I'm pretty sure Gayle cheated, peeking through her fingers when she was counting," Maggie said, "but I still won."

"Only because you're so small and fit between those two big rocks."

We'd played hide-and-seek for a couple of hours. It was usually a game I liked, but I wasn't ready to be alone yet. I wanted to stay within sight of the others, so I kept picking bad hiding places. Maggie was really good because she could stay still forever without so much as a twitch or a squirm.

But the best part was that none of the kids mentioned Virginia or asked about what had happened. All they cared about was who was "it" and where to hide. For a little while, I was able to forget about most of the bad stuff.

"Do you think we'll get in trouble?" Maggie asked, as walked along Miller Road.

"For what? Playing hide-and-seek and getting dirty? We do it all the time." Or at least we used to.

"No, for being late. Look, it's getting dark, and Momma said to make sure we were home well before the streetlamps came on."

I looked up at the sky. We still had a bit of a distance between us and home, and night fell fast when it was cloudy.

"If we stay on the road, we'll be even later," I said, "but if we cut through the back there, we'll get home quicker.

We could stay on Miller and walk down to French Street or cut across the open area in front of us, which would get us home in half the time. The only problem was being farther away from the houses meant walking in the dark because the light didn't reach that far.

"I don't know, Rose. Maybe we should stay on the road." Maggie looked back and forth between our options.

If I'd been alone, I would've stayed on the road for sure, but I wasn't and I really wanted to be home before it was fully dark. We also hadn't had dinner and I was starving.

.

"Come on, we'll stay together and be home in no time," I said.

"Fine," Maggie said.

As soon as we stepped off the road onto the worn path, a bank of clouds floated across the moon, blocking out the little light we had.

"Slow down, Rose! I can't see you," Maggie called out.

"Here, take my hand." Maggie grabbed my hand, which made me feel better, even though hers was kind of damp. We slowed down to get around the old railroad ties that had been dumped in the area years ago. Normally I walked on them to test my balance, but this night I was just trying not to bang my shins into them.

"I remember Virginia telling me if you went up the hills around Los Angeles at night, you could see the whole city lit up like daylight. Even in the hills it glowed so it was never completely dark." It made me feel less nervous if we just talked like normal.

"I wish it was like that here, or that we had a torch, like the kind they always have in castles and hidden caves in the movies." Maggie giggled.

"Yeah, like the Frankenstein and Dracula movies." We'd seen a double feature at Halloween that gave me nightmares. Olive told Mom not to let us see them anymore because my bad dreams kept her up at night.

"Ohhh, don't say that. I don't even want to think of Frankenstein." Maggie gripped my hand extra tight.

"Ouch, dang it." I stopped quickly, bending over, and Maggie walked into the back of me.

"What is it?"

"Stupid rail tie. I stubbed my toe." I leaned over and rubbed my throbbing big toe.

"What's that?" Maggie squeaked in my ear.

"What?" I stood up and squinted into the dark.

"Over there. I don't know. I thought I saw something move."

"Over where?" I couldn't even see where she was pointing. "It's just your imagination thinking about Frankenstein," I said and tried to hide the quiver in my voice.

"Stop it, Rose. I did see something." Her voice cracked. I peered really hard into the dark but didn't see anything.

"It's nothing, Maggie, come on."

"Ooof, damn." A voice came from the darkness. It was a man's voice.

"Rose?" Maggie whispered and pinched the back of my arm.

I froze, unsure if we should run or hide. The man's footsteps and muttering got closer. I reached my hands out in front of me and felt the railway tie. It was high up, so it must have been one on top of the other. I turned to Maggie and pushed her shoulders.

"Duck down. We'll hide until he passes," I whispered.

"What? Wait, but…"

"Just do it." I shoved her hard just as the moon broke fully through the clouds, lighting up the field enough to see the form of a man only a few feet away, and he could see me too. I'd practically turned to stone, unable to move even a little bit. The shape was just like the one that chased me down the hill. A faceless man in the dark.

"Hey, you!" he called out, "You there, little girl. Are you real?"

His step was unsteady as he moved towards me, and I heard the slur in his voice that meant he'd been drinking. One of the town bootleggers lived not far from here. It must have been where he'd come from.

"Come here. Who are you?" That's when I recognized his voice and was so relieved I almost cried. It was Mr. Clarke, our vice-principal, and even drunk he wasn't someone to be afraid of. I almost giggled with relief. This would be a great story to tell the other kids when we went back to school in the fall. How I'd seen the vice-principal drunk as a skunk. I stepped away from the railway tie where Maggie was still crouched down. Mr. Clarke was bent over at the waist with his hands on his knees, squinting at me.

"Hello, Mr. Clarke," I said in that sing-song voice you always use for teachers.

"Oh, it's you, the Boyle girl. What's your name again? Daisy? Petunia?"

"It's Rose, Mr. Clarke."

264

I took a step forwards, and the smell of alcohol coming off him was so strong I took a step back.

"Rose, that's right. What are you doing here, alone in the dark? It's not safe. Didn't you know there's a murderer on the loose?" He shook his finger at me.

"Yes, sir, I know."

He stood up straight and swayed side to side. "I guess you would, wouldn't you? It was your mom that died, wasn't it?"

"My sister, Virginia." My first thought was he knew, but he couldn't have, and people were always getting our family relationships confused. It was most likely just the drink that muddled his brain.

"Right, your sister. So sad. Poor, sweet Ginny. She was such a beautiful girl." He dropped his hand heavily on my head. I couldn't even turn my head. His voice was thick, like he might cry.

"Yes, sir." I knew enough about men who'd been drinking from seeing my dad and Angus. It was best to just agree with them and stay quiet. Then they'd forget all about you or just fall asleep. Mom did that with Dad plenty of times.

I almost floated up when Mr. Clarke lifted his hand off my head, but then he grabbed my arm as he stumbled backwards, pulling me with him. His ankles hit a rail tie and he fell backwards onto his bottom. He still held my arm which yanked me towards him hard.

"Oopsie." He burped and pulled me closer in. "Here, have a seat." He patted his thigh.

I didn't want to climb up onto his lap as if he was a smelly Santa Claus, but the word "no" just wasn't something you said to an adult, especially your vice-principal. So, I let him pull me onto his lap.

"I knew Virginia. Did you know that?" His arm laid heavy over my shoulder keeping me in place. His breath was sour when he spoke.

"You were her teacher?"

"Yes, I was her teacher, but I'm married now." His gaze drifted to the side, like he was looking past me. I hoped Maggie was still hidden.

"And you have a baby. A girl, right?" I tried to make conversation, wondering how I could slip away.

"Who told you that?" He snapped his head around with a cross look.

"Umm, everyone knows Mrs. Clarke just had her baby." I was confused and beginning to get a little frightened. Mr. Clarke had never snapped at me or even paid me any attention before.

He squinted at me like I was a puzzle he was trying to figure out. The smell of booze mixed with his body odour made me want to cover my nose with my hand. Instead, I just leaned backwards as far as I could and wished I'd listened to Maggie and not taken the shortcut.

"Yeah, a daughter. My wife Lorelei had a little girl, and she's my daughter." He smacked his palm on his chest. "Why did she have to come back here, eh? Why couldn't she just have stayed away? Let sleeping dogs lie. Why?" The hand wrapped around my shoulder gripped me tighter.

"Ow, Mr. Clarke, you're hurting me," I said, but he didn't seem to hear me.

"I'm a respectable man. I'm going to be the principal. Even dead, Ginny could ruin everything for me."

I tried to wriggle and pull away, but he was too strong.

"Look what happened to her, Rose. Such a waste, such a beautiful waste."

He let go of my shoulder, then grabbed both my arms so I would face him square on.

"You know, you kind of look like her." He stared at me like it was a bad thing.

I stayed silent while he looked me over. It felt like I wasn't even a person to him, just something he was trying to figure out what to do with. I wanted to kick him, or scream and run away, but I head mom's voice in the back of my head: "Be polite," "Don't embarrass me," and "Don't talk back."

"What am I going to have to do with you, Rose?" He hiccupped.

"What about me?" Even to my own ears I could barely hear my voice.

"You could ruin everything for me too, couldn't you? You're a loose end. Why do you Boyle women want to hurt me, huh? I never hurt you, Rose. I left you alone. Why couldn't you do the same for me?" He practically growled at me.

"Please, let me go," I begged, choking on a sob.

"Jefferson!"

Both Mr. Clarke and I stopped moving, and a beam of light blinded me.

"Jefferson, it's Gene Kowalski. Let the girl go." His words were a command, and to me, it was the nicest voice I'd ever heard. "Come here, Rose, it'll be okay. Mr. Clarke won't mind, will you, Jefferson?"

Mr. Clarke stayed silent but still held on tight. I didn't think he would obey the officer, but then his whole body went droopy, and he lowered his arms. Very slowly, I took one step at a time backwards, not taking my eyes off Mr. Clarke, even though everything inside me screamed to run away. When I got near Officer Kowalski, Maggie's frightened face poked out from behind his leg.

Officer Kowalski reached out and put his hand gently on my shoulder. I flinched, and he pulled it back. Maggie grabbed my hand and pulled me towards her.

"I remembered Officer Kowalski lived close by. I ran and got him," Maggie whispered to me.

"Are you all right, Rose?" Officer Kowalski asked softly.

"Yes, sir," I lied.

"Good girl."

"Gene?" A woman's voice came from the darkness.

"Over here, Lily!" he called back.

Mr. Clarke never moved from the railway tie. Then he moaned and threw up, which made a splashing sound. Then he retched a few more times.

Mrs. Kowalski showed up carrying her own flashlight. "Are they all right, Gene?"

"Yeah, they're fine. Just had a bit of a fright, eh, girls?"

Maggie and I both nodded silently in the dark.

"Lily, would you walk them home while I take care of Jefferson here?"

"Of course. Come on, girls, your mothers will be worried sick. Here, Maggie, since you were so clever coming to fetch Mr. Kowalski, you can carry the light."

It was a heavy metal flashlight that Maggie needed both hands to hold. She kept pointing it right down at our feet instead of up ahead. We soon stepped out onto French Street. The lights from the houses made it so we didn't need the flashlight, but Maggie held on to it tightly. I was still shaking and clutched the arm of Mrs. Kowalski's sweater. I could smell brown sugar and molasses from her, which made me feel safe.

"Mrs. Kowalski?" I looked up at her.

"Yes, Rose?"

"I know I'm not supposed to say this, but I don't think I like Mr. Clarke very much anymore."

"That's okay, Rose. I won't tell anyone."

She walked us all the way home, then came inside to talk with my mom and June. Even though our moms weren't happy with us, they let Maggie sleep over. Olive was spending the night at her friend Cheryl's, so there was room in the bed. I was glad to have Maggie to snuggle with. I didn't want to be alone.

"That sure was scary, wasn't it, Rose?" Maggie lay facing me.

"Yeah, I guess we shouldn't have taken that shortcut."

"What'd Mr. Clarke say to you? He sounded mad."

"Nothing, really. Just a lot of nonsense."

"Yeah, then he puked." Maggie laughed a little then yawned. "I bet we get grounded tomorrow."

269

"Probably."

Maggie rolled over and in minutes – I could tell by her breathing – she was asleep. It wasn't as easy for me. I knew Mr. Clarke had been drunk, but still, the things he said tumbled around in my head. He'd called me a loose end, and he said Virginia should have let sleeping dogs lie. A thought came into my head that was just too awful to be true, and there was no one who could make any sense of it for me. Only Virginia would have been able to.

My hands clenched into little balls. There were so many questions, but no one to ask. I squeezed my eyes and my whole body tight to keep in the feelings that wanted to come out. It took a couple big breaths to make my heart stop pounding.

My hands shook as I pushed the blankets off my sweaty body. Then, as if someone had waved a magic wand over me and whispered *sleep*, I was suddenly very tired. All night I dreamt I was running through the dark, trying to get away from one person and go towards someone else, but the confusing part was they felt like the same person.

THIRTY-EIGHT

ROSE

Mrs. Kowalski stayed to talk with Mom and June after she brought us home. I don't know what was said, but Maggie and I didn't get in as much trouble as we expected. Maggie did have to stay inside to do chores with June, but all my mom said was to stay out of trouble, and then she left me to myself.

In the daylight, what happened with Mr. Clarke didn't feel as scary – just confusing. Since he was drunk, I decided most of what he said was just "the booze talking," as Mom would say. And I had been pretty scared, so I most likely misunderstood the things he said. But one thing just he said wouldn't go away: "Why do you Boyle women want to hurt me, huh? I never hurt you, Rose. I left you alone." When I played it over in my head, it made my insides go cold.

I didn't want to think what it could mean. He was speaking about me and Virginia, and I didn't want my brain go there. So, I did the thing I always did when I wanted to get rid of bad thoughts. I sang to myself.

"All we do is go out walking, When the sun shines bright and gay

But what do we do - what do we do, On a dew-dew-dewy day?"

I had Mom's first-aid kit beside me and, while I sang, I picked at the scabs on my knees. When they started to bleed, I smeared the salve on, then a bandage. It was gross when other people picked their scabs but fun when I did my own. I was almost done when I felt the back of my neck prickle. I froze, hunched over, but turned my head to see if someone was about.

"Rose…Rose. Pssst, over here."

The voice came from the shadows at the side of our house. I recognized it immediately and went over to say hi.

"Hey, Hugh, whatcha doin'? Olive isn't home. She stayed at Cheryl's last night."

"I know. I came looking for you, Rose."

"Me? What for?"

"I need some help with something really special and you're the only one I could think of to help me."

"Me? Really?"

"It has to do with Olive, and I couldn't ask any of her girlfriends. They'd spill the beans. Mikey and Joey are too immature, and Maggie is too young. Besides, I know you can be counted on to keep a secret."

"What is it?" I was a little nervous, as I didn't know how many more secrets I could keep inside me.

Hugh blushed. "I'm going to propose to Olive." He looked down at his hands.

I knew my mouth was hanging open, catching flies, but I was shocked. "Propose…like to get married?"

"Yeah, I figured if I proposed and she accepted, then she wouldn't go to Toronto. We'd get married and stay here in Creighton. I'd take real good care of her and make sure nothing bad ever happened to her."

"You really wanna marry Olive?"

"Sure, she's the most perfect girl in the whole world," Hugh said with the goofiest smile I'd ever seen, but I didn't laugh 'cause it was kind of sweet. "That's why I need you. I want to propose in the most perfect spot. She promised to join me for a picnic today up on Slater's Rock, and I want to do it right. I was hoping you could help me set everything up. Will you, Rose? Please?"

"Well, heck yeah! What do you want me to do?" I practically jumped up and down, I was so excited.

"First, you can't tell anyone, you understand? No one." He looked down at his feet. "Just in case, well, she says…" He shrugged, but we both knew in case Olive said no, which in my mind was possible. "And if we keep it a secret, then when she says yes, we can surprise everyone when we tell them." His smile came back, and I couldn't help but smile with him. "Can you meet me at Slater's Rock in ten minutes?"

"You betcha." Mom hadn't actually said not to leave the yard, just to stay out of trouble, and this was the opposite of trouble.

"Great, and don't tell anyone or it might ruin the surprise, okay?"

"I promise. Do you need me to bring anything?"

He thought about it, then shook his head. "No, I think I've got everything: the picnic blanket, the food...and the ring." He patted his shirt pocket.

A ring? I hadn't even thought of that. "Can I see it, please?" I begged.

"Okay," he laughed, "but not until we get everything set up. Then you'll be the first one to see it."

I was so excited, I thought I'd burst. I realized I wanted Olive to say yes and stay with us in Creighton instead of moving to Toronto. Even if it meant sharing a room with her a little while longer, at least until she got married.

"I have to grab a few more things, so I'll meet you at Slater's Rock in ten minutes, okay?"

"Okay."

Hugh looked around and then disappeared around the front of the house. I ran around back, picked up the first-aid kit, and went into the kitchen to put it away. When I turned around, Maggie walked in.

"Hey, Mom sent me over to fetch some soap for laundry. We ran out, and she's making me scrub everyone's socks as punishment." She wrinkled her nose like she could smell the stinky socks.

I just stared at her and gripped the first-aid kit to my chest.

Maggie squinted at me. "What are you up to, Rose?"

"N—nothing," I stammered.

"Yes, you are. You've got guilty face like you just sucked on a lemon. I know you're fibbing."

I couldn't hold back; it was just too much. I'd kept so many secrets, my head was overflowing, and I had to share this one, since it was a happy secret. I was sure Hugh would understand.

"Okay, but you can't tell anyone, promise?"

She held out her pinky for an official swear. "I won't tell."

Then I did exactly what I promised I wouldn't. I spilled the beans about Hugh, Olive, the engagement, the picnic, the whole thing. I couldn't help myself, I needed to share it with someone who would be just as excited as me.

"Ooooh, maybe we'll get to be bridesmaids or flower girls at the wedding!"

I hadn't even thought of that. It made sense we'd get to be in the wedding since we were family. Now I was even more excited. "I gotta go, but I'll tell you all about it when I get back."

"Oh, don't be too long! I don't know if I can stand it."

I sprinted out the back door towards Slater's Rock. The sun warmed the back of my neck, and there wasn't a cloud in the sky to break the glow. I had to squint; it was so bright. I could hear the thumping from the mine, and it played a beat, so I joined in the singing.

But what do we do - what do we do, On a dew-dew-dewy day?"

I'd never been to a wedding before but knew there was always cake. I crossed my fingers that Olive would say yes to Hugh's proposal. A year ago, I would have laughed if anyone suggested she'd marry Hugh McLellan, but a lot happened since then, and I'd seen them both change.

Hugh had grown a bit taller and filled out some. Although he still wasn't handsome, he didn't look as gangly as he used to. Also, since Virginia's death, he'd been there, right by Olive's side, like a real friend. It was obvious Olive depended on him. They'd gotten closer and were rarely apart. Sometimes she'd even reach out and take his hand. Maybe that was love.

When I saw Slater's Rock up ahead I realized the funny feeling in me was happiness. It had been so long since I'd felt it – or allowed myself to – that I hadn't recognized it at first. I pictured the whole family hearing the news that Hugh and Olive were engaged. June would cry, Dad would approve, Oscar would nod and smile. While Mom, well, she wouldn't say it out loud, but I knew this was what she had always hoped for. Hugh was a good person and would provide for Olive and take care of her.

It was exactly what our family needed. Something to celebrate and look forward to after what happened to Virginia. She should have been here to see Olive get married. She could have helped her pick out a dress and taken pictures at the wedding. I shook my head, not wanting to let anything bring me down. For just a little longer, I wanted to remember what it felt like to have something good to look forward to.

I climbed over the ridge and saw I hadn't beat Hugh. He was already there, standing by the edge of the rock. I looked around for the picnic basket and blanket, but it was just him, staring over the side of the cliff with his hands in his pockets and his shoulders hunched. All the excitement of earlier seemed to have been gone. It drained from me as well. I walked slowly over to him.

"Hugh, what's up?"

He turned around with a sad smile. "Hey, Rose. I've got some bad news."

THIRTY-NINE

VICTOR

I stared at my notes, looking for something, anything I may have missed. So many suspicions, but nothing concrete that would hold up in court. It had been three days since we told the town we were looking for a berry-stained shirt. As expected, a few articles of clothing were brought in: a man's dress shirt with tomato stains, a pair of trousers with grease stains, and two men's shirts with what could be blueberry stains, but both were small and insignificant. Not at all the amount we'd expected compared to Virginia's shirt. We were easily able to clear the owners with alibis. I knew it was a long shot, but I'd solved crimes with luck before.

Jefferson Clarke was playing hardball. After his stunt with Rose the other night, he'd climbed to the top of the suspects list, but he kept making up excuses for why he couldn't come back in for an interview. Just that morning, I'd let him know if he didn't show up voluntarily at the station by tomorrow, I'd come drag him in. He agreed to meet us at 9:00 a.m. the next day.

The ringing of the phone on Gene's desk startled me, and I jumped up to answer it.

"Hello, Detective Lapointe speaking."

"Victor, it's me." Gene's voice was clipped.

"What is it?" I tensed.

"You need to come to my house right away. Odert Heikki just brought a shirt over. It may be nothing, but—"

"It may be something," I finished. "On my way."

I knew that name. It was a hard one to forget. Odert was the honeyman who was emptying the outhouse the other day.

Now that I was so familiar with the town, it was a toss-up whether cutting through backyards or taking my car was quicker. I opted for the car, unsure what my next move may be. In minutes, I was slamming the door and taking the porch two steps at a time. Lily was there, holding the door open for me.

"They're in the back," she said, leading me through the living room and out the back door. Gene and Odert were standing by the clothesline. A single shirt hung dripping from pegs.

"Victor, this is Odert Heikki. He found the shirt."

I shook the man's hand, and as I suspected the first time I saw him, his grip was firm, with a sense of power that he held back on.

"Where did you find it?" I asked. The shirt may have been light-coloured at one time but was now filthy and stained.

"It was at the end of my run. I don't know what house it came from, sorry. I only know when I was dumping everything at the sewage pond, this floated to the top." He pointed at the shirt. "I remembered everyone talking, saying you were looking for a shirt. It could belong to anyone, but I think to myself, well, maybe. So, I come here to Mr. Kowalski, just in case. I want to help. Mr. Boyle is my friend, and it is so very sad." He shook his head.

"So, what do you think, Gene?" I stepped closer to inspect the shirt, then moved back when the odour hit me.

"We rinsed it off. It was pretty awful after being in the outhouse." Lily spoke up from behind me. She had her arms wrapped around her middle, like she'd taken a chill, even though the day was warm, without a breeze.

"So, this is not the original colour," I stated obviously.

Lily stepped closer, pointing at the clothing. "It's cotton, so it soaked up whatever was in the outhouse, but after a really good rinsing, you can see," she pointed to a large, darker area on the chest, "there is another stain underneath. It was probably there before being dumped."

"It could be anything," I said, as I attempted to play devil's advocate.

"Or it could be something," added Gene.

"Mrs. Kowalski, in your expert opinion, could you take a guess at what could have made a stain like that?" All three of us turned to Lily, waiting.

"Detective, I couldn't say for sure because I can't tell the colour, but there are very few stains that would make you throw out a garment. Most can be removed, but blueberry is a tough one. I had to turn one of the girl's shirts into rags last month because I couldn't remove the colour."

I looked over at Gene. There wasn't the excitement I would have expected from him, considering we may have just found the first substantial clue of the case. Instead, he seemed troubled.

"Gene, is there any way of knowing who this could have belonged to?" I was convinced he knew the answer. "Gene?"

Gene looked at Lily, who wore the same defeated expression.

"It's an expensive brand," she said. "It had to be ordered in. They don't sell that kind here in Creighton. I only know one family who would pay that much for their child's clothing." She stopped, unable to say out loud what she and her husband had already concluded.

"Child?" I prompted Gene.

"The McLellan's," Gene swallowed hard. "They always dressed Hugh a bit above the other kids in town."

I needed a minute to take it in.

"Hugh McLellan? That doesn't make sense." I began checking off everything I knew, comparing it to clues and facts.

"I know it doesn't. There could be a logical explanation for this. He was probably berry picking that day too. Lots of people ended up with stained shirts, I'm sure of it."

"But why would he hide it and not just throw it in the trash if it was ruined?" I asked.

Gene bit his lip. "Yeah, it doesn't make any sense. Victor, I can't think of any reason for Hugh McLellan to want to kill Virginia Boyle, none at all." He shook his head, trying to loosen the image that had crept in.

I closed my eyes and let the pieces lie undisturbed, allowing my mind to find a connection. Hugh and Virginia – what could be the connection? He was a boy. No, a young man. A very close friend of the Boyle family with no history of trouble. Could he have secretly fancied Virginia? It couldn't be a grudge; he'd only have been about eleven years old when she left for Los Angeles. Nothing fell into place.

"There's no reason I can think of." I said, "But that doesn't mean…"

"It couldn't be him," Gene said. "He's only a boy."

"Remember, Gene, anyone is capable of murder with the right motive."

Gene nodded. "Yeah, but what would that be? Why?"

"I don't know, but I also don't want to wait one minute more to rule him out, just in case. I'll go to the Boyles'. It's where he spends most of his time. You go to his parents' house in case he's there. Mr. Heikki," I'd almost forgotten the man in all the commotion, "please tell no one about this for now. We need to be sure."

The man nodded. "I am a man of trust, Detective. I won't tell." I felt certain he could be depended on.

I sprinted to my car and tossed gravel as I pulled onto the street. I couldn't think of a motive Hugh might have, but the fact that he was there when Nick Valenti was also injured felt like too much of a coincidence. I needed to talk to him right away.

FORTY

VICTOR

I slammed on the brakes, and the car skidded to a stop inches from a group of kids in the middle of the road. They stared at me, open-mouthed and frozen, while a ball rolled across the ground.

"Move aside!" I yelled out the window, and they did as if the hand of God himself had reached down and pushed them out of the way.

I pulled to a stop outside the Boyles' house and took the steps two at a time. My impatient knock went unanswered. Against everything the people in town had been told, they'd foolishly left their door unlocked. I poked my head in and called out, but there was no hint of movement. The house was empty.

"Detective?" I stepped back outside. June McFaye leaned out her front door. "Can we help you with something?"

"Yes, I'm looking for Hugh McLellan. Is he here?"

"No, we haven't seen him today."

Mrs. Boyle stepped out on the porch, followed by the youngest girl in the family.

"Is there something wrong, Detective?" Mrs. Boyle crossed her arms.

"I just need to speak to Hugh. Would you know where he might be?"

"Olive stayed at the Gastons' last night," Mrs. Boyle said.

"Yes, but Olive and Hugh haven't been speaking for the past few days, so I doubt they are together," June said, which appeared to be a surprise to Mrs. Boyle.

"Why? What happened?" I asked.

June rolled her eyes. "Oh, he got upset when Olive told him she was moving to Toronto. He's always been keen on her, and I guess he just doesn't want her to leave."

Her words stabbed at my brain, like a punishment for not seeing the possibilities earlier. I could have kicked myself for being so blind. I noticed the little girl, Maggie, fidgeting nervously and recognized the signs.

"Maggie? That's your name, right?" I said.

Her eyes opened wide as she nodded at me.

"Maggie, it's really important I find Hugh. Do you know where he is?"

The women looked down at Maggie, surprised, while the girl struggled. It was like a physical fight was taking place. Her lips were clamped tight together but twitching to let something out.

"Maggie, answer the detective!" Mrs. Boyle snapped.

"I'm not supposed to tell," she said, which is often the precursor to someone telling everything. "But...Hugh is going to propose to Olive today. He asked Rose to meet him up on

Slater's Rock to help him set up a picnic, but I promised I wouldn't tell anyone because it would ruin the surprise."

"Oh my, that is so sweet." June folded her hands across her chest.

"No, that is so foolish," Mrs. Boyle said. "You'd think Hugh would remember Olive works at the drugstore Friday afternoons."

"Maybe he forgot because she was off for a bit, you know, because of what happened."

My blood ran cold because I was pretty sure Hugh hadn't forgotten a single thing about Olive Boyle, and now he was alone with Rose up on Slater's Rock. There was no time to explain. I ran back to the car with the women yelling questions after me.

I swore as I navigated the winding roads. Nothing was straight in this town, and I was desperate to get to Slater's Rock. My mind twisted and turned, putting together a trail of clues I would never have seen if it wasn't for that shirt. And if I was right, then Rose was in danger.

I'd thought if I found Virginia's killer, somehow it would be a redemption for not bringing Margeaux's murderer to justice. But now catching a killer was secondary to saving a life – Rose's life. I stopped the car as close to Slater's Rock as I could and dashed out, cursing my lack of agility as my shoes slipped on the rocks.

FORTY-ONE

ROSE

Hugh looked like he had the weight of the world on his shoulders.

"What's the bad news, Hugh?"

"Rose, I always liked you. You and me, we're a lot alike. No one pays any attention to us, and they kind of forget we're even around, don't they?"

I thought that was a horrible thing to say. "I don't think so," I answered, but even to my own ears it didn't sound convincing.

"Yeah, Rose, it's true. Think about it – if you weren't here anymore, who would even notice? Would the whole town show up for your funeral like they did Virginia's? Would they bother to bring a detective all the way from Sudbury to investigate if something happened to you? They sure wouldn't care if I died."

He began walking towards me, and every word was like a knife. How could Hugh say such mean things? He'd always treated me like I mattered, unlike everyone else.

"Why are you saying these things?"

He squatted down in front of me with such a kindly look that I couldn't stop the tears.

"Because it's true and you know it. You see, there are some people in the world who are golden. They don't even have to try, but they sparkle all the time, and you can't take your eyes off of them. Virginia was like that, and Olive is too, right?"

"I guess." I wiped the snot away with my arm. Hugh held out a handkerchief, which I took and wiped my eyes.

"You and I," he poked me lightly in the chest, "we're not golden. We're shadows. Even out in the sunlight, we don't shine. We're the people the world forgets about, but it's not all bad. Do you know why?"

I shook my head, unable to answer.

"Because the golden people, they need us. We give them purpose, we care for them, protect them, support them, and worship them. Without us, well, they'd be lost." He laughed lightly and shook his head. "Like Olive. Oh my, without me…well let's just say she doesn't make the best decisions, does she? Olive needs me to protect her from the bad people who would take advantage of her."

"Is that why you're going to propose to her today?"

His eyes opened wide, like he'd just remembered something. "Oh that, right. I already proposed to Olive a few days ago. She said no." Hugh smiled and rolled his eyes like it was no big deal.

"So why are we here then, if she said no?"

"It's like I said, Olive needs me. She's a silly girl who doesn't know what's best for her, but she is *my* silly girl." He emphasized the "my" in a way that made me uncomfortable. "Olive needs persuading. First, she was going to go to Los Angeles with Virginia, but I couldn't let that happen, could I?" He stood up and began pacing with his hands in his pockets. "Those Hollywood types, they'd ruin Olive."

I couldn't imagine Virginia letting anything happen to Olive and I was pretty sure Olive could take care of herself. She'd always been strong-minded. Something was off about Hugh. I'd never heard him speak so much or about his feelings. It just wasn't like him.

"Your family, Rose, they just don't have any sense. I asked Virginia to change her mind and not take Olive away, but she tried to tell me it was the best thing for Olive and that she would never be happy in Creighton." He turned to look at me, and his eyes were hard like stone. It changed the way his whole face looked. "Virginia shows up and thinks she knows better than *me*," he slapped his hand on his chest, "what is best for Olive. It was all her fault, you know. I didn't plan on hurting anyone, but she just wouldn't listen to me. Then later I realized it was the right thing to do."

My mind was spinning. What he was saying was unthinkable. He couldn't be saying what I thought he was.

"After that," he continued, "Olive stopped talking about leaving, and she needed me like never before. I was her rock. You saw it, didn't you?" He pointed at me. "She needed me, didn't she? Virginia's death was just what Olive needed to see that."

"What are you saying, Hugh?" I whispered, my voice caught in my chest.

"We were even closer than ever," his mouth twisted like a snarling dog, "but then Nick Valenti came around again, trying to sweet-talk her. I even heard from Cheryl that he was going to ask her to go steady with him, just so he'd have a girl in the stands rooting for him at every game. He didn't deserve a girl like Olive, and I couldn't take any chance she'd be so foolish. Olive's head is easily turned."

I looked and realized Hugh was standing between me and the path down. There was no way for me to get around him.

"But now, she's talking about leaving again." He laughed harshly. "I can't let this happen. Olive needs to realize Creighton is the place for her. I need to convince her of that. She has to stay here with her family, and with me. She needs to stop being so selfish by leaving the people that love her most. But our Olive," he shook his head, "feather-brained Olive, she won't listen to reason. She needs a grand romantic gesture," he yelled and threw his arms wide. Then, as if he just remembered I was there, he ran over and grabbed me by the arms.

Up close, his eyes were feverish, like he couldn't focus on me, even though we were close enough I could feel his breath on my face.

"You, my sweet, invisible Rose. You will be the sacrifice that finally brings Olive to me. But don't worry — it won't hurt, and it will be over so quickly." He scooped me up into his arms.

"No!" I tried to scream, but my face was pressed against his chest, and he held me so tight, I could barely breathe. He was stronger than I ever would have guessed. When he lifted me up, my legs swung free and I tried to kick him, but my bare feet didn't do any damage. I couldn't see anything, but I knew where we were going. He was taking me towards the edge of the rock. Hugh was going to throw me over.

I was terrified but also mad. Hugh was wrong. I wasn't forgotten or invisible. Virginia had seen me. She was golden and she loved me, which made me special. No matter what he had said, I knew I'd be missed. For all that I'd longed to see Virginia again, I wasn't ready to go yet. If I died, it would break my mom. She'd never recover if she lost one more of us. And Maggie – who would look out for her, share secrets, and put on shows? What about Angus... I was the only one who knew he was in love; that was something. The more I thought of my family, the angrier I got.

"Just close your eyes, Rose. It's almost over," he whispered in my ear.

At first, I tried to think what The Shadow would do, but I didn't have super powers, and The Shadow wasn't real. Instead, I thought of the detective. I didn't want him to think I was a victim. What would he do? He'd fight hard, any way he could, and wouldn't give up. Without a second thought, I chomped down on Hugh's chest where my face was pressed tight. It was all I had.

He screamed and grabbed where I'd bit him, letting go of me. I fell hard. We were both shocked and stared at each other for a few seconds. Then his face twisted, and he wasn't Hugh anymore. I scrambled backwards with my bare feet digging against the rocks, trying to pick up speed, but he was faster. He grabbed me by one ankle and yanked hard. My head bounced along the ground. The rocks scraped against my back as he pulled me back towards the ledge.

I didn't feel any of the cuts on my hands as I tried to grab on to something. When we reached the edge, it was clear he no longer cared about me being hurt or scared. He was going to toss me over.

I closed my eyes. "Virginia…Mommy…catch me," I whispered. I wasn't strong enough and knew I was going to die but was still so scared it would hurt. But instead of a yank over the edge, my leg dropped. My heel hit a pointed rock and bounced over the side, dangling, but the rest of me stayed right where I was.

"Hugh, step back." The detective's voice was firm and deep.

I opened my eyes and saw Hugh bent over me but looking behind me. I wanted to scooch backwards towards the voice, but I couldn't move my arms or legs.

Both Hugh and I were frozen like a moment captured in a photograph. Him hunched forward with his arms outstretched; me on my back, arms flung above my head. Only my eyes moved, looking for a way out, but afraid the slightest movement would cause Hugh to push me over.

"I will shoot you, Hugh. Do you understand me?" The detective's voice was now a few steps closer.

I never took my eyes off of Hugh. I could read everything going through his mind. His eyes flicked over the side of the cliff, then a shudder ran over his shoulders as he thought about jumping himself, but he wasn't brave enough. He couldn't make a wrong move without a gun going off, and he still wanted to live. He took two very small steps backwards and dropped his arms to his side.

I was yanked back, hard and fast. The detective stepped around me and pushed Hugh to the ground, away from the ledge. Hugh didn't put up a fight against the bigger man.

The detective kneeled with one knee in Hugh's back. He smoothly put his gun into the holster under his left arm and grabbed a pair of handcuffs from his jacket pocket, just like in the movies.

Once I was sure Hugh couldn't get away, I pushed myself up into a sitting position. Feeling flowed back into my arms and caused painful pins and needles. My back felt damp. I slipped my hand down the back of my shirt and it came back with smears of blood. Mom was not going to be happy about my bloodstained clothes. The worst pain was from my heel where Hugh had dropped it onto a sharp rock edge. I could see a chunk of flesh was missing, which made me woozy. I hurt, ached, and felt like I might throw up at any moment, but I felt something else: a lightness inside. I had survived.

"Are you okay, Rose?" The detective looked worried.

"Yeah, I think so," I lied, and my voice shook, but the detective smiled and winked at me.

"You sure are a tough kid," he said, as he pulled Hugh up with him, and I felt better just hearing those words.

Officer Kowalski came into view seconds after I heard his feet pounding up the hill. He slid to a stop, looking almost like a cartoon character. His eyes were so wide they could have popped out, and his mouth gaped open.

"Gene, help Rose. She's a bit banged-up, but she's going to be just fine."

When the detective said that, I knew it was true. I was banged-up and all, but I'd be okay. Officer Kowalski collected himself and came over to me. He gently picked my foot up and looked at the gash on my heel.

"That's gonna leave a scar, sweetie." He smiled so kindly, it broke the wall inside me. I started to cry and couldn't stop. He scooped me up in his arms. "Hang on tight," he said. It was a scary feeling to be carried down the hill, but I wouldn't have made it on my own, especially since I sobbed like a baby almost the whole way.

Through my tears, I could see Mom, June, and Maggie huddled together at the bottom of the hill. Officer Kowalski took me straight to them, and they surrounded me, each touching and patting me like they needed to be sure I was still in one piece. We were all piled into the back of the police car, and Mom insisted on holding me in her lap. I closed my eyes, and for the first time I could ever remember, I laid my head in the little crook of her neck. She smelled of soap and honey. Over and over, she rocked me, saying, "Shhh, it'll be okay, it'll be okay." Although I thought she was talking more to herself than to me.

June stroked my hair, and I even felt Maggie's small hand resting on my leg. Here I was, surrounded by three generations of Boyle women, and each of them reached out to hold on to me as if they were afraid to let me go. If I had died up on that rock, there would be a hole in our family that couldn't be filled, just like there was no filling in the places left behind by Virginia and even little Francis. Like a puzzle with a piece missing. No matter what, it would always be incomplete.

I kept my head buried in Mom's neck and never saw Hugh, handcuffed and defeated, get pushed into the back seat of the detective's car and driven out of town, never to return to Creighton Mine.

FORTY-TWO

VICTOR

I walked into the police station that had become so familiar to me. It had only been three weeks since I took Hugh McLellan to the Sudbury jail to await his murder trial, but it didn't take long for my perspective to change. The station seemed smaller than I remembered. Gene looked up from his usual place and grinned broadly.

"Well, look what the cat dragged in."

"Hello, Gene. How are things?"

The tables had turned for us over the past few weeks, and it was Gene who had to make the daily drive to Sudbury to wrap up the case, do paperwork, and be interviewed by the Crown prosecutor for the upcoming trial. There had been little reason for me to come back to Creighton during that time.

"Quiet. And I like it that way. What brings you back here?"

"Stopping in to see the Boyles and return something I promised."

Gene leaned back, his cheery demeanor vanishing. "This trial is going to be tough on them. I can't wait for it to be all over and get back to normal. I'm not sure how I'm supposed to keep running things around here while also being in Sudbury to testify and such."

"Well, you've got your partner back now, I see." I pointed at the desk that used to be mine. It was covered in papers, coffee cups, newspapers, and an ashtray overflowing with butts and ashes.

"True, Officer Greene has recuperated, and the bosses have decided to add a third officer. I guess Inco finally accepted that even Creighton Mine can have crime issues. You'll never guess who put their name in the ring for the position."

I shook my head.

"Angus Boyle."

"Doesn't he live in Copper Cliff?"

"He put in for transfer back here."

"Hmm, well, events like these can have that effect on people. Let me know how that goes. Don't worry. You won't get a chance to miss me. Before this trial is over, you'll be sick of the sight of me."

"Naw, it's been a real pleasure working with you, although it would be nice not to need your skills here in Creighton for the foreseeable future."

"I agree." I spun my hat in my hand, already feeling like a visitor. "Give my regards to Lily."

"Will do."

When I left the station, I was surprised by the amount of activity nearby and quickly realized both the high school and public school had just let out. During the summer, I'd never paid much attention to the two buildings beside each other.

Children of all ages laughed, shouted, and still exuded that start-of-school excitement that would fade in a few weeks. I got in my car and was more alert as I pulled out around the crowds and began the drive to the Dardanelles.

I didn't get very far before I recognized the familiar figure of Rose Boyle. She had an armful of books and walked with a slight limp, surrounded by several kids her age and Maggie. It made more sense that Maggie was really her cousin and not her niece, but we'd been able to keep a lid on that information. It had no bearing on the upcoming trial. The truth of Rose's parentage would most likely stay a family secret kept locked away. I pulled up beside the small group, who had all stopped to stare.

"Hey, Rose, Maggie. Want a ride? I'm going to your house."

Rose peered over at me with a muted smile. She'd faced a lot of grief and turmoil over a short span of time, but kids healed faster than grown-ups. Still, she'd be changed by what happened.

"Yeah, okay…c'mon, Maggie," she said.

The other kids called out their goodbyes and plans to walk together the next day. It looked like Rose had become a bit of a celebrity, which was to be expected. This case was the biggest thing to happen in Creighton Mine for probably a hundred years, and Rose was at the centre of it all. With the trial, she'd be in the spotlight even more as she testified against Hugh and his attempted murder charge, just one of the many he was facing.

"Are you happy to be back at school, girls?" I asked.

"Yes, sir," they answered in unison.

"Well, here we are," I said as we pulled onto their street. Maggie hopped out and ran into the house as soon as I came to a stop. Her voice carried into the street as she bellowed for her grandma. Rose moved a bit slower, stepping gingerly and using the car door to push herself up.

"How are you doing, Rose?"

"Fine. My foot still hurts. I had to get stitches. They feel weird."

"Have the kids at school been bugging you? Wanting to know all about what happened?"

She frowned and took her time to answer. "Yeah, but Officer Kowalski said I'm not supposed to say anything until after the trial."

"That's right." I was glad to hear Gene had directed her that way.

"I thought it would be different," she said, squinting up at me.

"What would be?"

"Well, now everyone wants to talk to me, and I always get asked to sit beside kids in class, like they now want to be my friend. I always wanted to be popular, but I wonder if once the trial is over, if it will all go back to how it was before, when no one noticed me."

"Rose, you should know it will never go back to how it was. Too much has happened. It is true. A lot of people will only want to be around because you're kind of famous right now." Her face screwed up in displeasure. "But I suggest you just keep being yourself, and the ones who stick around will be your real friends. And, hey, you've always got Maggie."

She chuckled. "Yup, because family has no say. They gotta stay." But she seemed rather pleased with that thought.

"I've got something for you." I held out the envelope I'd been holding. She frowned and didn't take it.

"It's Virginia's photographs. I promised, didn't I?"

Her eyes widened, and she snatched the envelope out of my hands, holding it tightly against her chest. She looked up at me with the intensity of someone twice her age.

"Thank you, Detective Lapointe…for the pictures and for saving my life. If you hadn't shown up, I'd be dead too." Her voice dropped to almost a whisper.

"You're welcome, Rose, but I was just doing my job. You were very brave, and your mom would be very proud of you."

She looked at me, startled, but understood who I was really referring to. It made her smile, shyly, like a little girl — and which I hoped she'd get more opportunities to be.

Mrs. Boyle opened the front door as if she'd been expecting me. "Detective, would you like to come in? Mr. Boyle is home too." She'd aged even more than when I first met her. Her dark hair sported more grey, and the circles under her eyes looked like they'd be there permanently.

"Come on inside, Rose, before Maggie eats all the cookies."

"Okay, Mom."

Mrs. Boyle's eyes lingered over Rose as if she was leery of letting her granddaughter out of view. That desire to keep her within sight would probably never go away.

I accepted her invitation and came inside. I spent the next hour explaining what the family should expect and what would be needed of them, and Rose, during the trial. Rose and Maggie stayed in the kitchen, presumably eating their cookies safe within their home.

EPILOGUE

ROSE

July 9, 1952

I sat alone on the back stoop. Maggie was inside, studying with her mom, which seemed unfair since it was summer, but June was teaching her Catholic things for her upcoming catechism. All I knew was that Maggie would get to wear a pretty white dress like a bride, and for that reason, I was jealous.

But I was glad to have some time alone. I'd been getting better at my picture taking. Virginia's camera was now mine, and I understood why she loved it so much. There was something special about looking through the lens that made the world look different. Things I'd never paid attention to looked interesting, even beautiful. In my back pocket, I had three rolls of unused film Olive had given me as a going-away gift.

She moved to Toronto in the spring. Although I missed her, I was glad she got to leave. Creighton wasn't a good place for her anymore. There were people who felt like she was to blame for everything that went on. That if she hadn't led Hugh on, none of this would have happened, which was just wrong. The detective explained to our family that some people were just bad, like something in their head wasn't right, and that it was no one's fault but Hugh's. He was the only one responsible for what he did. But the person who blamed Olive the most was Olive herself.

In the days after Hugh tried to kill me, she'd stayed by my side, fetching me treats, changing the bandages on my foot, and rubbing salves on my back and hands. She even read me stories at times because I was stuck inside.

I loved this new Olive who cared for me, but it was like having a beautiful bird in a cage. Having her with me made me happy, but you knew it was selfish because she should be happy and free. At times, I wished the old fiery Olive would come back.

If Hugh could see what she'd become, he wouldn't call her golden anymore. Would he even fall in love with this new Olive, enough to do what he did? We'd never know because Hugh would never see Olive, or any of us, again.

It was still hard to accept that the Hugh I'd always known was the same person described in the papers as the Creighton Mine Killer: cold-blooded, obsessed, and tormented. Even after what he tried to do to me, I had difficulty connecting that person to the one who had practically been like family.

It was no surprise when Hugh was charged with trying to kill me. I didn't look at him once when I had to go up on the stand to testify. Instead, I directed all my answers to my family, who sat in the front row: Mom, Dad, Oscar, June, and Angus. Mikey and Maggie weren't allowed to come, even though they begged, and Olive couldn't bring herself to be in the same room as Hugh.

Hugh was also found guilty of murdering Virginia, but they didn't try him for attempting to kill Nick. The detective said it wasn't worth putting everyone through another trial, and Hugh never admitted to it, even though I'd told them what he said to me up on Slater's Rock.

Some days it felt like this would never end. Today was one year to the day of when Virginia was killed, and in a few weeks, Hugh McLellan would be hanged from the neck until he was dead. I couldn't wrap my head around that, even after all he'd done. The McLellan's had packed up their house and left Creighton.

Jefferson Clarke also left Creighton. He'd got a new job as a principal at a school in London, Ontario. He, his wife, and new baby had left a few days ago, right after school ended. He and I managed to avoid each other most of the year. A few times, I'd see him coming down the hall towards me, but he'd quickly turn into the nearest classroom or pretend he didn't notice me, and I was fine with that.

It was all too much to think about, especially today. My feelings were all mixed up, and when it got to be too much, I'd grab my camera. I liked the distance I felt between me and the subject. All I had to worry about were things like shadows, light, and composition.

Eddie Szymaski had lent me some of his books and magazines on photography but said he didn't have time to teach me. In fact, he dropped the books off on our front step like I had the cooties or something. But still, it was nice of him to lend me his books.

I walked slowly around the side of the house and leaned up against it, peeking down the road towards the path. Besides being the anniversary of Virginia's death, it was also the first official day of blueberry-picking season. The two events would forever be linked in my mind. No one in my family was taking part this year. Mom's baskets and jars stayed tucked away in the pantry. There were no plans for preserves or pies to be made. It almost felt like we were being punished for what happened, but no one could bring themselves to venture into the berry patches. Mikey and Joey had gone to the movies. They invited me to tag along, but I felt the need to stay close to home.

I watched the shadows along the road lengthen. When I heard the first footsteps coming from the path I pulled back, hiding around the corner in the shade of the house, and lifted the camera to my eye. Mrs. Middleton, Mrs. O'Malley, and six kids between them came into view. They all talked excitedly, balancing their loads of berries. Even the littlest one had a small basket in each hand. As she swung her arms, a small trail of berries followed her.

When they neared the house, Mrs. Middleton shushed the children and nodded towards our front porch. It was out of respect, I knew, but it also annoyed me. I didn't want our family to be the one everybody pitied, that they spoke about in whispers. I didn't want them to forget either. Virginia deserved to be remembered.

They stopped in front of our porch. Mrs. O'Malley leaned over and whispered something into the little girl's ear, then pushed her lightly in the back. The child walked slowly and placed one of her baskets on the bottom step. She stared at it for a minute, like she maybe didn't want to give it up. I snapped her picture. When her mother called her name, she skipped back to the group, and I stayed hidden until they passed by.

Before I had time to think about why Mrs. O'Malley had given up one of her baskets, more pickers appeared. I recognized a loud group of teenagers, a few grades above me. When they got closer, they quieted down and kept glancing over at the house, whispering amongst themselves. They'd almost passed when one of the boys called them to stop and pointed at the little basket on the bottom step. A quick discussion took place. That same boy walked over and put one of his two jars, overflowing with large, fat berries, onto the step above the basket. I also caught that moment on film. The group moved on and continued laughing and talking over each other.

I stayed in the shadows at the side of the house, watching as more groups of pickers passed, paused, and gave up a portion of their bounty. I caught close-ups, wide shots, and group pictures. As I did, baskets, jars, and containers of every size filled the steps to our home, like offerings at an altar.

After some time, the shadows began to lengthen. I let the camera hang down on the strap around my neck and ran around the back and up the stairs, letting the door slam behind me.

"Mom, Mom, c'mon! You gotta see this!"

She was sitting at the kitchen table, folding a load of towels and clean rags.

"Please, Rose, not now." She sounded like she needed to go to bed and sleep for a week. The house had been so quiet all day that it almost felt like a sacrilege to speak out loud. Maggie had taught me what sacrilege meant from her church teachings.

"But Mom, you have to come out front and see what's happening."

"Just tell me, Rose. I don't have the energy today."

I put my hands on either side of her face. "Mom, this is something special. You have to see it. It's about Virginia."

She let me take her hand and lead her out the front door. I realized from my hiding place at the side of the house, I couldn't really appreciate the extent of the gifts that had collected. The berries fanned out from the top step all the way to ground, where they spread outward. Like a quilt of blue, intermingled with the colours from every different kind of container. It wasn't just what people had given up, which for some was a portion of their livelihood, but that they were paying tribute to Virginia and our family. As we stood and stared down, speechless, another group appeared. The last of the day. I recognized them immediately.

It was the Finnish ladies, carrying their huge baskets balanced on their heads. They were the same ladies who'd found me with Virginia's body that day. They stopped in front of us, and the lady with the biggest basket stepped forward, and with such ease, lifted it off her head and placed it on the ground, dwarfing the smaller jars and pint containers. She nodded ever so slightly at my Mom and pressed her hands over her heart.

I looked up at Mom, who nodded back while tears rolled down her cheeks. They left without a word. We stood silently together watching them go. Then Mom sucked in a big breath, wiped her face with her apron, and clapped her hands.

"Well, don't just stand there. Go fetch June and Maggie. We need to bring these berries inside before the critters think we're laying out a feast for them." She grabbed the ones closest to her and carried them into the house. I ran next door and whipped open the door.

"Maggie, June, come on! I need some help."

Within minutes, our house sang with activity. Mom and June banged away in the kitchen, dragging out pots and accessories for canning, flour, and ingredients for pie shells, while Maggie and I made trip after trip, retrieving the berries and bringing them inside. The jams, jellies, and preserves were a bounty that would sustain our family, fill our bellies, and feed the parts of us that needed filling throughout the winter and for years to come.

Trina Brooks was born in London, Ontario. Her book obsession began with Victorian orphans then moved through hobbits, elves, civil war heroines and onto World War two spies. With an interest in viewing history as it happened, she graduated from Broadcast-Journalism. With her other passion being theater, she spent several years on stage in Toronto, Canada and London, UK delivering the words from notables such as Shakespeare, Shaw and Simon until she came to the realization, she no longer wanted to speak other people's words. As a playwright most of her work has historically inspired themes, including her award-winning drama, Left Behind. After a lifetime of rolling her eyes every time her family members began waxing poetic about the "good old days" one day she chose to listen and concluded these stories were actually treasure troves of twentieth century life. These stories went on to inspire The Barren Hills of Creighton. Currently she resides in London, Ontario with her partner, Jim and her feline roommates, Rosey and Helen

You can follow her on Tik Tok or Instagram at trinabrooks_author where she posts Hidden History facts and updates on appearances and upcoming works, or visit her webpage www.trinabrooks.com to learn more about the town of Creighton Mine and the real people who inspired this story.